MY BEST FRIEND'S WIFE

A GRIPPING PSYCHOLOGICAL THRILLER

DINA SANTORELLI

Copyright © 2025 by Dina Santorelli

All rights reserved.

No part of this publication may be reproduced, distributed, or transmitted in any form or by any means, including photocopying, recording, or other electronic or mechanical methods, without the prior written permission of the publisher, except as permitted by U.S. copyright law.

This is a work of fiction. Certain public figures and/or long-standing institutions, agencies, and public offices are mentioned, but the characters involved are wholly imaginary. Any similarity between the characters and/or situations to actual persons, living or dead, and/or actual events is unintentional and coincidental.

ISBN: 978-1-7377394-9-4 (ebook)

ISBN: 978-1-964858-99-9 (paperback)

Book cover design by Bookfly Design

For Tommy

SANDRA

CHAPTER 1

Saturday, March 15, 10:30 p.m.

"The bride cuts the cake... The bride cuts the cake!"

Sandra slipped on her eyeglasses as she stood, searching the ballroom as she mouthed the song lyrics with about four hundred other wedding guests. She was hoping to make eye contact with Alex and duck out of there once the Venetian table was rolled out. She retook her cushioned seat and clapped absently as, on the dance floor, the groom shoved a mouthful of cream into the bride's mouth.

"So wonderful, isn't it? Young love?" asked an elderly woman across the table whose name Sandra had forgotten.

"Yes, it is."

"How long has it been for you and your husband, Alex?"

"Fifteen years," Sandra said.

"My goodness, that's a long time!" said the woman's husband, Clint, who began sipping his freshly poured coffee. Luckily, the old guy resembled Clint Eastwood or else Sandra never would have remembered his name either.

"Yeah, and we were together about eight years prior to that." Sandra always added that to give people a good jolt.

"Eight years!" Clint's wife said. "That's twenty-three years total. Quite a long time for such a young couple to be together."

At forty years old, Sandra wouldn't exactly call herself young, but she imagined that once you reached Clint's wife's age, youth was relative.

"What's your secret?" asked another wedding guest, a fifty-something woman who had called dibs on the table centerpiece.

Sandra shrugged. "Just luck, I guess."

"Excuse me, is this seat taken?"

Sandra glanced at the tall, athletic, and ridiculously attractive guy easing into the seat next to her. "Sorry," she said, "my husband is sitting there."

"Husband? Boy, is he a lucky man." He gazed at Sandra through glassy eyes. "You know, you're just my type. Beautiful, yet a wee bit scary."

"That's actually my Instagram bio."

"And now we ask that you join the bride and groom on the dance floor," the band leader said as couples squeezed themselves away from their tables and made their way toward the large crystal chandelier at the center of the room.

"May I have this dance?" Mr. Ridiculously Attractive whispered into Sandra's ear. "I'm sure your husband won't mind."

Sandra glanced at the others at the table who were already digging into their wedding cake, immersed in small talk. She sighed and put her eyeglasses on the table. "Oh, I guess so."

She walked with him to the dance floor, where he wrapped his arms around her in a bear hug.

"I think you're in my dance space." Sandra pulled back with a smile as they began to sway to the love song.

"I think you've seen *Dirty Dancing* one too many times." He leaned her back into a dip. "But, I must say, you dance divinely."

"As do you."

"It's like we've been dancing together for years."

"About twenty-three years, I'd say." She smirked.

His hands ran up and down her back. "I love these open-backed dresses when you don't wear a bra," he whispered. His breath smelled like whiskey.

"Well, I'm glad because I wore it for you." She kissed his warm cheek.

"Hey, Alex, one more shot?" someone called from the bar.

Sandra didn't recognize who was trying to pull her husband away from her, especially without her glasses, but she never did at these things. "I see you made some new friends. Surprise, surprise."

"Please, I'll never see these people again. That's my favorite part of weddings." Alex pulled her closer. "But I'm happy to stay with you, if you like."

She pushed him away playfully. "Go have fun. But let's get out of here in fifteen minutes."

"Got it."

"And don't forget to put the envelope in the mailbox near the dais."

"Yes, boss." He saluted.

She leaned toward him and whispered, "Okay, I'm going to walk back to my table real slow-like so you can gaze at the back of my dress."

"You're so good to me."

By the time Sandra was back in her seat with her glasses on, Alex was already at the bar with his arms wrapped around two people. He winked at her before throwing back a shot of something and yelling a hearty "Opa!" as everyone at the bar cheered, and the bartender, who had his arm around an ice sculpture of Eddie Van Halen, poured another round.

Sandra wanted to hate weddings. She really did. Dressing up in uncomfortable clothes. Calluses on the balls of her feet.

The same old song and dance routines. Forced small talk between people who had nothing in common beyond a passing acquaintance with the bride or groom. But going to weddings with Alex was always an adventure. He didn't quite get her out of her shell, but he got her to poke her head out of it every once in a while. She needed that. And, probably most surprising, she liked it, too.

"Your husband is so much fun!"

The bride was standing behind Sandra, shouting over the music into the top of her head. Sandra stood up and smiled into her young, happy face. She could barely remember her own wedding, but seeing the bride up close called to mind the flutter and excitement of the life yet to come. *This,* she wanted to say to Clint's wife, *is young.*

Instead, Sandra said, "We're having such a good time," and leaned in to hug the bride, whose name she had also forgotten even though she had been the one to write the check for the wedding gift. All of Alex's events were blurring together. "Thank you for inviting us."

"Are you kidding?" The bride still had a bit of wedding cake in the corner of her mouth. "Chuck can't stop talking about the way Alex has blown up his social media. Alex, Alex, Alex! And the band has three gigs booked the week after we come back from our honeymoon! Mostly thanks to your husband!"

"I'm so glad," Sandra said.

Chuck snuck up behind his new bride and gave her a hug. "It's been so wonderful to meet you, Sandra." He looked at the bar. "I see Alex is having a great time."

"Always." Sandra followed his gaze.

"It's a shame Blake couldn't make it," Chuck said.

"I know." Sandra missed him, too. Blake usually sat with her at these things while Alex schmoozed. He had given a weak reason for not attending, and Sandra planned to never let him live it down. It was weird being here without him.

"Well, look who it is!" Alex said, creeping between Chuck and his wife and handing them both a shot glass. "A toast to the beautiful couple and a kick-ass party!" They all threw back their heads, and Sandra spotted matching electric guitar tattoos on the bride and groom's necks.

"You're the best, man," Chuck said. "Thanks for coming. Let's chat when I get back."

"Definitely. I see good things coming your way, my friend." Alex leaned into Sandra as the bride and groom made their way around the table. "Ready to go, my love. I do believe you should drive."

"I do believe so, too." Sandra grabbed her purse and the Godiva chocolate wedding favors in the shape of music notes. "Let's go."

She grabbed Alex's hand, hoping to beat the valet rush, but it took nearly fifteen minutes to get from the ballroom to the lobby as people seemed to crawl out of the woodwork to say goodbye to Alex or to hand him business cards. She thought of Blake and how she and he liked to play *Guess how many people will shake Alex's hand* every time they left an event. She'd have to tell him tonight's answer. Twenty-three. Possibly a new record.

After tipping the coat check clerk and handing his ticket stub to the valet, Alex helped Sandra with her coat. "Looks like it's going to rain," he said. "When was the last time it rained?"

"It's been a while. Oh, by the way, Chuck mentioned Blake." She raised her eyebrows. "And he wasn't the *only* one." Sandra didn't know a lot about business, but she knew enough to know that it was bad business to not show up for your client's wedding.

"I know. A few people asked me, too. I told everyone that something came up."

"It's weird, though, isn't it? Blake canceling at the last minute. Especially for a client?"

Alex shrugged. "He knew I'd be here keeping everything under control."

"Oh, is that what you call it?" She playfully punched his arm. "No, seriously. Blake's been so absent lately, don't you think?"

"Not really. He's been in the office every day."

"That's not what I mean."

"You mean absent, like in school?"

"Alex..."

"Oooh, speaking of school..." He bent down to whisper in her ear. "How about we play school when we get home? I think I need detention."

Sandra rolled her eyes. She knew better than to have a serious conversation with Alex when he had been drinking. "Never mind. We can talk about this later."

"Seriously, I wouldn't worry about Blake," Alex said. "He's always trying to get out of these things anyway. That's the way we divide the company." He turned up his left hand like he was holding a melon. "He does more of the business-business stuff." He turned up his right hand. "And I do more of the getting-business and keeping-business stuff."

"Wow, you should teach a course at Harvard Business School."

"Trust me, he was probably happy not to come. He hates weddings more than you do."

"I don't *hate* weddings." Sandra smiled at several nearby guests as their car pulled up and she got into the driver's seat. She locked the doors after Alex got in and drove down the cobblestone path. "I just think weddings are a waste of money. Especially when the majority of marriages end in divorce anyway."

"Not all marriages end in divorce." Alex reached for her hand. His palm was warm.

"That's what I mean, Alex. We had a nice, relatively inexpensive affair with all our favorite people, and we didn't break the bank."

"We had an awesome wedding."

"And we didn't need ice sculptures . . ." She wriggled out of his hand and picked up the wedding favor. "Or customized Godiva chocolate."

"C'mon, San, life can be ugly. And unforgiving. You and I know a little bit about that. And Chuck has had some shitty things happen to him in his life and so has Beatrice."

Beatrice. That's her name.

"And they've had to scrimp and save just like your family did when you were a kid," Alex said. "But now they have some cash . . ."

"Thanks to you." She pinched his cheek.

"And the truth is, we don't know how much time we all have on this planet. Why not just say 'fuck it' every now and then?"

"I know what you mean. I married *you*, didn't I?"

"Ha! There's that sharp wit I love!" He tuned the radio to a classic rock station and turned it up. "I love this song!"

Shocker. Alex loved *every song* when he was drunk.

He began to sing.

Loudly.

And badly.

All. The. Way. Home.

BY THE TIME SANDRA placed her car keys and phone into the glass bowl on the entryway table, Alex was hoarse, but he was still crooning lyrics from Journey's "Don't Stop Believin'" at the top of his lungs. Those last shots of alcohol were probably kicking in.

"I wouldn't quit your day job, my love," Sandra said gently. "Maybe we should leave the singing to your clients."

"Hey, I could try using one of those voice-changing apps Blake's been experimenting with on social media. Give myself a Southern accent."

"Well, bless your heart."

"You're right. Awful idea. It's too bad. I would've made a terrific rock star." Alex locked the door and turned around with flair. "Ready for some drunk sex?" He dropped his suit jacket on the floor and loosened his tie. "I know how much you like it."

Sandra *did* like Alex's drunk sex. It was sloppy and fun. She was wondering if she should play hard to get, when her phone rang. She looked at the screen. "It's Blake."

"Ah, the prodigal son." Alex was unbuttoning his shirt now and looking at her alluringly.

"Maybe you should keep your shirt on," Sandra said. "It's a video call."

"Why?" Alex asked. "Blake has seen me naked. We used to take baths together."

"Um, that was when you were toddlers, and you're a lot hairier now. You don't want to scare him."

Alex grabbed Sandra in a tight hug and pushed the green Answer button on her phone. She held it up so they were both on the screen.

"Hey, Blake!" they said in unison.

"Hi, guys! How was the wedding?"

"Okay," Sandra said, while Alex yelled, "Great!"

"That's pretty much what I expected." Blake laughed.

"A lot of people asked for you," Sandra said.

"Yeah, I told them you had better things to do than make our clients happy." Alex smirked.

"Very funny," Blake said.

Sandra was scoping out the background of Blake's frame. He definitely wasn't at home, although it was neat and beige, Blake's two favorite colors. "Where are you?" she asked.

"Well, that's a good question," Blake said. "That's why I'm calling. First, to thank Alex for standing in for me tonight."

"Anytime, buddy!" Alex began peppering Sandra's forehead with kisses.

"And, second, to tell you that I had a very good reason for not attending Chuck's wedding."

"You won the lottery!" Alex said, moving down to Sandra's cheek.

"Well, sorta."

This got Alex's attention. He pulled the phone toward him. "You won the lottery, man?"

"Kind of." He thrust his hand into the camera lens, and just as the image focused on the gold band around his finger, Blake shouted, "I got married!"

CHAPTER 2

Sunday, March 16, 1:52 a.m.

"Married?!" Sandra asked. "What do you mean, *married*?"

"Don't be mad, San. It just all happened so fast. I can't wait for you to meet her. You're gonna love her!"

"I'm not... mad," Sandra said, but that wasn't entirely true. She *was* kind of mad. Blake rarely bought a dress shirt without sending of photo of him from a department store dressing room. Now he had gotten married?

"Well, aren't you full of surprises, my friend?!" Alex said. "Congratulations!"

"Thanks, buddy. That means a lot. San, please tell me you're happy for me."

"Of course, I'm happy," she said, but she knew she didn't sound or look happy at all. And she couldn't fake it. Blake knew her too well. "But who?" Blake wasn't seeing anyone as far as Sandra knew.

"I'll tell you all about it tomorrow. I mean, today." He laughed. "I want you to meet her! Can we meet for brunch?"

"Sure," Alex said. "Listen, buddy, I have to go. As you know, I have a small window until Sandra decides she's too tired for drunk sex. Text me the time, and we'll meet you tomorrow. And congrats again!" He ended the call before Sandra could say anything else.

"How could he have gotten married?" Sandra asked as Alex placed the phone on the table, lifted her up, and whisked her upstairs, firefighter's carry-style.

"Less . . . talking," he panted. "More . . . undressing."

Alex placed her on her side of the bed and began ripping off his dress shirt.

"Wait, Alex, don't you think this is weird?"

He was still humming the song "Don't Stop Believin'." Apparently, he was taking his own advice.

"How can he be married?" Sandra asked. "Who is this person? Aren't you at all curious?"

"Sex first, curiosity second." Alex wriggled out of his clothes and shimmied his way Morticia Addams-style toward her. She couldn't help but giggle.

"Ugh, okay, let's make it quick," she said. "We need to talk."

"Quick drunk sex?"

"Well," she corrected herself, putting her eyeglasses on the nightstand. "Not *that* quick."

SANDRA SNUGGLED IN ALEX'S arms with satisfaction. Quick drunk sex aside, their sex life had always been good, although trying to get pregnant all these years had put a weird pressure on them, making it feel more like work with a performance rating. She was happy they had decided to adopt. It had restored their lovemaking to its former glory.

"Maybe it's a joke," she said, running a finger through Alex's chest hair. "Blake has pulled this kind of thing before. Remember when he told us that he had cancer when we were in tenth grade? I still don't know how he could think that was funny."

"This didn't seem like a joke." Alex was sobering up. His voice was deeper, with more gravitas. "He seemed serious. And excited."

"But, I mean, how long has he known this person? Can you really marry someone you just met?"

"Who's to say he just met her?"

"He *must* have. Or else *we* would have met her. *Or* heard about her."

"San, not everyone is together for eight years before they tie the knot like us." He twisted her wedding ring. "You know how long Chuck and Beatrice knew each other? About five months. When you know, you know." He kissed the top of her head. "I'm thinking that maybe there's something else that's bothering you about all this?"

"What do you mean?"

"Like how Blake could go off and marry someone without having that person be approved by Sandra Wilson."

She turned to look at him. "He doesn't need my approval."

"Apparently, *he* knows that. But do *you* know that?"

"Alex Connor!"

"Blake's in love. It's a nice thing, San. And you know what's also nice?" He turned the lights off. "Sleep." He pulled her toward him and nuzzled his chin in her hair. "Oh, my God, is there any place in the world I'd rather be right now than right here? I think not."

Sandra settled in beside him. "Why is he hiding her from us?"

"Who says he's hiding her? You know Blake. He likes to keep things to himself. Remember when he got tickets to see the Spice Girls?"

"That's your point of reference? The Spiceworld Tour in 1998?"

"Um, you're the one who brought up the cancer from high school."

"That's true." She wrapped her arm around Alex and put her head on his chest, where the steady beat of his heart eased her tension. The soundtrack of her life.

"Did you ever think that maybe he feels a little left out?" Alex asked.

"Left out how?"

"Really, San? You have to ask that?"

She didn't think Blake felt left out. They had all been friends for so long they were like family to one another. Plus, Blake dated relatively often. First dates that sometimes turned into second dates, but rarely into thirds. Sandra always thought it was because Blake was picky. It took him twenty minutes to choose an avocado at the supermarket.

"I mean, we hang out with him all the time. Why would he be lonely?" she asked, but then stopped herself. Maybe that was the problem. She had always seen the three of them as the three musketeers. She never saw Blake as their plus-one. And maybe he was.

"It must be pretty shitty being the third wheel all the time," Alex said.

"But he's not a third wheel," Sandra stressed. "He's Blake. He's my best friend. And your best friend. He's the guy who was there with us when the pregnancy tests didn't go our way. When money was tight. When your mom got sick. When your father passed away. When I needed—well, *anything*. And we were always there for *him*. When he got mono. Got fired from his crappy job. Got into that big fight with his mom. At least, I *thought* he was our best friend until he decided to get married all on his own without telling his best friends . . . Right? . . . Alex?"

Alex's breathing had steadied. She looked up at him and ran her finger along his dry lips, where a tiny bead of drool was about to fall onto the pillow. She marveled at how he could always fall soundly asleep after some kind of bomb had been dropped into their lives. Like when he found out his mother had uterine cancer. Like when their doctor told them they would be unable to have biological children because Alex's sperm production was too low.

Our problems will be there in the morning, San, Alex always said. *Better to look at them with fresh eyes.*

Was Blake's new wife the latest bomb to be dropped into their lives?

Time would tell. For now, Sandra was sure of only one thing.

She wasn't going to sleep at all tonight.

CHAPTER 3

Sunday, March 16, 10:52 a.m.

Sandra gazed into the mirror on the sun visor.

"You look fine," Alex said, his face clean shaven and adorable with no signs of any hangover.

"You always say that."

"Because it's true."

"Tell that to the bags under my eyes." She flipped up the visor and put her glasses back on. "Ugh, I'm nervous."

"You? Why?"

"I don't know."

"Well, imagine how *she* feels. You know what it's like meeting someone's close friends. You think they're going to judge you. Not accept you."

"But she's already been accepted. By Blake. And we didn't have a say in it."

"Would you listen to yourself? Are we *supposed* to have a say in it? Did Blake have a say when the two of us fell in love?"

Sandra barely had a say in it. She had been so surprised at how she had been swept off her feet. By *Alex Connor*. The last person on earth she ever thought she'd be with. He was too cool. And popular. But he saw something in her that she hadn't seen in herself. And she had done the same for him. She thought of the elderly woman at the wedding. Maybe Clint had done the same for her. She smiled.

"There you go," Alex said. "A smile."

"I'm not smiling," she said, making it disappear. "Did you ever think that Blake didn't introduce us to this person because he's . . . I don't know, embarrassed of *us*?"

"Why would he be embarrassed of us?"

Sandra didn't know. She had thought all kinds of things while she was lying in bed last night, unable to sleep. That Blake was embarrassed of *her*. That Blake was embarrassed of *them*. That Blake had gotten this person pregnant and was forced into some kind of shotgun wedding. That Blake's new wife came from a Mafia family, and if he didn't marry her, he would sleep with the fishes. That last idea came to her at 4:00 a.m., just before she fell into a fitful sleep.

"Let me throw this out there." Alex turned into a parking spot in the restaurant's lot. "Alex met a woman and fell totally in love with her and knew on the spot that he wanted to spend the rest of his life with her." He reached for Sandra's hand. "I get that."

"Ugh, would you stop being so romantic for a minute?" She leaned over and kissed him on the mouth. "See what you made me do? Now I have to reapply my lipstick."

Alex stopped her from reaching into her purse. "You're fine. Everything is fine. Ready for this?"

"No, but I'm doing it anyway."

"That's the spirit!"

As they got out of the car, a sprinkling of raindrops fell onto Sandra's glasses. Normally, she didn't mind wearing glasses—in fact, she preferred them over contacts—but when it rained, they were a pain in the ass. She took Alex's hand. Not only was she hobbling on sore heels and calluses from the night before, but now she was practically blind.

April's Café was busy as usual. The place had a sophisticated but cheery vibe that Sandra always thought matched Blake and Alex's personalities. It wasn't surprising they had made the decision to go into business together there eight years ago.

As Alex said hello to several people at the bar, Sandra wiped the rain off her glasses and put them back on, searching the crowd. Blake was standing at the other end of the bar next to a woman who was facing him. She was in a long black coat with a designer backpack. Sandra tried not to read too much into this moment, that her first impression of Blake's new wife would be a turned back.

"There they are!" Alex said, and gently guided Sandra toward Blake with his hand on her back. Probably so that she didn't walk right out the door.

Blake's eyes were wide open with an almost childish excitement. Sandra had rarely seen him this way. He was the unflappable one. Never overly emotional. Never rattled. She had always joked that if a fire broke out in a building, in all the panic Blake would be the only one to have the wherewithal to find the fire exit and guide everyone to safety. Mister Calm, Cool, and Collected.

But not today.

"Guys," Blake gushed. "I want you to meet Tara. My *wife*."

The woman turned around, and her eyes met Sandra's. Unsurprisingly, she looked nothing like the Wicked Witch of the East that Sandra had convinced herself she must be. Although she was a bit older than Sandra had anticipated, probably close to fifty, she was quite lovely. She had a short bob of blond hair that cupped her oval face with long bangs swept elegantly to the side. Her piercing blue eyes were flanked by light wrinkles that Sandra hoped came from years of laughing and joy. Blake deserved that.

Sandra was immediately disarmed, her doubts and fears melting away. How silly she had been. Alex was right. (As usual.) She was totally overthinking this. And being selfish. Blake was *married*. And he seemed happy. She needed to be happy for him. There would be a fourth musketeer in their gang! Someone to inject sorely needed estrogen into their mostly testosterone friendship. Someone who might be a new best friend.

Sandra stepped forward and wrapped Tara in a bear hug. "So nice to meet you," she gushed.

But then the worst thing happened.

Tara didn't hug back.

Worse than that.

She stiffened.

As Sandra pulled back, Tara gave an uncomfortable smile. "Nice to meet you, too," she said without much conviction. She adjusted her yellow cable-knit sweater over her bootcut jeans.

Sandra struggled with what to say next, but, luckily, she didn't have to say anything as Alex cut in, saving the day. (As usual.)

"I'm Alex," he said, hugging her.

Sandra couldn't be certain, but Tara seemed to be hugging Alex back.

"It's so good to see you all together." Blake smiled broadly. "The people I care about the most in this world, all in one place." He put his hand on Sandra's shoulder. "C'mon, our table is ready."

Alex and Blake brought so much business to April's Café that their table was rarely *not* ready—ever since the two of them had written a quick business plan on a cocktail napkin and decided to start a marketing company, appropriately named Napkin Marketing. Blake waved to the bartender. "John, we're going to head to our table." He picked up a Bloody Mary that was on the bar and handed it to Alex. "For you, my friend."

"Just what I needed." Alex took a long sip as Blake reached for Tara, and the two began walking into the restaurant. Alex and Sandra followed behind.

"She seems nice, right?" Alex whispered into Sandra's ear, unaware that she would have trouble hearing him because of the alarm bells ringing in her head.

"Yeah. Nice," Sandra muttered.

"Remember, she might feel uncomfortable meeting us. Give her a chance."

Right. Of course. Maybe Sandra had overwhelmed Tara with her hug. Maybe it was too much. Maybe Tara was shy. Or didn't like to be touched—at least by other women. Sandra had been the same way until Alex had converted her into a hugging machine. That must have been it. Sandra had come on too strong.

When they reached the table, Tara appeared to be waiting for Sandra to choose a seat before selecting her own. How sweet. Sandra sat near the window, but then Tara elected to sit across from her. Not next to her. Um . . . *what the fuck?*

They smiled at one another as they scooched their seats in and Sandra hung her handbag on the back of her chair. She took a sip of ice water, and then, unable to control herself, blurted, "So, how did you guys meet?"

Alex kicked her under the table.

"I know, this must seem so sudden," Blake said.

"Not at all," Sandra said with sarcasm, lifting her foot as Alex tried to kick her again.

"How we met is a great story," Blake said.

"Tinder?" Alex asked, sipping from his Bloody Mary.

"Not quite," Blake said with a laugh. "We met at the library."

"The library? People still go to the library?" Alex asked. "Wait, I take that back. *You* still go to the library, Blake?"

"There was a Microsoft Excel class, intermediate level, that I wanted to take."

"But you know Microsoft Excel already," Sandra said. "You took it in college."

"Things change, San. I needed to brush up. I feel like I'm not utilizing it the way I can be. Tara and I sat next to each other that first day. And the rest is history."

Not much *history,* Sandra thought. "When was this?"

"Don't mind my wife," Alex said to Tara. "She's thinking about enrolling in detective school."

"I'm . . ." Sandra took another sip of water. "I'm just curious, that's all." She changed the subject. "So, why were you taking Excel, Tara? What do you do?" She hoped that was an appropriate question. She didn't know anymore.

"I'm a high school psychologist."

Tara's voice had a gravelly timbre. Very sexy. Blake had always liked Demi Moore.

"My school district just implemented Excel, and I was trying to figure it out," Tara said. "It wasn't going well."

"You were doing fine," Blake said.

"Wow, a psychologist," Alex said. "What are you doing with *this* guy?" He reached across the table and punched Blake in the arm.

"I can say the same to Sandra." Blake winked at Sandra, who was trying to relax. This was a new dynamic to get used to.

"That must be fun, working with kids," Alex said.

"Well, yes and no," Tara took a deep breath. "We had a fentanyl overdose last week."

"Oh my God," Sandra said.

"It happened in the student's car. He was with another student. That second student pulled him out and called for help. Probably saved his life. I've been counseling him. Our school district is partnering with the local police department to raise awareness about the dangers of fentanyl—and about buying pills on social media."

Sandra didn't know what to say. They sat around looking at one another. Where does one go from fentanyl?

"That *is* heavy," Alex said. It was weird to see him socially stymied. He avoided heavy topics of conversation like the plague.

"So..."

It took Sandra a moment to realize Tara was speaking to her.

"What do you do, Sandra?" Tara asked.

"I'm a writer."

"No, I mean for your job. You know, your profession."

Sandra could feel the blood drain from her face. "I'm sorry? That *is* my profession."

"Oh." Tara blushed and turned to Blake. "Blake said it was a hobby."

"A hobby, Blake?" Sandra said. Alex reached for her hand under the table and squeezed. *Relax.*

"I meant the novel writing was a side hustle to your business writing career," Blake said.

"Blake, you know as well as I do that novel writing is not a side thing and very much what I do. Writing is my *career*. I write novels, proposals, website content. Since when did you not know that? And since when are you not supportive of that?"

"Relax, San." Blake took a sip of his drink. "I *am* supportive. But I happen to know that the novels don't bring in that much revenue."

Sandra's cheeks warmed. "Well, I also happen to know how much *revenue* your business brings in. And my little *hobby* brings in about as much as half your clients."

"She does well," Alex said to Tara as Sandra continued to glare at Blake.

What? Blake mouthed to Sandra.

"It was Sandra who pretty much supported me in the early days of the business Blake and I started," Alex said.

Sandra appreciated what Alex was doing, but she didn't need him to defend her. Before she could say anything, Alex added, "We're all self-starters. Have the entrepreneurial spirit. Sandra has a rock-solid core of readers who buy every novel she writes."

"What genre do you write?" Tara asked.

"Romance," Sandra said.

Tara nodded, but didn't say anything, and Sandra wanted to take her smug high school–psychologist look and pour ice water all over it.

"It's the biggest genre in publishing," Alex said.

Tara looked unimpressed.

"Tara, you run a book club. Right, honey?" Blake said.

Honey? Blake never called anyone *honey*.

"Well, I'm not sure I would call it an official book club anymore. It's just me now. It started off with a bunch of teachers from school, but most of them left a few years ago."

"Sandra's always been a bookworm," Alex said.

"God knows Alex hasn't read a book since high school English," Blake added with a laugh.

"I read Sandra's books," Alex said. "Those are the only books I need."

"If you're interested in reading one, just let me know," Sandra said to Tara. "No pressure, though."

"Sure," Tara said half-heartedly. "Listen, I'm sorry about—"

"It's fine," Sandra said. "I overreacted."

"Sandra can be sensitive," Blake whispered to Tara.

"I am not, *Blake*."

"Blake," Alex said, clearing his throat, which Sandra knew was her husband's way of telling her to take a breath, "you should have seen the ice sculptures of the famous guitarists at the wedding last night."

"There was more than one?" Blake asked.

As Alex filled Blake in on Chuck's wedding, Sandra and Tara sat at the table spinning their water glasses. Tara's coming out party was turning into a disaster, and Sandra was feeling responsible. Maybe they should start over. She was about to say something, when Tara grabbed her menu and started perusing it. Sandra cleared her throat. "Hey, Tara."

Tara looked up.

"Maybe we can get a cup of coffee one day? You know, and chat. Away from these knuckleheads." Sandra gestured to Alex and Blake. "You know. Just us. Girl talk." She smiled.

"Maybe," Tara said. She wasn't smiling. *Why isn't she smiling?* For a psychologist, she was doing a shitty job of faking it.

"Speaking of parties," Alex said. "Tara, did you know you married the world's best surprise-party thrower?" He motioned toward Blake and raised his Bloody Mary in a toast.

"What can I say? I can lie well for a good cause." Blake clinked his glass with Alex's.

"Totally fooled me," Alex said.

"Hey, Tara, I told you that Alex and I knew each other as kids, right?" Blake said. "Our mothers met at some kind of Jazzercize class, and we used to play together while we waited for them. What were we? Three or four years old, Alex?"

"Yep. Three. Then our moms became best friends, and so did we," Alex said.

"So, how did you and your wife meet?" Tara asked Alex.

Alex? She's asking Alex? Sandra was sitting right there. Did she say *your wife?* What the hell?

"She and Blake were best friends," Alex said.

"Still are!" Blake raised his glass to Sandra, and Sandra returned the gesture by glaring at him.

"Blake and San met each other in Spanish class in middle school. Sandra would let Blake cheat off her, and in exchange Blake taught Sandra the lyrics to every Radiohead song." Alex chuckled, and that adorable dimpled chin bobbed up and down. "When we got to high school, I was failing biology, and Blake was tutoring me at the library. Sandra would come and do her homework there because she didn't like staying home."

"Why didn't she like staying home?" Tara asked, like the snooping psychologist she was.

Sandra cleared her throat. Was that a question for *her*? How thoughtful. And unusual. "My mom babysat, so there was always a lot of noise."

"So that's when I met San," Alex said. "At the library. Hey, the same place you and Blake met."

"That's right! What a coincidence." Blake squeezed Tara's hand.

"That's not when I first noticed Alex, though," Sandra said.

Alex grinned. "She noticed my muscled arms on the football field."

"Not quite." Sandra couldn't help but smile. "I noticed his long fingers in typing class. Can you believe our high school still had typing? We had just gotten our first computers." She glanced at Tara, who still seemed unimpressed. "Anyway, Alex had been the only boy in the class. It was hard *not* to notice him. I thought it strange at the time, that the high school's star running back would use one of his electives to take typing."

"See?" Alex said. "I told you. Sandra noticed me on the football field."

Sandra rolled her eyes. "It was only later I found out that Alex's mother had worked as a secretary and insisted that he know his way around a keyboard. Turned out to be good advice. Alex wound up supporting himself through college by doing medical transcriptions."

"Ninety words a minute, baby," Alex said with pride.

After the server came and took their orders, April, the restaurant's owner, appeared as she usually did when Alex and Blake were there, wrapping them in a friendly hug. While they chatted, Tara was folding and refolding her napkin. Yet again, Sandra took the initiative.

"So, where are you from, Tara? Did you grow up on Long Island?"

She nodded. "Sayville. Suffolk County. I live in Seaford now."

"Seaford?" Sandra said. "Hey, that's not too far from Alex and me."

Tara nodded and returned to her menu, leaving Sandra to stare at the April's Café logo. Wasn't Tara the one who was supposed to be trying to fit in? This was too much work.

When April left, Blake said, "Alex, I forgot to tell you. Missy called the other day." He turned to Tara. "Missy is the lead singer of a band up in Maine that we contracted with about a year ago. They're an '80s cover band."

"They do it all," Alex said. "George Michael. Joan Jett. Tom Petty. They put on a great show."

"Missy said we can use her parents' time-share at the ski resort again," Blake said. "This weekend. Her sister just had a baby, so they won't need it, and if we don't use it, it'll go unused."

"I love that place," Sandra said. "That's exciting."

"Lots of exciting news today, it seems," Alex said with a smile.

"Adopting a baby is exciting, too," Tara said.

Mic drop. Sandra's insides clenched again. She looked at Blake. "Yes, it is." Sounded like he and Tara had done a lot of talking. About Sandra's career. About Sandra and Alex adopting a baby.

"Sorry," Tara said. "Did I say something wrong?"

"Not at all," Alex said.

"How's that going?" Blake said. "The adoption?"

"Good." Alex took Sandra's hand. "Well, not so good, but we're hopeful." He looked at Tara. "We're not going through an adoption agency, which makes it a little harder."

"Why not?"

"We just don't have the money for that kind of thing," Alex said. "Plus, my uncle is an adoption lawyer, so he's been helping us, but no luck so far. We have an interview this afternoon, though. Out in Stony Brook. Thank God San's a writer because we have to write up these whole biographies about ourselves and why we think we'd be a good fit for a baby. I never know what to say."

Sandra had been so preoccupied with meeting Tara that she had forgotten about the adoption interview. Her heart began to race. She always got her hopes up before an interview, thinking this time would be different, but she had been disappointed so many times before.

"That's amazing," Blake said. "Maybe we can celebrate next weekend and ski."

"I don't think we'll hear anything on the spot," Sandra said.

"But we can celebrate anyway," Alex said.

"Alex would celebrate the sun rising every morning if he could," Sandra said to Tara, and, lo and behold, she thought she saw Tara smile. Just a little.

"Plus, it might be a nice way we can all get to know one another," Blake said. "You know, get away from things. What do you think, San?" Blake had that look in his eye, like *Please.*

"I've been trying to get Sandra to ski for *years*," Alex told Tara.

"Usually, I just go up there and write," Sandra said. "I don't see the point in strapping two sticks to your feet and throwing yourself down a mountain."

"Don't knock it till you try it, my love." Alex kissed Sandra on the cheek and then said to Tara, "As you can see, Sandra is the more conservative one in the relationship."

"I'm not conservative," Sandra said. "I'm sensible."

"She's also clumsy," Blake said.

"I am not!" Sandra demanded, but even she laughed a little. She *was* clumsy. Tara smiled again. It was at Sandra's expense, but at this point, she'd take anything.

"Then it's a date." Blake raised his glass in the air. "To friendship."

"And to new beginnings," Sandra said, raising her glass.

"Hear, hear," Alex said.

As they all drank, celebrating this weird, new dynamic, Sandra couldn't help but watch Tara out of the corner of her eye. To her surprise, or maybe not so surprising, Tara was watching her right back.

CHAPTER 4

Sunday, March 16, 3:00 p.m.

"Well, that went well," Sandra said, slamming the car door closed and wiping the rain from her glasses. The sky had opened up while they were in the restaurant; she could barely see through the front windshield.

"You were a little intense." Alex started the car, and the windshield wipers kicked on.

"Can you blame me?"

"Tara seems okay."

"She hates me."

Alex fastened his seat belt. "She doesn't hate you, San. Maybe she feels like you're coming on too strong. You can send her one of your books and get to know her more."

"Like she would ever read one of my books." Sandra shook her head. "Did you see her face when she found out I write romance?"

"What face?"

Men were so obtuse. "It was clear she didn't like me or what I do."

"It wasn't clear to *me*." Alex pulled out of the parking spot.

"Let's face it, Alex." Sandra threw up her hands. "You're the only one who loves me."

"Blake loves you."

"Yeah, well, let's see for how much longer."

Alex smiled. "Could it be that maybe you're a little nervous about the interview today and you're taking it out on Tara?"

"I'm actually not nervous about the adoption interview at all."

"You're not?"

"No, because I don't expect it to go well."

"Sandra . . ."

"No, really, Alex. How long have we been trying to adopt a baby? Every prospective birth mother we've met has seemed so nice and kind, and we got along really well, and I got my hopes up, and then *splat*. There go my hopes and dreams. I told you. No one likes me. And I'll probably make a terrible mother anyway, so what does it matter?" Sandra looked out the window so that Alex wouldn't see her eyes water.

"You'll make a wonderful mother, Sandra, and you know it." He put his hand on Sandra's, and she squeezed it. She loved that hand—and the man attached to it—more than she ever thought she could love anyone or anything.

Alex pushed a few buttons on the dashboard to set up the GPS. "Do you have the address?"

"One Twelve Piccolo Court." She had memorized it months ago, like she did with all the others, as if it did her any good. Maybe one day, on her deathbed, Alex could quiz her about the addresses of all the families that denied her having a family.

"Stony Brook, right?"

She nodded. "How long is the ride?"

"About forty minutes. Without traffic, at least."

They pulled onto the street, got onto the entrance to the Southern State Parkway a block down, and immediately came to a halt. The red taillights led all the way around the bend.

"Did you say *without traffic*?" Sandra asked. "You do know we live on Long Island, right?"

"I'm sure it'll clear up. Do you want to practice our mock interview questions? We haven't done them in a while."

"Do you mind if we just listen to music?" Sandra asked.

"As long as you promise not to sing." He pinched her cheek.

"I'll try to contain myself."

Alex turned on the radio and switched to a love song station. "Maybe your schmalzy music will cheer you up."

"Nothing like a good love song to bring out the potential mother qualities in you."

"Exactly!" he said.

As usual, Alex was right, and their traffic speed picked up pretty quickly once they drove past a family on the side of the road fixing a flat tire—a family of four with two small children, whom the mother was clutching. Sandra might have been stuck in traffic, and might have a best friend whose wife hated her, and she'd probably never be a mother, but, hey, she didn't have a flat tire. Things could always be worse.

Ugh, Alex's optimism was rubbing off on her.

They were mostly quiet for the rest of the way, and as much as Sandra didn't want to practice her mock interview skills, questions swirled around her brain.

Tell me about your marriage. What do you love most about your significant other?

What are some of your hobbies?

How would you describe your personality?

Why do you think you would be a good mother?

Why do you want to adopt?

What do you think your parenting style will be?

She tried to remember the answers she had come up with, but it had been a while since their last interview. She thought about taking Alex up on his offer to practice, but she was worried that would only serve to make her more panicky.

Just be yourself, she thought. *After all, look how well that went with Tara!*

Sandra's phone rang, and Blake's name appeared on the dashboard screen. Alex pushed the Answer button. "Hey," he said.

"So . . . what did you think of Tara?"

Alex looked at Sandra. He mouthed, *Be nice*.

"She was nice!" Sandra cooed.

"Wasn't she?" Blake said, sounding relieved. "I knew you guys would hit it off."

The car's GPS noted the next turn.

"Blake, we gotta go, buddy. We're almost at the house."

"You'll make a great mother, San," Blake said.

The tears welled in her eyes again. "Thanks, Blakey." Was she even allowed to call him Blakey anymore?

"Bye, brother." Alex clicked off the call as the GPS announced their arrival and they pulled in front of a beautiful Tudor-style home that was the size of Alex's office building.

"Nice house," Alex said.

"Is that what this is? I thought it was city hall." Sandra had done a bit of research on Stony Brook. It *was* a nice neighborhood, and she didn't know whether the fact that she and Alex couldn't afford to live there on their salaries worked for or against them. Probably against.

"Well, here goes nothing, right?" Alex said. "We're ready, San."

She was not ready. But she kept smiling.

They got out of the car and approached the front door, which opened before they had a chance to knock. That's what happened in nice neighborhoods, she guessed. If a strange car pulled up in front of your house, you immediately noticed.

The woman standing before them was around Sandra's age; her designer clothing probably cost more than Sandra's last car payment.

"You must be Alex," the woman said, reaching to shake Alex's hand.

Breathe, Sandra, breathe.

"Yes, and you must be Mrs. Burke," Alex said. "It's a pleasure to meet you. This is my wife, Sandra."

The woman shook Sandra's hand. "Nice to meet you. Come in."

Before Sandra and Alex even made it into the entryway, Mrs. Burke said, "I feel I must tell you that we've already made a decision regarding the adoption of my grandchild, but my brother-in-law thinks very highly of your uncle, who apparently is a wonderful pickleball player." She wrinkled her nose. "So . . . I thought I would offer the courtesy of seeing you. I mean, you never know, right?"

Sandra knew. There was no way this woman was going to hand over her grandchild to them. There was no perfect interview answer that would ever make that happen. She handed

Mrs. Burke her folder anyway. "Here are my written documents."

Mrs. Burke placed them under her arm like a football. "Follow me upstairs. Casey is expecting you. But we shouldn't stay for long. She needs her rest."

So did Sandra after the day she was having.

Alex took Sandra's hand, and they followed Mrs. Burke upstairs past an array of family photos. Casey appeared to be an only child, judging by the number of family photos that showed three people: Mrs. Burke, presumably Mr. Burke, and presumably Casey, who seemed lovely, at least in two dimensions. Apparently, the Burke family had done a lot of traveling together. The other photos were all of Casey alone. Casey in a bejeweled dance leotard. Casey in a baseball uniform, squaring up. Casey surfing. A tiny Casey standing on a stage with a graduation cap tilted on her head.

"You have a beautiful family," Sandra said, which sounded corny and very "please like me," but she meant it. Her insides were squeezing with jealousy.

"Thank you," Mrs. Burke said in that way that showed she agreed. She knocked on a bedroom door that had sketches of clothing designs taped to it. It looked like Casey wanted to be the next Donna Karan. "Casey, they're here." She opened the door.

Sandra couldn't help but smile when she walked into the teenage girl's bedroom. There were posters on the wall of guys and bands and selfies of Casey with a bunch of girls. By the looks of it, Casey Burke seemed very popular. The girl was sitting on her bed, her legs crossed beneath her.

"Casey," Mrs. Burke said, with a grand gesture, "this is Alex and Sandra Connor."

"Sandra Wilson," Alex corrected. "Sandra uses her maiden name."

"Oh... very progressive," Mrs. Burke said, and then directed her attention to her daughter. "Would you like me to stay?"

"No, that's all right, Mom."

Sandra was expecting Mrs. Burke to hand her folder to Casey, but she didn't. "I'm just down the hall if you need anything," Mrs. Burke said. Then she closed the bedroom door softly as if she were afraid to wake the unborn baby.

"Please have a seat." Casey indicated her desk chair. She looked a lot like her mother, with short blond hair that fell straight around her face. Alex pulled out the chair for Sandra, and he leaned against the wall.

"If you'd like a chair, too," Casey said, "I can get one from—"

"No, I'm fine here," Alex said with a smile, putting his hand on Sandra's shoulder.

"How are you feeling?" Sandra asked.

Casey shrugged. "Better now. The first trimester was rough. I think I missed, like, every first-period class because I was in the nurse's office."

"It must be hard to keep up with your classes when you're not feeling well," Sandra said.

"Unfortunately, my mom is good about getting me the notes," Casey said with a laugh. "I've managed to maintain my straight-A average even while pregnant."

"Wow, that's amazing," Alex said. "I couldn't even maintain a B average my high school senior year—and I wasn't pregnant!"

Sandra inwardly frowned. Was it a good idea for Alex to mention he wasn't a top-notch student? Sandra had a feeling academics would be important to the Burke family. At least the mother.

"I don't think I have a choice," Casey said. "I've already been accepted to Princeton. Early decision."

"Congratulations," Sandra said.

"That was before we found out about this little guy." Casey pointed to her belly.

Sandra let out a gasp. "Oh my gosh, you're having a boy?"

"I'm sorry. Did you, like, not want to know?" Casey asked.

"No, that's fine. It's just . . . I don't remember the sex of the baby being mentioned in the paperwork."

"I just found out last week. Mom thought it wasn't a good idea to find out, but I bribed the lab tech to tell me."

"Nice!" Alex said with a laugh. "What did you bribe the tech with?"

"Reese's Peanut Butter Cups."

"That's all?"

"The lab tech's daughter has a peanut allergy, so she's not allowed to eat peanut butter at home. She feels guilty buying them, so I figured if I bought them, then they would be a gift. No guilt necessary. She agreed." Casey smiled, and Sandra couldn't help but admire her teeth, which were whiter and straighter than most celebrities'. Had Sandra even remembered to brush her teeth that morning? The odds weren't good. "I also gave her some Altoids so her breath didn't smell when she got home."

"That was very thoughtful," Sandra said.

"More like *devious*, but who am I to quibble about adjectives?" Alex said. "Sandra's the writer."

"Oh, really? What do you write?"

Sandra hesitated. She had already gotten the look of condescension from Tara that morning. She didn't want to get the same look from a teenager. She had a feeling sweet romance novels weren't Casey's cup of tea. She seemed too cool for them somehow. "I'm a business writer by day . . . and write romance novels at night."

"Really?" Casey's eyes went wide.

"Not *that* kind," Sandra said with a laugh. "I tried once, but I couldn't get past first base. I don't know why I thought it would be easy."

"Because they say you should write what you know." Alex winked at her.

Oh, God! Alex! This isn't the time for your blue humor. She smiled as demurely as she could for Casey, who laughed out loud, but then she suddenly cleared her throat and turned serious.

"As I was saying," Casey said, "I feel very strongly that my baby has a good family and gets a good education."

What? Casey hadn't been saying that. And she was no longer looking at Sandra. She was looking behind her. Sandra turned around to see Mrs. Burke standing there.

"How's it going in here?" Mrs. Burke asked.

"Great," Alex said. "You have a wonderful daughter."

Mrs. Burke was flipping through Sandra's painstakingly written documents like she was skimming a magazine at the doctor's office. "Yes, she is." She paused. "It says here that the two of you went to college locally? On Long Island?"

"Yes," Sandra said.

"Neither of you wanted to go away?" she asked.

Sandra glanced at Alex, who, for the first time, appeared injured, and Sandra's protective instincts emerged. "Alex got a football scholarship for Ohio State, but decided to go to a local school so he could take care of his mom, who was sick."

This seemed to have gotten Mrs. Burke's attention. She looked up from the folder. "Oh, I'm sorry to hear that. My condolences."

"No need," Sandra said when Alex didn't say anything. "She's still with us. Alex's mom fought cancer and beat it."

"Kicked its ass, actually," Alex said with a smile.

"That's amazing," Casey said.

"And for me . . . Well, Alex and I were dating at the time I was applying to schools. He and I were having too much fun for me to think about going away. There are good schools and good people on Long Island. I went to Adelphi University and graduated with an English degree."

"Which has served her well," Alex said. "She has some long-time freelance clients who pay her well and does the business writing for my company. Honestly, Sandra is, like, half the reason we've been so successful."

"Well, a third maybe," Sandra said.

"So, tell us why you decided to adopt?" Mrs. Burke asked Sandra pointedly.

Sandra froze. *What had she written down as her answer for that one?* Mrs. Burke's unfriendly face was like a barrier to her memory. Luckily, Alex picked up on Sandra's hesitation and answered the question. As he talked about their inability to get pregnant, a feeling of anxiety coursed through Sandra. It really wasn't fair. Couples who could get pregnant didn't have to deal with these kinds of interviews or judgments. Sandra had always hated the feeling of wanting to get picked. Whether it was for dodgeball in junior high school. Or a freelance job. Everything was a popularity contest. Sandra never minded being unpopular. Until that morning with Tara. And until she tried to adopt a baby.

"Interesting," Mrs. Burke said when Alex finished. She shuffled her feet. "I don't know if Casey told you, but we feel very strongly about two things. Right, Casey?"

Casey seemed to be sitting up straighter than before. She nodded dutifully at her mother.

"The first is that our baby is raised by two parents, which, obviously"—she gestured toward Sandra and Alex—"is not an issue here. The second is that we are interested in having an open adoption. We want Casey to be a part of her baby's life. Would that be a problem?"

"No," Sandra said. "It's important for the baby to know who his biological mother is."

"His?" Mrs. Burke glanced at Casey.

"It slipped," Casey said.

"Hmmm . . . Lots of things seem to be slipping around you lately," Mrs. Burke said, and Sandra couldn't help but wonder if she was referring to contraception. "Okay, last question before I let you go . . ."

Wait . . . Were she and Alex leaving already?

"May I ask why you're not working with an adoption agency?" Mrs. Burke asked. "That's very risky, no?"

"And also very expensive, unfortunately," Alex said.

"Well, some things are worth it, no?"

"It's just a decision that we made together," Sandra said. "A private decision."

"I see." Mrs. Burke nodded slowly.

"Well." Sandra stood up. She had had enough. She didn't know if it was because of the whole Tara thing, but she was tired of acting like a dancing monkey in front of people and hoping they liked her. There were other babies out there for whom she and Alex wouldn't have to jump through hoops to prove themselves, other families who could see they were good people. And if there weren't, that was okay, too. She didn't need an Ivy League pedigree to prove she could love a child. She took Alex's hand. "Thank you so very much for welcoming us into your home." She turned to Casey. "You're a lovely young woman, and I know you'll do great at Princeton. Thank you for taking the time to see us."

Mrs. Burke wasted no time. She set Sandra's folder on Casey's desk and said, "I'll see you out then. We appreciate you both coming down. Right, Casey?"

"Yes, thank you," the young woman said, standing up and shaking Sandra and Alex's hands. "It was lovely to meet you."

Mrs. Burke led them down the stairway. "I wish you the best of luck."

"Same to you and Casey," Sandra said politely.

As she and Alex walked down the carefully power-washed brick path past the perfectly manicured lawn, Sandra couldn't get into the car fast enough.

"Well, what do you think?" Alex said as they buckled themselves into the front seat.

"What do I think? Well, how do you feel about getting a dog instead?" she asked with a smile.

Alex wasn't smiling.

"What's the matter?" she asked.

"I'm so sorry, San."

"Sorry for what? There's nothing to be sorry about, Alex."

"Maybe we can look at a sperm bank or—"

"I told you. I don't want to go to a sperm bank. I don't need a biological child. I just want a child who needs us, who needs a loving family. We decided we would give a needy baby a home. If it's not Casey Burke's baby, that's okay."

"I love you. You know that?" He kissed her on the mouth as Sandra's phone pinged. She looked at the phone number. She didn't recognize it.

"Who is it?" Alex asked.

"I don't know." She pressed the number and read the text:

Are you free this week? I'd love to get together and talk some more.

"I don't know who it is," she said. "Wait . . ."
"Wait, what?"
"Could it be Tara?"
"See?" Alex said, perking up. "I told you she liked you."
Impossible. Every cell in Sandra's body told her otherwise. Could she have been this wrong about a person? She sighed. Yes, she *could*. When Alex had asked her out, she thought it had been a joke. She had no idea her heart could hold so much love and her life could become so much bigger. She wasn't always right.

She looked over at her husband who, despite himself, was singing along to one of her schmalzy songs. Maybe he was right. Sandra was so busy trying to make a good impression and so busy being mad at Blake for not telling them about Tara, that maybe she hadn't realized that Tara was cool and wanted to be friends. She wrote:

Sure, my schedule is flexible. What day/time? And where?

"Pretty soon, you and Tara will be best friends." Alex made a right-hand turn, following signs toward the highway.

Sandra's phone pinged again. "I don't know about that."

"What do you mean?"

"Turns out, it wasn't Tara who texted me," Sandra said.

"It wasn't?"

"It was Casey."

Alex stopped at a red light and looked at her. "Casey?"

"She must have gotten my phone number from the paperwork Mrs. Burke left on her desk. She wants to meet with me again."

"Alone?"

Sandra shrugged. "I guess. She didn't say."

"When?"

"This Friday. She's asking if I'm free around eleven. What time are we leaving for Vermont?"

"We can leave anytime you want. Go meet her."

"Honestly, Alex, should I even bother? You saw how Mrs. Burke was. There's no way we're getting this kid."

"What's the harm? Meet her. Chat. Have a bite to eat."

Sandra sighed and texted Casey back a yes even though she knew it should be a no. There was no point in letting this drag on. Why should Sandra punish herself any more than she already had? Casey texted back immediately.

"She wants to meet at some place called the Langford Tea Room in Stony Brook at 11:00 a.m."

"Oh, I think that's right by the Long Island Music and Entertainment Hall of Fame. While you're lunching, I can stop by and drop off those flyers for Chuck's upcoming gig in June. And then when you're done, we'll hop on the ferry and head to Vermont. Easy peasy."

Alex thought everything was easy peasy. It was part of his charm. "So, let me get this straight," Sandra said. "I'm trying to be friends with a woman who wants nothing to do with me."

"You don't know that."

"And I'm trying to impress a young woman whose mother will never let me adopt her child."

"You don't know that either."

"Maybe. I do know something, though . . ."

"What's that?" Alex asked as he turned onto the highway.

She reached for his hand and squeezed.

"Me too, baby," he said, squeezing back. "Me too."

CHAPTER 5

MONDAY, MARCH 17, 9:00 A.M.

THE LONG ISLAND RAIL Road train rumbled into the elevated station, and Sandra tilted down her umbrella to watch the sausages of steel come to a halt. The train cars appeared crowded even though it was the tail end of the morning rush hour. Maybe the rain had slowed people down.

She watched the passengers' bored faces, imagining herself sitting next to them on her way to New York City for the day. She had never regretting not working in Manhattan—something Mrs. Burke probably wouldn't understand—but had always wondered if she was missing out on something. There was a certain cache that came with working there—and also a certain bump in salary that she and Alex could use. She had said no to a few corporate writing jobs in the City so that she could spend more time helping Alex grow his company, but that had been her choice. And, truth be told, she wanted to stay close to home because she thought she'd have a new baby to come home to at night one day. Sandra's body suddenly wrenched with longing.

She balanced the three cups of coffee in her hand as she opened the door to Napkin Marketing's office building. As she stepped inside, she placed the coffees on the floor and wiped her glasses. Why did she even bother carrying an umbrella? The rain always managed to find her lenses. She picked up the coffees and the mail that had been left on the floor and walked up the stairs, admiring, as she always did, the eleven-by-fourteen photographs of the musical acts that Blake and Alex worked with. Jack and the Trippers, a lighthearted group that did '70s covers. Angel Sass, a rhythm-and-blues singer from out east that, according to Alex, was slowly building a following. The photo at the top of the stairs featured Axe Handle with Care, a metal band that Alex had somehow picked up while she and he were having dinner at a Mexican restaurant once—Sandra's ears were still ringing from the performance of theirs they attended five years ago.

As she rounded the landing on the second floor, she glanced at the photo of Chuck onstage with his band, Rockknot, sweat spraying from his hair like a propeller. He had such joy on his face when he performed. She had seen that same joy when he was on the dance floor with his wife, Beatrice, Saturday night, which made Sandra like Chuck even more.

She opened Napkin Marketing's office door.

"Is that you, babe?" Alex called.

"Yeah, it's me."

She walked into the first office and plopped the letters into Blake's inbox, which was empty and looked like it had been wiped clean. It probably *had* been. Blake was notoriously fastidious about his space—unlike Alex, who never met a dust bunny he didn't like. Blake was sitting at his desk, reaching for a sheet of paper from the printer.

"Hey, San, how are you doing?" he said with concern.

"I'm fine, why?"

"It's just... Alex told me about the meeting with the Burkes yesterday. I'm sorry it didn't work out."

"Who says it didn't work out?!" Alex called from the next office.

Sandra had no idea why there were even walls in this place. You could hear everything that went on in every room. "Let's be realistic, Alex," she called back. "It didn't work out."

"Casey wants to see you on Friday, right?" Alex yelled.

"Yeah, but we don't know why. She seemed interested in writing. Maybe she wants some advice." Sandra shrugged and looked at Blake. "You know Alex. The eternal optimist."

"You would make such a great mother, San," Blake said. "Tara thinks so, too."

Sandra swallowed a sneer. How could Tara think she would be a good mother? She barely knew her. And she had missed an opportunity to *get* to know her the day before. Sandra placed Blake's coffee in the coaster on his desk and left the room. She didn't want to talk about Tara as much as she didn't want to talk about babies.

By the time she got to Alex's office, he was already out of his chair and wrapping her in one of his patented "it will all be okay" Alex hugs.

"I'm fine," she said.

"I know, but . . ."

"Don't say it."

"I just want you to know that it hasn't *not* worked out yet." He scrunched up his face. "Hasn't not? Is that right?" Double negatives always confused Alex. She squeezed his chin with her hand.

"Yes, and I know," she lied. "There's always hope." There was no use going against Alex's optimism, which was like Kryptonite.

She wriggled out of Alex's embrace, went into her office, and plopped into her chair. She was happy Blake and Alex had given her her own space to use; she had to share it with a copy machine and a bunch of file cabinets, but she didn't care. It was a nice change of pace to working from home, even with its uninspiring view of the parking lot. She thought of Tara spending her days in the halls of a high school, with all the activity and chatter and laughing that came with that, and she was a bit jealous. Maybe Sandra should have chosen a career where she worked with children. The way the adoption process was going, it might be the only way she would be able to spend her days around them.

Alex came in and sat in the chair in front of her desk. Blake followed. She giggled. Having an office was great, but she got way more work done at home where these two clowns weren't around. Blake was holding the paper he had printed out in his hand.

"What's that?" she asked.

"We just got invited to a pop-up event for Axe Handle with Care on Wednesday."

"*This* Wednesday? Talk about last minute," Sandra said.

"I think that's part of the allure," Alex said. "These things just pop up out of nowhere, and the lucky ones find out about it through text, email, or social media."

"Are you going?" Sandra asked.

"We have a conflict," Blake said. "That's the night of the local marketing association meeting."

"To quote my wife . . . *ugh*," Alex said, resting his head on the top of Sandra's desk. "Those things are *so* boring."

Sandra reached over and mussed Alex's hair.

"We already RSVP'd for two, though," Blake said. "We don't want to make a bad impression."

"Wait... I have an idea," Alex said. "We can split up and go to both."

"I really don't want to go alone," Blake said.

"You don't have to. San, you can go with him, right?" Alex suggested.

"Me? Why would I want to go? They're *boring*."

"They usually have some speaker there that talks about marketing," Alex said. "You know—social media best practices, writing press releases, how to get social influencers interested in your clients, etc."

That did sound interesting. And Sandra didn't have anything planned for Wednesday. She rarely had anything planned at all. She had caught up on quite a few Netflix shows over the years as Alex was out and about acquiring clients. "Are you sure?" she asked, looking at Blake. "What about Tara? Would she want to go?"

"Probably not. After a day spent talking about her school's zero-tolerance bullying policy to a bunch of bullies, she likes to kick off her shoes at night, put her pajamas on, and watch Netflix."

So far, that sounded like one of the only things that she and Tara had in common. A streaming service.

"C'mon, Sandra," Alex pleaded. "Don't make me go to this and learn things."

"Oh, all right." She stuck out her tongue at her husband.

"Great," Blake said. "It's settled. Sandra and I will tackle the marketing association. It'll be good. Lyle Mathers, the guy who operates all those high-end pizzerias on Long Island, will be there."

"Since when did you guys start working with restaurants?" she asked. "I thought you were doing the music thing."

"Can't we do both?" Blake asked.

"Of course, you can. I just didn't know." Sandra thought of Tara. She didn't know about a lot of things lately.

"Like you, San," Blake said. "You write romance, and you write social media posts, and you write press releases and emails. You're a regular Renaissance woman! We're taking our cues from you." He smiled.

Sandra looked at Alex, who shrugged. "Blake thinks we should diversify," he said.

"You know, be more than just a music-client company," Blake said. "Tara and I were talking . . ."

"About Napkin Marketing?" Sandra asked.

"Yeah, why not? I mean, you talk about the business with Alex, right?"

Sandra shrugged. Blake had a point, although Sandra was connected to the business; her name was on the bank account so she could make deposits.

"And Tara was saying that diversity might be the way to go," Blake continued. "She had a lot of really interesting ideas."

"But being really good at one thing makes you an expert," Alex said.

It wasn't hard to detect the disagreement in Alex's voice, mainly because Alex rarely disagreed with anyone. "What do you think, San?" Alex asked.

Sandra didn't like getting involved with Blake and Alex's decision-making. *Unlike Tara, apparently.* "Well, I can see both your points."

"Surprise, surprise," Alex said with a smile. "When are you running for office?"

"What I mean is, I agree with Alex that having a specialty might be good," she said, "and yet I also think it might be a good idea not to keep all your eggs in one basket. Maybe you can have two divisions. Blake oversees food, and you"—she squeezed Alex's arm—"oversee music." Before either one of them could react, she continued. "And . . . now that that's settled" —she pulled toward her desk—"I better hire a photographer for Wednesday night's pop-up."

"See if José is available," Alex said. "He's awesome."

"Got it." Sandra picked up her phone and was about to call José, when she heard a "yoo hoo" come from the hallway, followed by the smell of freshly baked cookies.

CHAPTER 6

Monday, March 17, 9:30 a.m.

Pam Connor blew into Sandra's office with vigor and a smile.

"I should have known you'd all be in here. I don't know why you bother having more than one office. You're always all together." She wrapped Alex in a hug and kissed his head. "Hello, handsome. I made your favorite." She pointed to the oatmeal raisin cookies.

"Thanks, Mom!" he said, kissing her cheek.

Pam used to be the type to never smile too much because it caused wrinkles. Since the cancer, she smiled hard all the time. "Hello, lovelies!" she chirped to Sandra and Blake. She looked as put together as ever in a tan double-breasted pants suit with a black V-neck and cropped blazer. Even when she was fighting cancer, vomiting into the bucket Sandra was holding beside her bed, her mother-in-law never lost her zest for appearances. She had Sandra bring her makeup and business suits to the hospital: "They make me feel like myself," she had said. Sandra had known Pam practically as long as she had known Alex, and even *she* had never seen Pam wearing anything that didn't need to be dry-cleaned.

Alex offered his mother his chair. "Where you off to today?"

"Oh, you know, the usual boring meetings." Pam plopped into the chair. As a longtime vice president of Capital Bank, she made her own schedule, which gave her the chance to stop by Alex's office as much as she liked, her favorite activity. She crossed her shapely legs and indicated the black pump on her foot. "Aren't these great, San?"

Pam's open schedule also allowed time to shoe shop, her second favorite activity. Sandra had gone to many a clearance shoe sale with her mother-in-law, flipping through bins for just the right style and color. It was that same perseverance and patience that got her through chemotherapy.

"They're great," Sandra said.

"But enough about me, I'd much rather talk about you." Pam set her gaze on Sandra. "How did it go yesterday?" Before Sandra could answer, Pam turned to Blake. "Actually, Blake, talk to me. How's business?"

Sandra had never met anyone as intuitive as Pam Connor. She could probably tell with just a glance that Sandra didn't want to talk about yesterday, so she wouldn't make her. She adored her mother-in-law for that. She was kind that way, putting Sandra's feelings before her own curiosity. Pam Connor would make a far better grandma than Mrs. Burke.

Before Blake could answer, Pam stood up and grabbed his face, moving it from side to side. "Hmmm . . . are you okay? You don't look too good."

"I'm fine, Pam," Blake said, although Sandra could see him shrink a little. "In fact . . ." He showed her his hand. "I got married over the weekend."

"Married? Very funny!" Pam glanced again at Sandra, who forced a smile. Then Pam glanced at Alex, who smiled, too. "Wait, you seriously got married?"

"I seriously did," Blake said.

"Why do I not know this person? Why haven't I met this person?"

Sandra had the urge to yell *See!* to Alex. Even her mother-in-law thought all this secrecy was weird.

"Mom, you don't have to know *everything*." Alex pulled the plastic wrap from the plate of cookies and avoided making eye contact with Sandra.

"Yes, I do have to know everything, but that's beside the point." Pam pulled Blake into a hug. "Well, congratulations. I would say married life looks good on you, but you look like you're coming down with a cold." She squeezed him a little harder. "And you feel like you're losing weight. Does your bride cook?"

"Yes." Blake patted his stomach. "Very well."

"Well, you'll have to invite her to the house one of these days. We'll have a big dinner and all get to know one another."

"Alex and Sandra met Tara yesterday," Blake said with a smile. "Right, San?"

"Right." Sandra avoided her mother-in-law's piercing gaze. "Tell her, Alex." *Please!*

"She's really nice, Mom," Alex began, and as he waxed poetically about yesterday's brunch, Sandra decided to take a good look at Blake.

Pam was right. Something *did* seem off with him. He looked kinda pale. And, yes, thin. Ugh. Sandra had been too busy feeling sorry for herself because of Casey, or Tara, or both, that she hadn't noticed. What kind of best friend was she? Maybe he *did* have a cold. Or, blah, COVID. There were a few expired tests lying around the office. She could get him to take one.

"Well, I'd better be off," Pam said. "I have a ten-thirty meeting in Plainview and a coupon for DSW Shoes. Love you all, especially you." She pointed to Alex.

"I'll walk you out, Mom." Alex took another cookie and left the office with his mother.

"You know, you do look a little rundown," Sandra said to Blake when they were alone. "Have you been sleeping well?"

"Not really."

"Too much excitement?"

"Too much sex, probably."

Sandra rolled her eyes. "This is a conversation I do *not* want to have."

"Seriously, San, I can't remember when I've had this much physical activit—"

"Alrighty then . . ." Sandra scooted Blake out of her office. "Out, out, out. I have photographers to hire and social media posts to write."

Blake smiled. "Don't be jealous."

"I'll try not to be." Sandra started up the computer on her desk.

"Are you really okay with coming with me Wednesday night to the marketing association meeting?" he asked.

"Sure. I'll be working from home, so send me the address and I'll meet you there."

"It's a date," Blake said, and left the office.

Sandra logged in to her computer. Was it sad that she was looking forward to a boring marketing meeting? Probably. She needed to find some friends. Other than Tara, of course, who didn't seem to want to be friends. There was a very good chance that she and Alex would never be able to adopt, and she had to be okay with that and make room for other things in her life. Where did forty-somethings go to meet people? There had to be an app for that. Was she supposed to swipe left? Or right? She had no idea. All she knew was she would probably get more warmth from a two-dimensional profile than she had from Blake's new wife.

CHAPTER 7

WEDNESDAY, MARCH 19, 6:00 P.M.

THE LONG ISLAND SMALL Business Marketers Association's monthly meeting was being held in a historic building in Amityville, and Sandra counted her lucky stars that it wasn't the infamous Horror House, which was the only historic building she knew in the area.

She pulled open the heavy wooden door of the old bank and ducked inside. She didn't know what to expect when she got there and was immediately surprised by the dozens of people in attendance, most of them women.

"San!" Blake waved from the refreshment table. He looked handsome in his khakis and sweater, but Sandra couldn't get what Pam said out of her mind. She had asked Alex earlier how Blake was, and he seemed to think he was fine, but there was still a dullness to Blake's complexion, like he had applied the wrong shade of foundation.

"Hey," Sandra said when she got to him. "Are you sure you're feeling okay?"

"Never better, San." Blake handed her a bottle of water. "Is this still about Pam? You know Pam. If we don't dance or have bright smiles on our faces, she thinks something's wrong."

"That's true." Sandra looked around. "So, what's the mission here?"

"You know, our favorite thing. Networking." Blake rolled his eyes.

"This is like the blind leading the blind," Sandra said with a laugh. "What was I thinking? We should be the ones at the pop-up. Going temporarily deaf from the heavy metal music would be a better time than striking up a conversation with a bunch of strangers."

"Yeah, well, maybe it's time we learn, right? We can't lean on Alex our whole lives. I think we just need to come up with a plan."

Sandra looked around. "Okay, so what do you think?"

"You take that side of the room. I'll take this side. I'll meet you in the middle."

"That's your plan?"

"You got anything better?"

"Nope. Looks like I'll meet you in the middle," she said, and they fist-bumped one another and went their separate ways.

Sandra cracked open the bottle of water Blake had given her and took a quick sip as she began walking. She wasn't sure if she should make eye contact or listen for a familiar topic of conversation and then lean in. Unfortunately, everyone already seemed to know one another. She held on to the water bottle for dear life. Talking to people—especially without Alex—was not her strong suit. She had become a writer to avoid this kind of thing.

Within fifteen minutes, she had made it all around the room without managing one conversation. That had to be a new record of some kind for a networking meeting.

"Well, you look about as excited to be here as I am," said a young woman with jet-black hair and long jet-black fingernails to match.

"It's that obvious, huh?" Sandra said, embarrassed. "Sandra Wilson." She extended her hand.

"Viola Gomez." She shook Sandra's hand. "Nice to meet you. What do you do, Sandra Wilson?"

"Well, I'm a writer, here representing Napkin Marketing, which is my husband's marketing firm."

"Is that your husband over there?" She pointed to Blake, who was talking to a middle-aged bald man with a clearly dyed goatee. Sandra wondered if that was Lyle Mathers, the pizza guy. "I saw the two of you together."

"Oh, no, that's my best friend . . . er, my friend Blake." Sandra had to keep reminding herself that she was no longer a teenager. "What do *you* do?"

"Well . . ." Viola's cheeks tinged red. "I'm a deejay, and I'm here, I guess, trying to figure out how to market my business. I'm ashamed to say, but I'm a TikTok virgin."

"Yeah, I'm not the greatest at it, either," Sandra admitted. "But I'm sure you'll pick it up quickly. And, if you don't, my husband is a whiz at TikTok."

"Really?"

"Yeah, I'm supposed to be the business's marketer, but he picked it up in no time. You should check out the company's profile at *Napkin hyphen Marketing*."

"I think I'll do that. Do you have a business card?"

"I actually do." Sandra was happy she had grabbed a handful of Alex's cards before she left. She took a pen out of her purse and wrote her phone number on the back, handing it to Viola. "Here you go. I jotted my number on the back or you can call Alex directly here." She pointed to the front of the card. "When you reach out to Alex, just let him know that we spoke tonight. I think you'll love him. Everyone does."

"Thanks, Sandra. I'll be in touch."

As Viola walked away, Sandra could hardly believe that she had given away one of Alex's business cards. Just then a woman in a graphic T-shirt clapped her hands at the front of the room.

"Attention, everyone. I'm so happy to see such a tremendous turnout tonight. We'll be starting the program shortly, so please grab a coffee, tea, or water, and take a seat."

Sandra made her way toward the back of the room and sat down. If Alex had been there, he would have preferred to be up front, but she knew that Blake, a fellow wallflower, wouldn't mind. When he sat down next to her, he put a business card on Sandra's leg. She looked down. It read Lyle Mathers, Long Island Restaurant Group.

"Victory," he said. "I think I made a good initial sales pitch. He wants me to send over a proposal in the morning."

"Tomorrow morning? Looks like you'll be up all night."

"It'll be worth it, San. One large account like Lyle's is worth ten of these rinky-dink music groups. Did you meet anyone?"

Sandra was reluctant to say she had just pitched another rinky-dink music person. "Not sure," she said.

"No matter. I'm really looking forward to this weekend."

"Me too," Sandra lied.

"Liar." Blake smiled, plucking a hair from the lapel of Sandra's blazer. "Can you try? For me? Tara really doesn't have any family. No real friends. Show her a little of that Sandra magic."

"It's just . . ." Sandra took a swig of water, which she knew was a tell that she was uneasy. "I mean, I'm happy for you, Blake. I really am, but don't you think this whole marriage thing was a little fast?"

"Not if you know what you want, San."

"And you want Tara?"

"I want to be happy." Blake's smile disappeared. "I was hoping you would approve."

"I do, I mean . . . Alex says I'm being selfish. Maybe I am, but it doesn't seem like Tara is trying to meet me halfway."

"You're more sociable than she is."

"Okay, now that's just sad." Sandra couldn't help but laugh.

Blake laughed, too. "It is, kinda."

The woman in the graphic tee got to the front of the room and began talking. Sandra was trying to pay attention, but Blake leaned over.

"This reminds me of Spanish class, the two of us in the back of the room."

"Yeah, and how many times did you get me in trouble for talking while the teacher was speaking? I see old habits die hard."

"If you could reach out to Tara, San, I'd really appreciate it. She's too shy to call or text you."

"Oh, all right. If I'm going to make a fool of myself, I might as well do it for my best friend."

"Awesome. Thank you," Blake said as a social media marketer was introduced at the front of the room and began to speak about the strategy of turning followers into superfans.

Maybe Sandra would pick up a few tips on how to get her best friend's wife to do the same.

CHAPTER 8

Friday, March 21, 11:00 a.m.

THE PICNIC-STYLE TABLES OUTSIDE the Langford Tea Room were overrun with teenagers. So was the restaurant, which looked like a school cafeteria. A bunch of girls were piled into a corner booth near a back exit and laughing hysterically over something on one of their phones, glancing at a group of boys at a nearby table. Was there some kind of school holiday that Sandra didn't know about?

The hostess appeared behind her podium, harried and maybe even a bit perturbed as she glanced around at the few remaining tables. Sandra had a feeling a lot of these kids bought a scone that they shared between them for hours, leaving no room for the paying customers. How bright-eyed they all seemed, though. And confident. She wondered if she and Alex had looked that way in high school. She certainly hadn't *felt* that way. Even after the high school football star asked her out on a date. Even after she married him.

"One?" the hostess asked, her carefully trimmed eyebrows raised.

"Two." Sandra held up two fingers. "I'm waiting for someone."

The hostess nodded and quickly brought Sandra to a two-person table tucked near the windows. When she sat, the hostess placed two menus down. "Your server will be right with you."

Sandra glanced out the window and could see where Alex had parked the car. She thought the car would be empty and that Alex would have already gone into the Long Island Music and Entertainment Hall of Fame, but Alex's bare feet were on the steering wheel, his long toes curled around the top. *Looks like he hasn't made it in yet.* A good song was probably playing on the radio. Or he was napping. That guy could sleep anywhere.

A Mercedes filled with teenagers pulled out of a parking spot nearby, and a BMW pulled in right after them. Parking certainly was hard to come by in this place. The BMW's door opened, and Casey emerged. She was wearing a cute pastel green shirt that was loose around her waist and fell over a pair of ripped jeans—if they were maternity, they certainly didn't look like it. A matching sweater hung over her shoulders. Casey waved to a group of girls who were standing near the handicapped ramp. They didn't wave back. And as she made her way into the tea room, the girls seemed to giggle and roll their eyes.

Sandra did *not* miss high school.

Casey walked in and drew the attention of the girls in the corner booth, but when their eyes met, she seemed to ignore them as she scanned the restaurant. When she saw Sandra, she smiled and walked over.

"Sorry I'm a little late," she said. "My AP Gov teacher wanted to see me after class."

"Is everything okay?"

"Yeah, he went to Princeton and wanted to give me some literature."

"Oh, that was nice. Did he give you a recommendation?"

Casey nodded. "I think that one might have done the trick." She ran her hand along her belly. "Sometimes I wonder if he wants to take the recommendation back." She smiled.

Casey may have been smiling, but Sandra wondered if there was concern behind her comment. "I doubt it. I don't know him, but it's clear you're a solid student."

"I try." Casey picked up the menu. "They have a great tea service here. A little of everything." She seemed relaxed and glowing, as a new mom should be.

"Hi, Casey," said a young girl who walked toward their table with a boy in a hoodie. Sandra assumed they were friends of

Casey's, but Casey responded coolly, and the couple stood there awkwardly.

"Hi," Casey said, and kept looking at her menu.

"How are you feeling?" the girl asked.

"Great. How are you?" Casey's eyes stayed on the menu.

"I'm . . . um, good, I guess," the girl said.

"Great. Nice seeing you." Casey drew her attention to Sandra as the girl and boy eventually walked off.

"She seemed . . . nice," Sandra said.

"Yeah, well, I thought so too until she went on Snapchat and told everyone I was pregnant."

"That's terrible. How did she find out?"

"I was an idiot and told her." Casey rolled her eyes. "I thought she was my best friend."

"Do you have a lot of friends?" Sandra asked.

"*Had* a lot of friends." Casey shrugged. "I seemed to have lost a few when this little guy came onto the scene." She rubbed her belly. "I guess you really don't know who your friends are until you get pregnant. Now I'm just some weird sideshow for people. Or maybe a cautionary tale."

"I wouldn't sweat it. You're gonna put this place behind you in a few months. You're due at the end of June, right?" Sandra knew Casey's due date and probable date of conception by heart, but she didn't want to appear obsessed.

Casey nodded. "I head down to Princeton in mid-August."

"That's amazing." Sandra tried to keep herself from getting too excited. There was *no way* Mrs. Burke was going to let her adopt Casey's baby. *No way.* She glanced outside the window. Alex was sitting up now and playing drums on the steering wheel. She could only imagine the rock concert going on inside her car. She hoped he didn't get any of the teens' attention; he might wind up going viral on social media. On second thought, he probably wouldn't mind.

"Thank you for coming," Casey said.

"Of course. Is everything okay?"

"Everything is fine. It's just I don't really get a lot of alone time with the . . . like, prospective parents . . . when I'm at home, and I wanted to talk a bit more with you."

"I got the impression from your mom that you had decided on the family who was going to adopt your baby."

"Nothing was signed, if that's what you mean." Casey put down her menu. "Was your husband okay with you coming alone?"

"My husband is actually in the car." Sandra pointed to the parking lot. "He's the one pretending to be Dave Grohl."

Casey appeared alarmed. "He didn't have to stay in there!"

"It's totally fine," Sandra said. "Trust me, he doesn't mind. In June, one of his clients is having a concert at the Long Island Music and Entertainment Hall of Fame right down the lane, and he had to drop off some flyers anyway. And even if he didn't, we tend to give each other a lot of space. Believe it or not, I think it helps to keep us together. And happy."

"You might have a point." Casey unfurled her cloth napkin, causing the silverware that had been wrapped inside to clink and drop onto the table. "My parents are rarely apart. And rarely happy."

Sandra remembered the family photos on the walls of Casey's home. She wanted to kick herself for being fooled by the smiles and tight hugs. Social media should have taught her that things are seldom as they seem.

The server came and placed two wet glasses of water on the table. Beads of condensation slid down their sides. "Are you getting the tea service, ladies?" he asked with a British accent that sounded authentic. Wow, they went all-out here.

"Yes, and I'll have the blueberry vanilla decaf," Casey said.

"And I think I'll try the almond sugar cookie tea."

"That's a good one," Casey said.

"Scones?" the waiter asked.

"Chocolate chip for me." Casey folded her menu and set it aside.

"I'll have the same," Sandra said.

"Sorry to make you drive all this way to meet," Casey said as the server hurried away. "But it's the only place that's near the high school and I can get away."

"There *is* school today, right?" Sandra motioned around them. "I can't imagine what this place would be like on a weekend."

"A lot of seniors have off this period. We like to come here instead of going to the cafeteria. The food's better. And there's a coffee shop next door, too. Was it a long drive for you?"

"Not at all," Sandra said. "We're heading up for a ski weekend in Vermont anyway, and this was on the way. We're taking the ferry."

"That sounds fun!" Casey said. "I love to ski."

"I actually don't," Sandra said with a laugh. "But I go up there to write."

"Romance novels, right? And not the steamy kind."

"Exactly." Sandra could feel her cheeks warm. "Like I told you, I tried to write spicy romance once. It wasn't pretty."

"Does Alex ski?"

"Yeah, and so does my best friend, Blake. That's the reason we're going away for the weekend. Blake just got married, and I think he wants me and Tara—that's his new wife—to become besties."

The server placed the teas and a beautiful tiered tray of desserts and sandwiches on the table. Casey tore into the chocolate chip scone on the bottom level. As she ripped off a big piece and slabbed some raspberry jelly on it, she studied

Sandra. "Why do I get the impression what's her name is a problem? Tara, is it?"

Sandra plucked her scone onto her plate. "Wow, am I that transparent?" She ripped off an equally sized piece and dropped it into her mouth. So much for British etiquette.

Casey picked up her teacup. "Go ahead, like, *spill* . . . you know, the tea," she said, taking a sip.

"Well . . ." Sandra stopped herself. Was she really about to tell the woman—*girl*—whose baby she wanted to adopt that she was getting the impression that someone didn't like her? Wasn't she supposed to be giving Casey a highlight reel? She figured what the hell. "Blake sort of didn't even tell Alex and me that he was getting married. Or that he was even dating anyone. It was really weird. But I'm trying to put that aside and accept Tara as my new friend. It's just . . ."

"It's just what?" Casey looked intrigued, her top lip smudged with chocolate chip.

Sandra shrugged. "I'm getting a vibe, you know. That Tara just isn't interested in being friends with me."

"What does Alex think?" Casey shoved another piece of scone into her mouth and then reached for a finger sandwich of cucumber and vegetable cream cheese.

"He says I need to give her a chance." Sandra sighed. "He said that maybe she's just nervous about meeting Blake's friends. To be honest, Alex is usually right." She dropped another bite of scone into her mouth. "It's pretty annoying," she said with a laugh as she chewed.

"Well, just because Alex is right doesn't mean that you're not, too."

Sandra smiled. Whatever she thought of Mrs. Burke, the woman seemed to have raised a thoughtful daughter.

"Can I ask you a question?" Casey asked.

"Of course." Sandra reached for a deviled egg sandwich. She had already decided she was going to save the quiche and mini-croissant for Alex.

"Why did you refer to Blake as your best friend? Wouldn't Alex be your best friend?"

"That's a great question." Sandra took a bite of her sandwich. "It's a holdover from when we were all kids. Alex, Blake, and I have been friends for so long. I met Blake when we were about eleven or twelve. And Alex knew Blake even longer. He and Alex took baths together when they were kids." She laughed. "When Alex and I got together, which, trust me, was as surprising to me as anyone, we didn't want Blake to feel like a third wheel. Ever. We always refer to Blake as our best friend, which he is. Mine and Alex's." She took a sip of her tea. "I know a lot of couples refer to each other as best friends, but . . . I think what Alex and I have goes so much deeper than that anyway. We are . . . Well, I think of us as an eleven."

"Eleven?"

"Yeah." Sandra didn't often get the chance to talk about Alex to someone who didn't know him. *Everyone* seemed to know Alex. Maybe one day she would be able to talk to Tara like this, too. "You know how some people use math to describe married couples? Like 1 + 1 = 2?"

Casey nodded.

"Or, for the really hard-core romantics, it's like 1 + 1 = 1? You know, how each individual person sort of morphs into this new being?"

"Yeah. Blech."

"Exactly. Well, I don't see it that way. I see marriage as more of a 1 + 1 = 11. Alex and I have remained committed to who we are as individuals as much as we are to each other. Like an eleven."

"Eleven till heaven," Casey said with a gleam in her eye.

"Yes." Sandra smiled.

"I like that." Casey took another bite of her sandwich. "I see why you write romance now. It suits you."

"Really?" Sandra never really thought it did, but after she met Alex, she thought she understood a little something about love.

"Why were you surprised that you and Alex got together?" Casey asked, patting her mouth with her napkin. "Sorry, I have a habit of being, like, intense and pretty aggressive with my questions. My mom says I can be *a lot*."

"No, it's fine," Sandra said. "As for why I was surprised, I guess it's the age-old story, right? Quiet, shy, studious girl. Friendly, popular, incredibly gorgeous athlete."

"My God, you're an eighties movie!" Casey fake-wiped a tear from the corner of her eye. "Seriously, though, that's the sweetest thing I ever heard."

Sandra was taking a sip of tea when Casey added, "So, like, Alex is the only one you've had sex with?"

Sandra started coughing, tea dribbling down her face and dripping onto the elegantly decorated table.

"Oh, I'm sorry." Casey handed her one of the paper napkins the server left on the table. "That was too personal, wasn't it? There I go again."

"No, no, no, it's okay." Sandra removed her eyeglasses, quickly wiped her face, and put them back on.

"I just figured, you know, that you were so young when you met. It's none of my business, really."

"Honestly, Casey. I mean . . . I want to adopt your *baby*. It doesn't get any more personal than that, right?"

"I guess."

"And, no, Alex wasn't really my *first*. Believe it or not, Blake was."

"The best friend?!" Casey was super-interested now. She scooted forward on her bench seat, as much as her belly would allow, and rested her chin in her palms. "Do tell!"

"There's nothing to tell." Sandra shrugged. She seriously needed some friends her own age. "We both just didn't want the weight of virginity hanging over us. We had been best friends since we were kids, so we went for it."

"Not very romantic."

"Not at all." Sandra laughed. "The sex between us lasted . . . I don't know . . . a few minutes? I'm sure Blake would even tell you that it was nothing to write home about, although I like to joke with him that the reason he's had such trouble finding the right woman is because I've ruined him for all women." She laughed again. "But, seriously, that's what I thought sex was, really. Nothing special. That it was all blown out of proportion. Until . . ."

"Until you met Alex."

Sandra could feel her cheeks warm again. "Yeah. That was when I really understood what the term 'making love' meant."

"Oh my God, you guys are adorable!" Casey took another large bite, this time of quiche. On her plate, there were big bites taken in every dessert and sandwich. "You haven't asked me about, you know . . ." She pointed to her belly. "How a smart girl like me could let this happen."

Sandra didn't know how to respond. She didn't want Casey to feel uncomfortable. She had to admit she was curious, but she only wanted Casey to say what she wanted to say. "It doesn't really matter."

"It does to me," Casey said. "I'm not, like, slutty or anything. I had been dating a guy for a few months. We met last summer. He told me he loved me. Stupid me believed him."

"Being vulnerable, letting your feelings show, doesn't make you stupid," Sandra said. "It makes you brave. I would want to live my life that way more than any other way."

"That's kind of you to say. Anyway, he told me he was wearing a condom. He wasn't. Dopey me didn't know the difference."

"How could you? It was your first time."

Casey shrugged. "My mom wasn't too happy about it. She wanted me to get an abortion. But I didn't want to. I figured my mistake could be someone else's blessing."

"That's beautiful," Sandra said. "It must have been hard to go against your mom's wishes."

"It was. She can be pretty opinionated."

"Yeah, I got the feeling when I was at your house that your mom had a strong opinion about me and Alex. And it wasn't good."

Casey laughed. "Yeah, I can confirm that one. Please don't take it personally. My mother doesn't like anyone. Including me sometimes." Her eyes drifted. "My mom . . ." Her eyes widened. "Oh, shit. *My mom . . .*"

"What do you mean?"

"My mother!" Casey pointed. "She's outside the window."

Sandra turned and saw Mrs. Burke walking toward the tea room with another woman, both of them dressed in yoga pants and a T-shirt.

"I gotta go!" Casey jumped out of her seat. She grabbed at the remaining food on her plate and began sticking everything into her napkin.

"Wait. What do you mean you have to go?" Sandra said.

"My mom can't catch me cutting class."

"Cutting class?! What do you mean? You said you had off this period."

Casey was ducking below the window and putting the napkin filled with food into her backpack. "No, I said a lot of seniors do. But I don't. Listen, I'll Venmo you the money for the food."

"No, no, it's on me." Sandra looked out the window. Mrs. Burke was just about to enter the restaurant.

"There's a back way out," Casey said.

"Hurry. Go. I'll take care of the check."

"Really, thank you! It was nice chatting!" Casey ran toward the rear of the restaurant.

Sandra flagged the server, and he brought the check. With any luck, Mrs. Burke would be seated on the other side of the restaurant, and Sandra could skulk out undetected. As she quickly calculated the waiter's tip, she heard someone clear her throat.

"Sandra Wilson?!" Mrs. Burke exclaimed. "Is that you?"

So much for luck.

Sandra looked up and feigned surprise. "Hi! Mrs. Burke. How nice to see you."

"What are you doing here?" she asked incredulously, as if Sandra had crossed some turf boundary between the south and north shores of Long Island. She was looking at the table, where, to Sandra's horror, there were crumbs scattered all about and pieces of food everywhere.

"I heard so much about this place that I thought I'd give it a try," Sandra said innocently.

"Looks like you were hungry." Mrs. Burke raised her eyebrows in what looked like disgust.

Great, an unfortunate second impression to go with the first. "Oh, yeah, really hungry. I'm about to head up on vacation to—"

"Well, it was nice to see you again. Good luck to you." With that, Mrs. Burke and her lady friend followed the hostess toward the back of the restaurant.

By the time Sandra was in the parking lot and walking to the car, Alex spotted her and rolled down the driver's-side window. "Hey, how did it—"

"Shhhhh," Sandra said. "Not here." She quickly got into the car and slid down in the passenger seat. "Go, go, go. Act natural, but go, go, go."

Alex pulled out of the spot without saying another word and drove toward the shopping center exit. "What's going on?" he whispered.

"Mrs. Burke showed up while I was talking to Casey."

"You're kidding."

"Oh no, I'm not. Casey freaked and then snuck out of the back of the restaurant because, it turns out, she was cutting class to meet me, and now I'm sure that Mrs. Burke will not only think I'm a slob but also a terrible influence on her daughter when she finds out that we met for lunch, because one of those little catty teenage girls is bound to tell on Casey."

"Why will she think you're a slob?"

Sandra was about to explain the look on Mrs. Burke's face when she spotted the crumbs Casey left behind and all the food that had been ordered, when Alex said, "Oh no, wait, I've seen you eat. Never mind."

She punched him in the arm as he grabbed her hand and kissed it.

"Here, Wise Guy. I saved you some finger sandwiches." She placed the doggie bag the server had given her on the console.

"You're so good to me." He shoved his hand in, pulling out the quiche.

"Were you in the car the whole time?"

"Just about. Chuck was leaving the Hall as I was about to go inside, so I gave him the flyers. And . . ."

"And?" Sandra watched as Alex made a left turn. "Wait, where are you going? The ferry is that way." She pointed east.

"I invited Chuck to come with us."

"You did? Wait, isn't he on his honeymoon?"

"They had to postpone it. Beatrice's mom is sick. Really sick. She had to go out of town for a few days, and instead of Chuck moping around with nothing to do, I thought he could come with us and have some fun." He looked at her. "You don't mind, right?"

The truth was that Sandra *didn't* mind. She liked Chuck. Blake would probably be pissed since this was supposed to be a couples thing; he was more of a symmetry kind of guy. "Nah, the more the merrier, right?"

Chuck was standing outside his small, pretty home that still had its Christmas lights up. He had a duffel bag slung over his shoulder and was pretending to hitchhike. Sandra had forgotten how much Chuck was a slip of a man. Slender. Very Mick Jagger. His wedding tuxedo seemed to have given him some bulk, but standing there in his ripped jeans, he looked like an overgrown kid. Which is probably why he and Alex got along so well.

Alex stopped in front of him, and Chuck got into the back seat. "Thanks for letting me tag along, Sandra," he said. "I don't know how many men like me have their wives leave them less than a week after they get married."

"Yeah, but yours is coming back." Sandra smiled. "Glad to have you along."

"Next stop, Vermont!" Alex said, setting the GPS for the ferry and pulling into traffic.

As Alex and Chuck began to chat, Sandra leaned back in her seat and glanced at her friendly and easygoing husband. She wasn't sure how things would go in Vermont—whether Tara would come around, whether Blake would be mad, whether she would get any writing done—but she knew that as long as Alex was by her side, she would be ready for anything.

CHAPTER 9

Friday, March 21, 5:00 p.m.

The state of Vermont seemed to have forgotten that spring was here. About a half foot of snow covered most of the sides of the roadway, and the piles got taller the higher the latitude and elevation. Sandra looked at her phone screen. Despite all the pit stops—Chuck had a very weak bladder—they had made good time and managed to get to the hotel before dark.

Sandra opened her window to let in some of the cold country air, which helped drown out Chuck's snoring from the back seat.

"Beautiful country, isn't it?" Alex said.

"Yes. No mountains on Long Island."

"Are you going to give Tara a ring?"

"A ring?" Sandra asked. "Are we suddenly British now?"

"I am." Alex cleared his throat. "Pip-pip. Cheerios."

"It's cheerio. Not Cheerios."

"You know what I mean, and I think you're deflecting."

Sandra was. She had already texted Tara twice after telling Blake she would and gotten no response. Alex knew that.

"She probably forgot," Alex said, reading her thoughts, like always. "It happens, right?"

Sandra shrugged.

"This weekend is a good opportunity for the two of you to bond. Maybe at dinner tonight, you can start." He looked over at her. "C'mon, San . . . Promise me you'll give her a chance."

She gave him her best puppy-dog eyes. "Do I have to?"

"Yes. For me."

She laughed. "Okay, I promise, but I don't think she's giving *me* a chance."

"Well, you can be the better person."

"So, who is this Tara person?" Chuck asked, sticking his head between the two front seats. Dried up saliva dotted the corners of his mouth. "Do I have to break a few kneecaps?"

"I don't think so," Sandra said. "At least not yet, but I'll keep that in mind." She was beginning to like Chuck more and more.

They drove through the quaint little village of shops just outside the ski resort. Sandra had visited the cute boutiques before and, for a moment, thought maybe Tara might want to go shopping with her tomorrow. She doubted it, but she told

Alex she would try, and she would. She decided to ask Tara at dinner.

As they drove through the entrance gates of the resort, Sandra gazed up at the beautiful hotel that sat on a majestic mountain. The Hamlin Hideaway was the perfect setting for a romance novel. She had been meaning to set one of her novels there.

The parking lot was full, but someone was pulling out right near the entrance, and Alex deftly turned the car into the spot.

"This must be our lucky day." He threw the car into park.

"This place is adorable," Chuck said, getting out of the car. "Beatrice would love it." His mouth turned down.

"You'll get your time together, don't worry," Sandra said. "You have a whole lifetime together." Sandra's phone pinged. "It's Blake." She was surprised he hadn't texted sooner. She typed:

We just parked.

Sandra wrapped the straps of her briefcase around her shoulder and pulled her luggage out from the back of the car as Alex and Chuck reached for their duffel bags. It amazed her how little Alex could pack for a weekend. Basically, he brought his toothbrush, a turtleneck and ski bib, a change of underwear, and the same assortment of his favorite worn T-shirts, most of which he had been wearing since high school.

It was drizzling a little, a mix of rain and snow, and Sandra's glasses fogged. She tilted her head up to find a dry spot on her lenses and spotted Blake, who was surveying the parking lot until his eyes landed on them.

"Guys!" Blake waved wildly at them. "You made it!"

Tara was standing dutifully beside him. Sandra hated to admit it, but she looked lovely in a brown puffer jacket and matching hat.

"Hi." Sandra kissed Blake on the cheek. Her eyes glanced at Tara, who seemed to be watching. Sandra went to hug her—that's what friends did, right?—but instead of extending her arms, Tara gave a quick wave and said a short hi. "Hi," Sandra said, gently dropping her arms.

"Hey there!" Alex said.

Blake's broad smile faded when he saw Chuck, but just for a moment. Sandra could tell he was disappointed that she and Alex hadn't come alone, but he was courteous enough not to let Chuck see that. It would be bad manners. And in this case, also bad business. "Chuck, what a surprise!" he said.

"I hope that's all right." Chuck looked from Blake to Alex.

"The more the merrier, right?" Alex said.

"Always." Blake swiveled and extended his hand to Tara. "I'd like you to meet my wife, Tara."

Chuck glanced at Sandra before shaking Tara's hand. *Why are men so obvious?* Tara smiled, and Sandra hoped she didn't notice.

"So nice to meet you!" Chuck said. "Although I'm not sure what you see in *this* guy." He elbowed Blake in the ribs. Tara smiled sheepishly as Sandra placed her briefcase on the cobblestone entryway.

"I didn't know this was a working vacation, San," Blake said.

"It's not. But I'm working on this new book I'm excited about." She nudged Alex. "You know I get up about four hours earlier than Alex. This gives me something to do."

"Ah, a fellow early bird," Chuck said. "I do my best songwriting in the morning."

"You guys are nuts," Alex said. "Night owls rock. I don't know about you, but I'm ready to party."

Sandra didn't doubt him. Even after driving for hours, Alex could keep going all night.

"I got us a reservation at the hibachi place for dinner tonight," Blake said, "but only for four." He looked at Chuck. "Chuck, I'm sorry. I didn't know you were coming."

"That's all right," Chuck said. "I'll order room service or grab a slice somewhere."

"Can't you change it?" Alex asked Blake.

"I doubt it. Look around. This place is mobbed. People are trying to get in a few more runs before the season ends."

"Please don't go to any trouble for me," Chuck said. "There was a nice little town just outside the resort. I'll head there."

To Sandra's surprise, Tara took a step forward. "I'm feeling a bit tired anyway. You all go to dinner. I'll head back to the room."

Sandra glanced at Alex. So much for her and Tara getting to know one another at dinner.

"You don't have to do that," Chuck said.

"No, it's been a long day at work," Tara said.

"Tara's a high school psychologist," Sandra explained.

"Wow, I wish our high school had a psychologist..." Chuck seemed to stop mid-sentence. Sandra wondered if he was going to add *who looked like you*.

Blake kissed Tara on the cheek. "Are you sure, honey?"

"Don't worry, Tara," Alex said. "The food sucks there anyway." He eyed Sandra strangely.

What, she mouthed.

Oh no . . . He doesn't want me to . . . Ugh, he did . . . Sandra cleared her throat. "Tara, I'd be happy to grab something with you for dinner. We can let the men do their he-man thing."

"I think that's a great idea!" Alex said.

Of course, he did.

"So do I," Blake said.

"Oh," Tara said, "that would really be nice, but . . ." She glanced at the wet ground.

But what?

But I hate you?

But I think you're annoying?

But we'll never be friends?

"I'm just really tired," Tara said. "I wouldn't be much company. I hope you understand."

"Of course." Sandra tried to keep the relief out of her voice. Was she a bad person for being happy that Tara was declining her invitation? Probably.

"All right, friends, let's get you all checked in and something to eat," Blake said.

"And drink!" Alex said. "Don't forget drink!"

"How could we?" Sandra playfully punched Alex in the arm. "*You* never let us."

CHAPTER 10

SATURDAY, MARCH 22, 8:00 A.M.

Vivian had never felt this way before. She may have been only eighteen years old and had only dated Robby Hill next door, if you could call a drunken night of letting him claw under her bra dating, but this was the first time she had that little flutter in her belly that all her friends liked to talk about when they were around a guy. Stefan ... er, Professor Markus ... was so kind. And sympathetic. And passionate about dead writers. So what if her best friend, Chrissy, said he was old? Love was ageless, wasn't it? Boundless. Sometimes no one else could see what you did.

Sandra sat back in her hotel desk chair. *Ugh, this is horrible.*

The light of her computer screen illuminated her hands, making them look ghastly in the dark of the room. First drafts sucked. Well, *hers* always did. She had to keep reminding herself the writing would get better with each revision. She looked around at the large suite they were staying in, a charming set of rooms that was nearly bigger than her condo. The suite had a wonderful log cabin feel; she could almost smell the wood-burning stove. Outside a sliding door on the back wall was a large porch with a small table and a trio of lounge chairs with a view of the sun coming over the snowy mountain. Sandra always felt extra-inspired when she was writing in places other than home, getting out of her routine, but this was pretty special. And there was something clandestine about typing away in a room where two other people were sleeping, one of them not her husband. She felt like she was doing something illegal, which added to the thrill and also the theme of her novel, forbidden romance.

"Oh, Vivian," she whispered into the warm, heated air. She reached for the mug of tea she had made for herself at the suite's coffee bar and drank the rest. "Who are you? What do you want?" An image of Casey sitting in the Langford Tea Room came to mind. Sandra had been so inspired by her. Such a strong young woman. Someone who had something unexpected happen to her, but instead of erasing her mistake, she was turning it into something beautiful for someone else. Maybe she would have the character of Vivian resemble Casey, who had chocolate-brown eyes and a small mouth with perfect pearly white teeth. That was the best part of writing a novel. She could stuff so much of her life into a book, little things she thought or did, and because it was fiction, readers were none the wiser. She could hide in plain sight.

A phlegmy cough from behind her interrupted her thoughts. Chuck sat up on the squeaky cot the hotel had provided for them. "I hope my pecking didn't wake you up," she said apologetically.

"Not at all. I think it was the ice cream sundae from last night." Chuck patted his stomach. "Sometimes I forget I'm not eighteen anymore."

"Well, I can see why you and Alex hit it off so well then." Sandra smiled. "He forgets all the time."

"I heard that!" Alex said, slapping at his pillow. "What time is it?"

"Early," she said. "At least for you. Around eight."

"We need to get up anyway," Alex said, flopping onto the floor. "A quick breakfast. Want to hit those slopes early before the crowds come."

Chuck padded across the room toward the bathroom, scratching his belly like a chimp and still wearing the jeans he had been wearing the day before. He seemed comfortable around Sandra, like he had known her for years. Normally, she didn't like that, but she was comfortable with Chuck. He seemed like a good guy, although she *had* slept with her bra on. She wasn't *that* comfortable. When the bathroom door closed, Alex crawled toward her, reached for her, and pulled her back into a hug.

"Good morning," he said, nuzzling his face into her hair.

"Good morning to you."

"You've been so great about Chuck," he said. "Thanks for being a good sport."

"I really like Chuck. It was fun getting to know him last night at dinner. And finding out how many quarters he could balance on his elbow and catch."

"Too bad Tara couldn't make it, right?"

"I really like Chuck," Sandra said again with a smile.

"Very funny. You should try calling her again."

"Alex..."

"Ask her if she wants to get some breakfast with us or a cup of coffee."

"Honestly, Alex... How many more times do I have to make an effort?" She rolled her eyes, picked up her phone, swiped to her text thread with Tara, and showed him the screen. "Look. These are my texts from the past week. All unanswered."

Monday: Hey, Tara. Do you want to get that cup of coffee this morning? Would love to chat and get to know each other.

Wednesday: Hey, Tara. Not sure you got my previous message from Monday, but I have some free time in the afternoon and thought we could grab a cup.

"Maybe the third time's a charm," Alex said hopefully.

"I don't even like coffee," Sandra said.

"Maybe Blake gave you the wrong number."

"Don't let *him* hear you say that." She laughed. "Blake is the most organized person we know. He's a regular Marie Kondo."

Alex tightened his arms around her and peered at her computer screen. "What are you working on?"

"Oh, you know, that forbidden love story I wanted to try."

"The young girl and the old geezer professor?"

"Um, she's eighteen, and he's far from an old geezer. He's an attractive middle-aged guy. You know, like you."

Alex's arms stiffened. "Middle-aged? Me? Are you kidding? Forty-two is the new twenty-two."

"Tell that to your chiropractor."

He released her and switched on the lamp on his nightstand. Reaching into his suitcase, he pulled out a clean pair of underwear and his ski bib, and did a quick change. "Why is their love so forbidden?" he asked.

"The professor is married."

"Aww, poor kid." Alex ran his fingers through his hair, which was as close as his hair ever got to a comb. "Maybe you should throw in a murder. You know, make it a thriller."

"Being married to you is thrilling enough."

He walked toward the window, his bibbed legs making a swishing noise as they rubbed together. "It looks like a beautiful day," he said as Chuck came out of the bathroom. "You gonna ski in those jeans, man?" Alex asked him.

"It's all I have. I'm not so fancy-schmancy like some people." He motioned toward Alex's bib.

"You can wear my bib," Sandra said, digging into her suitcase at the foot of her bed. "I can't believe I'm saying this, but I think you're probably my size."

"Don't you need it?" Chuck asked.

"Not really. I only brought it in case I want to take a lesson." She handed the bib to him.

"But she never does." Alex smiled.

"Thanks," Chuck said, and slipped one of his legs easily into the pant leg. "I think you're right. It'll fit." When he stuck his other leg in and pulled up on the waterproof nylon, he lost his balance, and his arm swung out, knocking Sandra's mug onto the wood floor.

"Shit!" he said.

"Are you okay?" Sandra asked.

"I'm fine. But I don't think I can say the same for your mug." Chuck reached down to survey the damage. "It's not that bad. It broke in only two places." He picked up the pieces and placed them on Sandra's desk. "Is it a bad omen to break a ceramic mug before skiing?"

"Only if you throw it against a mirror while walking under a ladder," Alex said with a smile. His phone pinged on the nightstand, and he reached for it. "It's Blake. He said he and Tara are going to skip breakfast and meet us by the boot rental." He kept reading. "And he said Tara volunteered to pick up some coffees for me and Chuck." He looked at Sandra. "Isn't that nice?"

"Coffee? How thoughtful," Sandra said. "I wonder where she got the idea of having coffee. Hmmm . . ."

"Am I missing something?" Chuck said.

"Don't ask," Alex said.

"No problem." Chuck adjusted the straps on his bib. They might have had the same-sized thighs, but he was way taller. "I may only be married for a week, but I know when I need to mind my own business." He looked out the window. "This place is really something."

"I know," Alex said. "I can't believe we get to stay here for free."

"Does that mean I'm not your favorite client?" Chuck put on a faux-sad boo-boo face.

"You'll always be my favorite," Alex said, and then they did some weird long-ass handshake. Men.

"Let's grab a quick breakfast." Alex rubbed his stomach.

"I'm still full from last night," Chuck said.

"Alex starts thinking about breakfast as soon as he finishes dinner," Sandra said.

"I might check out the hotel and meet you at the boot rental." Chuck looked at his watch. "Around nine a.m.?"

"Sounds good." Alex pulled at his bib straps. "C'mon, San, get dressed. You're buying me breakfast."

THE HOTEL BUFFET WAS a lavish affair. Four omelet stations with vegetarian options. Two carving stations for steak and pork. A soda fountain touting an array of concoctions including fifteen different types of milkshakes. Alex was practically salivating. He showed off his platinum hotel bracelet, which allowed them to walk right into the room and bypass a long line of hungry faces. Sandra hadn't even walked ten paces before Alex grabbed a plate and began piling food onto it.

"I'll find us a table," she said.

She chose one near the soda fountain, since she figured Alex would be up there at least three times. She caught his eye and waved to let him know where she was, and then she dropped her things down, picked up a plate, and made her way around the buffet. By the time she got back, Alex was sitting with two plates in front of him piled high with food.

"Is that all you're having?" she asked, sitting across from him.

"This is just round one, of course."

Sandra poured maple syrup on her pancake. "I can't stop thinking about Casey."

"You like her. I can tell," Alex said around a mouthful of sausage.

"I do. And I would love to get the chance to raise her baby. I'm not even sure I'm into open adoption, but with Casey, it would be a pleasure."

"How about with Mrs. Burke?"

Sandra rolled her eyes. "Yeah, that wouldn't be fun. Anyway, I don't expect to hear from her."

"Hey, isn't that Blake?" Alex asked. "Blake!"

Across the restaurant, Blake and Tara were walking hand in hand, eyeing the omelet station. Blake waved and started to walk over, but Sandra could tell that Tara initially seemed reluctant.

"Hey there!" Alex said when they finally reached the table. "I thought you guys didn't want breakfast."

"We don't, really," Blake said. "Just passing through. Where's Chuck?"

"He wanted to check out the hotel and the grounds. You want to join us?"

Sandra saw Tara nudge Blake from behind. A subtle tug.

"No," Blake said. "Thanks anyway. We're going to head over that way." He pointed outside the window. "Check things out, too. I'll see you in a bit."

Sandra watched them go.

"Don't say it," Alex said.

"C'mon, Alex. Don't you think that's weird? When did you know Blake to pass up a meal?"

"Maybe his hunger is being satisfied in other ways." Alex smirked.

"Please, I'm eating." She threw her napkin at him. "And don't you think he looks a little weird?"

"Weird how?"

"Like gaunt? Pale? His coloring is off a bit."

"Blake is always pale. He hates the sun."

"I know, but this is different. Maybe he needs some supplements, speaking of which . . ." Sandra reached into her handbag. "Don't forget this." She handed Alex a bottle of calcium supplements.

"Do I really need that?" He looked around, embarrassed.

"The doctor says your calcium is low. It's really not a big deal."

"I never had to take anything before."

"I know, but that's the way it goes, right?" she said. "I take thyroid medication every day. I don't love it, but this kind of stuff comes with getting older, and that's a gift, right? Some people don't get the chance to get older. Especially with someone they love."

"Ah, you should have been a saleswoman." He opened the bottle and popped a vitamin into his hand, glancing at his watch. "I'd better hurry if I'm gonna have another round of breakfast before I go." He shoved the supplement into his pocket and handed the bottle back to Sandra. "I'll take this when I'm done eating." When Sandra glared at him, he gave the Boy Scouts' three-finger salute. "I promise."

As Alex ate like it was his last day on earth and then hurried back for some more, Sandra speared a piece of pancake with her fork and swished it around in the syrup.

"I love this place," Alex said as he returned, placing another milkshake and a large stack of pancakes on the table.

"Did you leave some food for the other guests?"

"Ha." He poured the rest of the syrup on the stack, stuck his fork into the top pancake, and stuck the entire thing in his mouth.

"Lovely," Sandra said with a laugh.

"So." Alex swallowed. "Are you gonna—"

"Alex, don't say it."

"C'mon, San. Are you going to ask Tara?" He slurped his milkshake.

"Ugh. Quit browbeating me. Yes, I'll ask her if she wants to get a cup of coffee later today. But only for you." She reached for his hand.

"That's my girl."

Alex inhaled the rest of his second breakfast and then patted his mouth with a paper napkin. "Time to ski." He got up from the table, picked up her briefcase from the seat beside her, and extended his hand. "Shall I help you up?"

"You shall," she said, reaching for his hand. "You have pretty amazing manners for a guy who just ate an entire breakfast without the use of his teeth."

"My skill set continues to amaze you, I see."

She fixed one of his bib straps, which was turned over. "Play nice with the other children, okay?"

"I will."

"Does Chuck even ski?"

Alex shrugged. "He seems to think so."

They both laughed as Alex put a tip on the table.

"Make sure Chuck doesn't get himself killed out there." She shoved Alex's Def Leppard T-shirt into the sides of the bib.

"Try and play nice with your new friend, Tara." He squeezed her chin.

"She's not my—"

"Sandra . . ."

"I will," Sandra said, making a face.

"Really, San. Promise me you'll give her a chance."

"Ugh, I promise."

"Good." He slapped her butt before handing her the briefcase. "I love you, baby." Alex reached forward and planted a soft, wet kiss on her lips.

"I love you, too. So much. Now go have fun."

As she watched Alex sashay his way toward the exit after making yet another pitstop at the milkshake station, Sandra glanced at her phone. She let out a huge sigh and typed:

Hey, Tara, do you want to grab some coffee later today after you guys ski?

She began walking as her phone pinged.

Sorry, I'm not sure I'll have time. I'm trying to see if I can go snowmobiling.

"Seriously?" Sandra said aloud. She would have happily joined Tara for a snowmobile excursion if she had asked. But she didn't. She hadn't said anything at all.

Idiot, she doesn't want to go snowmobiling with you. Or have coffee. Or do anything. That's why she didn't ask.

Sandra adjusted her briefcase on her shoulder.

Fine.

Who needed Tara when she had Vivian, an eighteen-year-old who was about to make a pass at her middle-aged comparative literature professor? That sounded way more fun than trying to pass the time with a real-life high school psychologist.

CHAPTER 11

SATURDAY, MARCH 22, 9:30 A.M.

SANDRA GAZED OUTSIDE THE third-floor balcony. The line for the ski lift was already twenty-skiers long. *See, Alex? Lots of morning people.* And what a morning it was. Not a cloud in the blue sky. The sun warmed Sandra's face even though the cold breeze blew through the weaves of her bulky sweater.

Sandra watched the tiny dots at the top of the mountain whiz down the slopes and wondered if Alex was one of them. The man loved to ski. Probably almost as much as he loved her. She could never understand his infatuation with it, but Alex loved everything about it. The speed. The wind. The adrenaline rush during a run. She was happy it made him happy, and was even happier that he didn't mind that she didn't love it, as much as she tried to.

To Sandra's left, beginning skiers were standing in a semicircle with an instructor who was explaining how to grab hold of the rope pull without falling down. Sandra should have taken that class.

She readjusted her briefcase strap around her shoulders and went back inside, looking for a good place to write. She wanted somewhere with a bit of background noise, but not too much. A place with enough activity for people watching, but not too many distractions. She walked and walked until she got to the immense lobby of the resort, where a long line of people were checking out. Off to the side, near a bar that was closed, was a sprinkling of tables, an out-of-the-way area she would have mostly to herself. It was near a large window that looked out onto the slopes. Perfect.

She sat down and opened her laptop. A chill was coming from the glass of the window, and Sandra thought about changing seats, but the scenery was so beautiful and the light was helping to put her in a better mood, so she decided to stay. Trying to stop thinking about Tara, she plunged into writing:

Did love really exist across the years, Stefan wondered. He tried not to watch Vivian as she worked on her midterm essay, but he was drawn inexplicably to her. Why? Was it simply her youthful beauty? The soft curve of her face, the way her dark bangs fell just below her forehead, covering a freckle over her left eyebrow. He knew this was wrong. He was married, a father of two, a tenured professor, but it didn't feel wrong. His marriage had felt wrong. Since the beginning. He had lived for years feeling numb until Vivian Woletsky walked into his classroom in late January. And why was Tara being such a bitch??

Sandra sat back.

Ugh.

She deleted the last sentence from her screen, but she was having less success deleting it from her mind. What was Tara's problem? Were some relationships never meant to be? *Focus, Sandra.* She took a deep breath and imagined Stefan's wife at home, caring for her two boys, unaware that her professor husband was swooning over a student who hadn't even been born at the time of their wedding. Could Stefan turn off his feelings? Simply deny them? Where did unrequited feelings go? And what if Tara *never* warmed up to Sandra?

She took a deep breath.

If some love stories were forbidden, what made them forbidden? Would Vivian and Stefan ever consummate their love? If so, where? Sandra looked around the vast lobby area with its wooden beams. Maybe Vivian and her comp lit professor could run away together to a ski resort. Hmmm . . . Hot, forbidden love blooming in a cold place? A tingle ran through her, which often signaled a good idea. Her fingers began pecking at the keys. Hey, this novel just might write itself, after all.

"Excuse me?"

Sandra startled. She wasn't sure how long she had been writing, but a young man was standing nearby with a concerned look on his face. "Can I help you?"

"Are you Mrs. Connor?"

He was very young, with a tapered haircut that was neatly trimmed on the sides. His skin was so soft and smooth that he looked like he had never shaved at all. He had to be sixteen—seventeen, tops. She blinked her eyes a few times, trying to switch gears. Sometimes it took her a while to disconnect from a scene when she was writing. Alex liked to call it her "coming out" period. "Mrs. Connor?" Sandra asked. "Um, no ... Well, yes, I am, technically, Mrs. Connor, but my last name isn't Connor. It's Wilson, I go by my ... I'm sorry, you didn't need to know all that. Can I help you?"

The young man pointed to the hotel logo and name badge on his white shirt. "Ma'am, my name is Mitchell. We've been trying to page you." He pointed up to a brown loudspeaker on the ceiling that was barely noticeable among the wooden beams.

"Sorry." Sandra's cheeks began to burn. "Sometimes when I'm in the middle of writing," she pointed to her laptop, "the whole world can be coming apart around me, and I wouldn't notice." She gave a little laugh. She also wanted to say that if someone was paging a Mrs. Connor, she might not have heard, even if she *wasn't* writing. She had already been at the doctor's office and angered the nurses because she didn't respond to her married name, which she had to use for insurance purposes. As far as Sandra was concerned, Mrs. Connor was Pam, her mother-in-law. Even after all these years of marriage. "How can I help you?"

"Um . . ." The young man pulled at the side of his khaki trousers, stumbling for words.

"Is this about the broken glass in the hotel room?" Sandra asked, trying to help him along. "I'm sorry about that. It was a freak accident."

"Glass?" He seemed perplexed. "No . . . no, it's not." He looked behind him, and Sandra could see two more members of the hotel staff hurrying toward them.

"What's going on?" Sandra said.

When the two reached them, they were out of breath. One was looking outside, and that's when Sandra realized the ski lift had stopped. No one was coming down the mountain.

"Has there been a blackout?" she asked but then noticed the lobby lights were still on.

One of the two hotel employees, a young woman named Laurel, according to her name badge, pulled out a walkie-talkie. "We found her," she said, speaking into it. "In the dining hall annex."

"Found who? Me?" Sandra pointed to herself. "What's going on?"

"Um, we need you to come with us," Mitchell said.

"Come with you where?" Sandra said. "I don't understand."

Laurel reached for Sandra's hand. "Something has happened, Mrs. Connor."

"Her name is Ms. Wilson," Mitchell said.

"They're not married?" asked the third employee, whose name badge read Rick.

"No, they're married, but with different names," Mitchell explained.

Frustrated, Sandra stood up. "I'd like someone to please tell me what's going on."

The three employees looked at one another and then behind them, as if waiting for something or someone.

"We really shouldn't say," Mitchell said, and turned to Laurel. "Did you call Daryl?"

"Who's Daryl?" Sandra asked.

"You really need to come with us," Rick said.

Sandra slammed her laptop closed. "I'm not going anywhere with you until you tell me what's going on."

The two young men looked at Laurel.

"Laurel, tell me," Sandra said.

Laurel took another look behind her before inhaling deeply. "Your husband . . . he's been in an accident."

Sandra felt the blood drain from her face. "What do you mean, an accident?" She tucked the laptop under her arm. "Where is he? I need to see him."

"No, I'm sorry," Laurel said, her face turning bright red. "I didn't say that right. You misunderstood. We really should wait for—"

"Misunderstood how?" Sandra asked. "Was he in an accident or not?"

She was about to leave, when a tall man in a suit appeared at the far end of the lobby, striding in Sandra's direction, followed by a team of others. Rick, Laurel, and Mitchell took a step back.

"Mrs. Connor?" the man asked, breathless, when he arrived.

"I'm Alex Connor's wife, and I'd like to see him," Sandra said.

The man took a deep breath. "I'm so sorry, Mrs. Connor. My name is Daryl Winters. I'm the manager of the resort. There's been a terrible accident. Your husband suffered an injury while skiing."

"I know. They told me." She pointed to the hotel workers.

"Is there someone we can call for you? Is there—?"

"No, I need to see my husband. Take me to where the accident happened."

"I'm afraid that's not possible at the moment."

"What do you mean? I demand to see him now. Where is he?"

"I'm..." Mr. Winters's brows furrowed, and a deep vertical line appeared between his eyes. "I'm afraid... afraid the coroner has already removed the body."

CHAPTER 12

Saturday, March 22, 12:00 p.m.

Coroner? All sensation left Sandra's body, replaced by a numbness. Daryl Winters was talking. His lips were moving, but she could no longer hear his words. A hand was on her shoulder. And then another hand. She could feel herself being pulled. Someone took the laptop out from under her arm. Someone was leading her forward. She didn't know where. Then, in the distance... a familiar shape. Running toward her. Arms waving wildly.

"San!" Blake wrapped her in a hug. "Oh my God, Sandra. Where have you been?" Tears were streaming down his face. The familiar smell of his cologne nearly made her break down and cry. She closed her eyes, and an image appeared of Blake buying cologne at the mall, with Alex dabbing every sample along his arms.

When Sandra opened her eyes, she noticed Tara standing there too, looking sad and unsure.

Sandra looked Blake in the eyes. "What's going on, Blake? It's not true, right? This is a joke, right? One of your jokes?"

Blake shook his head sadly. "I wish it was."

"Where is he?" she asked.

"They brought him into a room. It's not far. I'll take you to him."

"I'll stay here," Tara said. "I'll take Sandra's things back to the room for her."

What things? Sandra didn't remember having *things*. She didn't remember anything anymore.

"Please, Mrs. Connor, follow me," Daryl Winters was saying to her.

Sandra leaned into Blake as they began to walk. "What happened?" she asked him.

"I don't know," he said. "You know Alex. Normally, he likes to be the first one down the mountain, but he and Chuck were singing some song, and they were chatting and laughing, so Tara and I went first. We waited and Chuck came down and asked where Alex was. I told him he never came down."

"Where's Chuck?" Sandra asked.

"He's talking to the police officers."

"*Police officers?* Why are there police officers?"

"When there's a death on the premises, Mrs. Connor, we typically contact the police to report the death," Daryl Winters said. "It's just protocol. We do it for all . . . er, incidents." He put his hand on her shoulder, and Sandra wanted to tell him to take it away. She didn't want anyone to touch her. Ever again.

As they walked toward the lobby, she felt like she was leading a funeral possession as people stood on the sidelines, watching. Some were wearing ski bibs. Others, sweaters. Women had their hands in front of their mouths in shock and sadness, and Sandra held back a powerful wail as she realized they were sad for *her*. Feeling sorry for *her*.

"I don't understand," Sandra said. "Alex is an excellent skier."

Daryl Winters answered. "Unfortunately, many deaths that take place on the slopes occur to experienced male skiers," he said.

"How could that be?" she asked.

Daryl Winters shrugged. "They hit a tree going too fast, sometimes."

"Is that what happened to Alex? That can't be. Right, Blake?" She needed Blake to tell her she was right. That this made no sense. "Tell him, Blakey. Tell him that Alex was a confident skier."

"Yes, he was very confident," Blake offered. "The best skier I knew."

"The best skier you *know*," Sandra corrected.

"Yes, *know*. You're right, Sandra," Blake said.

"We don't know what happened, Mrs. Connor. Sometimes experienced skiers push boundaries," Daryl Winters said. "They ski faster, closer to the trees, they..."

"Show off?" Sandra asked. "Is that what you mean?"

"Yes, unfortunately." He cleared his throat. "We take great pains to make sure that our terrain is safe to use."

Sandra suddenly felt affronted. Daryl Winters was speaking as if he were at a deposition. Everything he said related that Alex's death couldn't have been the ski resort's fault. He was trying to pin all this on Alex.

"He was wearing a helmet," Sandra said, defensively. "I'm sure of it. He always wears a helmet."

"The data shows that, unfortunately, that doesn't make much of a difference if the impact is great," Daryl Winters said.

"Then what are helmets for?!" she screamed, and everyone around them seemed to startle and glance at each other.

"I'm so sorry for your loss," Daryl Winters said quietly as they arrived at an area with two police officers and another man in a long coat standing off to the side.

"Sandra..."

Someone was saying her name.

Chuck.

He ran toward her and hugged her tightly. She wanted to tell him that she didn't want to be touched, to get away from her, but the smell of his body brought her back to that morning when she, he, and Alex were in the suite together. Talking. Laughing. She didn't want him to let go.

"I'm so sorry," he whispered into her ear with a sniffle. He pulled away, and she could see tears streaming down his face. "I don't know what happened. One minute, we were at the top of the mountain, laughing and singing, and the next . . ." He couldn't say any more. He adjusted the jacket that someone had placed over Sandra's shoulders. Who had placed it there? And whose was it? She didn't have a jacket with her.

"Are you Mrs. Connor?" the man in the long coat asked her as she approached.

She nodded.

"My name is Detective Miller. I'm very sorry for your loss," he said, and opened the door to a room.

"Do you want me to come with you?" Blake asked.

"No. I need to be alone," she said.

He nodded as she stepped inside.

A body was lying on a table in an empty room. The first thing she saw were the skis, crossed in an X, feet twisted. Then the Def Leppard T-shirt, the ski jacket hanging open. Had CPR been administered? Had Alex been alive, asking for her? She couldn't bear the thought. She gazed at the black bib she had helped him zip up only hours before. What was the last thing they had said to each other? Who knew that when someone walked away, that it might be for the last time?

She had a thought.

Maybe this was all a mistake. Wasn't it possible that someone else could be wearing a similar T-shirt? And black bib?

She knelt beside the body and looked at the swollen face, the blue lips, the head wound filled with dried blood, and her heart melted.

It was Alex.

Her Alex.

The love of her life.

And he was gone.

CHAPTER 13

Wednesday, March 26, 7:30 p.m.

Sandra stood at the front of the funeral home's viewing room, nodding and hand-shaking, for what felt like hours. Blake had gotten her water, tried to get her to eat, but she wasn't hungry. *Would she ever be hungry again?*

She looked back at Alex's mother, who was crumpled in a Queen Anne chair in the first row, surrounded by Alex's aunts and uncles. They had lost Alex's father only two years ago. And now Alex. It seemed too much for one family to bear.

"Are you okay?"

Sandra's mother hugged her.

"No," Sandra said.

"Do you want to take a break? Maybe step outside?"

"No. I want to stay near Alex." Sandra looked at the open casket, at the barely recognizable face of her beloved. The funeral parlor had done all they could to make him look like he had, but the one thing they couldn't bring back was the life in Alex's cheeks. "Plus, I'm afraid if I leave, I'll never come back."

"It'll be all right," her mother said. "I promise it will."

It would never be all right. Never again.

Her mother kissed her cheek and went to check on Pam, who was now being comforted by Wallace, Blake's mother. Sandra was happy they all had each other. Longtime friends. They had been through a lot together. In the row behind, Sandra's father was sitting. He smiled sadly at her. She smiled sadly back.

Sandra took a step forward and straightened the New York Jets baseball cap on Alex's head. He had always said he wanted to be buried with that cap on so he could cheer the team from the grave. She held back a sob.

"You okay?"

Blake approached Sandra, and they stood quietly side by side, looking at Alex's body.

"No," she whispered.

"I know." He put his hand on her shoulder and sighed. "Well, leave it to Alex to leave this life in some badass way like a skiing accident. He died like he lived. Enjoying life to the fullest."

Sandra nodded. Probably the only other way Alex might have chosen to go was while on top of her in bed. The thought made her let out a tiny laugh.

"It's nice to see you smile a little," Blake said.

Sandra adjusted the items she had stuffed in the casket. Some of Alex's favorite things. His Journey T-shirt, which had been packed for their trip to Vermont. His favorite pair of ripped sweats. The first dollar Napkin Marketing had ever made, which Sandra had plucked from the wall of Alex's office. A photo of Pam. And, in the corner, a photo of Blake, Alex, and Sandra next to Alex's favorite photo of him and Sandra on their wedding day—the one of them on the dance floor for their first dance.

She reached out and touched Alex's face. So cold. Alex was never cold. Even after taking a cold summer shower.

"Goodbye, my love," Sandra said.

A waft of air rushed into the room as a door opened, and more people came and left. Sandra and Blake stepped away from the coffin to allow others some time with Alex, and she continued shaking hands and accepting condolences, all the faces blurring into one another, all the words meaningless, as Blake retook his seat next to his mother.

Someone let out a cry from somewhere in the middle of the room, and Sandra turned to see Chuck, seated next to his wife, Beatrice. Chuck's head was buried in his wife's shoulder. Beatrice gave a tiny wave, her eyes filled with tears.

Then Sandra suddenly had a thought. She looked around for Tara but couldn't find her. She wasn't seated, nor was she on the long line snaking through the viewing room, all the way out the exit door.

"I'm so sorry," said a woman Sandra didn't know who embraced her in a hug. "I knew Alex from the time he was a little boy. I'm friends with his mother." She pointed to Pam, whose face was obscured by a tissue. "He was always kind to me."

"Thank you for coming," Sandra said, and then scanned the room again for Tara. Where *was* she?

After what felt like dozens of hours of being consoled by friends, family members, and strangers, Blake came up to Sandra. "It's almost over," he said. "Is there anything you need?"

Yes, she thought. Two things. First, she needed to know why Alex had been taken from her. And, second, she needed to know where the hell her best friend's wife was and why she couldn't find it in her heart to be there for Sandra when she needed her the most.

CHAPTER 14

Thursday, April 3, 5:00 p.m.

Sandra sat on the couch, staring at the dark television screen.

What did people do in the evenings? Watch TV *alone*? Who would there be to comment that he was much more attractive than Chris Pine? Eat *alone*? Who would chew with his mouth open so Sandra could say he looked like the schnauzer she had as a child? Life seemed empty without Alex—and yet suffocating. Her phone pinged, and Sandra picked it up, happy for the distraction.

Don't forget to eat, San.

Another text from Blake. He was really trying. He had volunteered to come over every day since the funeral, trying to help. As much as she appreciated it, seeing him reminded her of Alex. There had been the three of them for so long, and now there were only two.

Oh, and Tara.

But Sandra hadn't seen or heard from her. *At all.*

The last time she had seen Tara was at the ski resort. Standing there, looking like she cared, but did she really? If she *had*, she would have come to the wake or the funeral. If she *had*, she would have called. She certainly had Sandra's number.

For the past two weeks, Sandra contemplated saying something to Blake about it, but she didn't know how. Was it possible to say *Your wife is an insensitive, callous, elitist bitch* without offense? There *must* have been, but even though Sandra did PR writing, she couldn't come up with one. When Sandra was feeling charitable, she reasoned that maybe Tara had a thing about funerals or didn't know what to say to Sandra, so she didn't say anything at all. But why not tell Sandra that? Surely, Blake thought it was odd his wife would skip the funeral of his closest friend.

Her phone rang, and she glanced at the screen.

Pam.

Sandra sighed and let the call go to voicemail. She didn't have the strength to talk with her mother-in-law. Their daily cryfests were draining her. She pulled at the blanket lying on the couch and wrapped it around her, glancing around the house. She knew she had a lot to do but couldn't even think about doing any of it. Paying bills. Food shopping. Cleaning. She hadn't been in the bedroom since the morning she left for Vermont. She couldn't face Alex's clothing or his smell or the way he always left the bedsheets rumpled. That was *their* bedroom. They had never slept apart—in all the years they had been married. And Sandra didn't want to start now.

Maybe she would have to get the room fumigated and the furniture replaced. Or move out of this condo altogether. But where would she go? And what could she afford? Her income wouldn't be enough to support herself without Alex's. Would she still work for Napkin Marketing? She was, technically, at least on paper, an owner of the company. She didn't want to move back home, although her parents would probably love to have her.

Why did you leave me alone?

The doorbell rang. It had been ringing every day since the funeral. Friends. Family. She finally had to tell her parents to please stay home, that she would be okay. Her refrigerator was stocked with lasagnas and casseroles, and the living room had so many peace lily plants from the funeral parlor. They would probably die in a few weeks. Sandra had a black thumb. Alex would tease her about it if he were here.

But he wasn't.

She got up, bringing the blanket with her, and padded to the door. She peeked through the peephole. Two men were standing there. The one on the right looked familiar, but she couldn't remember from where. "Who is it?" she asked.

"It's Detective Miller and my associate, Detective Menendez."

Detective Miller? Sandra continued to stare through the peephole at the detective's features and, in her mind's eye, could see him standing in the lobby of the ski resort. She opened the door.

"Detective?" she asked.

"Sorry to come unannounced." He was looking past her, at the inside of her apartment. "May we come in?"

Sandra hesitated. She was pretty sure she remembered the detective, but what if she was mistaken? What if these two strange men were looking to ransack her apartment? Maybe they had read Alex's obituary in the newspaper and wanted to rob or scam her. *Or worse.* She had never lived alone before. *Is this how single women lived?* In perpetual fear?

She opened the door wider.

Let them murder her. Then she could be with Alex.

"Come in," she said.

The detectives walked in and stood near the couch.

"Sorry for the mess," she said, dropping the blanket around her into a pile on the side of the room. She was about to close the door but decided to leave it open. Just in case she needed a way out. *Clearly, I don't want to be murdered.* "What can I help you with?" she asked. "You're a long way from Vermont."

"Well . . ." Detective Miller was still looking around the apartment. "Mrs. Connor, I'd like to get right to the point, if that's okay."

"Sure, and please call me Sandra. Or Ms. Wilson. I usually go by my maiden name. My married name makes me think of my mother-in-law. Not that that's a *bad* thing. She's amazing." She gave a small smile.

The detectives glanced at one another, which made Sandra nervous. Had she said something wrong?

"Well, Ms. Wilson," Detective Miller said. "We believe there is some suspicious activity surrounding the death of your husband."

"Suspicious activity?"

Detective Miller looked at his partner again. "We believe that your husband's death may not have been an accident."

Sandra stared at Detective Miller's strong jaw and no-nonsense expression as his words fought their way into her brain. *What did that mean?* "I don't understand."

"There was a toxicology report done on the scene," Detective Miller said. "It's standard stuff. It showed his blood alcohol level was high, which, frankly, is surprising and not surprising. Surprising, because it was early in the morning. Is he a morning drinker?"

Before Sandra could answer, Detective Miller continued, "But not surprising because alcohol seems to be a major factor in skiing-related injuries and deaths."

"Alex was a social drinker, Detective," she said defensively. First, the ski resort manager—what was his name? Winters?—was eager to blame Alex for his own death, and now the detectives were trying to do the same. "Alex liked to have a good time. That's not a crime." She wiped her eyes. "I'm sorry. I shouldn't have said that. I'm just . . . well . . ." She cleared her throat. "No, he was not drinking that morning. But we were out late the evening before. And he did have quite a bit to drink after dinner. But he's always been good about holding his liquor."

Could Alex really have been that drunk that morning? It didn't seem possible. Sandra had seen him inebriated more times than she could count. He seemed fine. Unless that milkshake station in the ski resort's restaurant was spiking drinks. And, yet, a part of Sandra wished that maybe Alex *had* been drunk; this way, his blood alcohol level could shield him from any pain from the accident. She would rather think Alex simply drifted off into a deep, inebriated slumber. "But I don't understand. Why would a high blood alcohol level be a crime?"

"It's not," Detective Miller said. "But there's more. The coroner didn't just order a routine toxicology screening. We conducted additional screenings based on some eyewitness accounts."

"Whose eyewitness accounts?"

Detective Miller ignored her question. "And those findings showed traces of a drug."

"What drug?"

The detectives glanced at each other again. "Fentanyl," Detective Miller said.

"Fentanyl? That's impossible."

"Why is that impossible?" Detective Menendez asked.

"Because Alex wasn't a recreational drug user. He drank, yeah, but not drugs. Never."

"You sure about that?"

"I'm positive," she answered defensively again. "Wait, is *that* what you're trying to tell me? That someone slipped Alex some fentanyl?" Sandra's heart began to pound. "And that's what caused the accident?" Her breath was getting lodged in her throat. "Are you saying . . . Are you saying that someone *else* was responsible for Alex's death?" Feelings she couldn't describe were bubbling up inside her. Relief? Fury? Despondency?

"I'd like to show you something." The detective reached into his pocket, pulled out his phone, and held it up. "Can you identify the people on this screen?"

Sandra took the phone and stared at the image. "That's a photo of my husband and me. At breakfast that morning at the resort."

"It's not a photo, Ms. Wilson," Detective Menendez said. "It's a video. Will you please press Play?"

She pressed Play and her eyes went immediately to Alex. Alive. Laughing. His eyes glued to Sandra. She had always loved the way his eyes bored into her, like he was searching for buried treasure. But then, on the screen, Sandra was reaching into her purse . . .

"What is this?" She handed the phone back to Detective Miller.

"*You* tell *me*," he said.

"Is this security footage?"

"What was in the pill you gave your husband, Ms. Wilson?" Detective Menendez asked.

"It wasn't a pill. It was a dietary supplement." She began telling them about Alex's calcium deficiency when she stopped abruptly. "Wait, you can't possibly think . . ."

"Were you and Alex having trouble?" Detective Miller asked.

"Trouble? No, why?"

"Apparently, you two were trying to have a baby, yes?"

Sandra nearly gasped, but she was having trouble sucking in oxygen, as if the air had suddenly left the room. "Who told you that?"

"I would appreciate you answering the question, Ms. Wilson," Detective Miller said.

How could she? She had suddenly forgotten how to speak.

"I . . . We . . ." Sandra's thoughts were swirling, and none of them were making it to her mouth. "Alex and I . . ."

"Did you tell your late husband . . ." Detective Miller pulled out a notepad and began to check some notes. "Did you say to him, 'I should just find a man who has good sperm'?"

Sandra almost fell to the floor as if she had been sucker punched. She *had* said that. The memory of that night came flooding back. The yelling. The tears. That had been the worst thing she had ever said to Alex. That had been the worst thing she had ever said to *anyone*. There was no excuse for it. Even in the heat of the moment. And she had apologized profusely. And Alex had forgiven her. She was sure of it. But she had never forgiven herself. "How did you know that, Detective Miller?"

"Please just answer—"

"That was more than two years ago, Detective. We were having trouble conceiving. But we decided to adopt . . ."

The adoption process. Sandra had forgotten all about it. She would have to call the birth parents and pull their applications from the lists. Unless Alex's uncle had done it already. The detectives continued standing there, waiting. And watching.

"Listen, I loved my husband. I don't know why there was fentanyl in his toxicology report. Maybe he picked up someone's drink at a bar. Maybe someone spiked something he was drinking after we had breakfast. I don't know. Isn't fentanyl a big problem, like, in . . ."

"Like in what, Ms. Wilson?" Detective Menendez asked.

She was about to say *in schools*. She remembered what Tara had said the day she had met her. That there had been an overdose of fentanyl in the school she worked in.

"Is something wrong?" Detective Miller asked.

Sandra nearly laughed. A wild, frenzied release of sound. "*Everything* is wrong, Detective. My husband is gone, and my life is over. I would never have done anything to harm him, if that's what you're getting at. It would be like harming myself." She reached for her purse, pulled out the vial of vitamins, and handed it to him. "Here. Take these. These are the calcium tablets I carry for Alex, since he always forgets to take them. I'm sure you can check his medical history. You'll see that his doctor prescribed calcium."

Detective Miller took the calcium tablets from her hand.

"I know you don't know me. And you didn't know *us*." Tears were streaming down Sandra's cheeks now. "But Alex and I were about as close as two human beings could possibly be. We had a wonderful life and have been together so long that it was difficult to know where he ended and I began. He was an amazing, amazing person, and it's bad enough thinking that he died by some stupid skiing accident, but to think that he mistakenly drank something or that somebody tried to hurt him is . . . just . . ." She took a long breath. "Well, it's just fucking shitty." She wiped away her tears. "Normally, I'm very polite. If Alex were here, he would tell you that. But he's not. And, I'm sorry, but unless you want to arrest me or take me down to some police station, I need to ask you to please leave."

The room was quiet as Detective Miller and his partner assessed her. She was sure she didn't do herself any favors by having this little meltdown, but she didn't care. After a long moment, Detective Miller put his notepad back into a pocket of his long coat. "Well, sorry to have disturbed you, Ms. Wilson." He reached into another pocket and pulled out a card. "If you think of anything, please give us a call. We'll see ourselves out."

Sandra took the card, placed it on the coffee table, and watched the detectives leave. She waited until their footsteps left her front porch and a car engine started somewhere nearby. Then she hurried to the door, closed it, and threw herself onto the couch, sobbing uncontrollably.

CHAPTER 15

Friday, April 4, 9:00 a.m.

Sandra flung open the front door of the office building and flew up the stairs. She could only imagine what she looked like. Messy hair. Yesterday's clothing. When she had awoken on the couch that morning, she prayed that the encounter with the detectives had been a dream. But then she saw Detective Miller's business card on the coffee table.

Blake wasn't answering her texts or calls, so she got into her car and drove straight to Napkin Marketing. When she got upstairs, he was on the phone in his office. With just one look at her, Blake said, "Sorry, Lyle, I have to run. I'll be in touch in a day or so." He clicked off the call. "What's wrong?"

Sandra could hardly breathe. "The police came to see me."

"The police?" Blake stood up. "Why?"

"They think Alex's death may not have been an accident."

"What?!"

"That's what they said. And . . . and . . ."

"And what?"

She burst into tears. "And they think it might have been *me*."

Blake appeared stunned. "It might have been you that what?"

"Me, Blake! They think I tried to poison Alex."

Blake furrowed his brows. "Why the hell would they think that?"

"Because, because . . ." She was starting to hyperventilate now.

"Here." Blake pulled a water bottle from a stack he kept neatly on a side table, opened it, and handed it to her. "Breathe, Sandra, breathe. We both know how ridiculous that is."

Sandra took a sip. "They said they found traces of fentanyl in Alex's system. Why was there fentanyl in Alex's system?" she asked and then began choking down more water as if to drown the words in her throat.

"Fentanyl in his system?" Blake shook his head as he took the bottle from Sandra's hands. "That's impossible. Alex has never taken a drug in his life."

"Exactly. That's why they think someone probably gave it to him." She pointed to herself. "Me! They think *I* gave it to him."

"Why would they think that?"

"Because they saw me give Alex a calcium tablet on some security footage they took at the restaurant where we had breakfast that morning."

"What security footage? At the ski resort?"

Sandra nodded.

"San, this is insane. I'm sure it's all one big misunderstanding. You *loved* Alex. Anyone knows that. They're probably just covering their bases."

Sandra couldn't get out of her mind the way the detectives were looking at her. Like she was a criminal. Like she belonged in handcuffs and an orange jumpsuit. "Yeah, but fentanyl, Blake? How the hell would he have fentanyl in him?"

"That stuff is insidious. And it's becoming a real problem. Just ask Tara. She told you about the incident at her school, right?"

Sandra wouldn't exactly say that Tara had told *her*. She told everyone at the table that day at April's Café, and Sandra happened to be there.

"Stupid high school kid was snorting fentanyl powder. What did he expect?" Blake shook his head. "These street drugs are more dangerous than ever."

"I can't get that stupid ski resort manager out of my mind. How high and mighty he was." She dropped her briefcase on the floor. "Basically, trying to pin the blame for Alex's death on Alex. Blame the victim, right? *He must have been going too fast.*

He must have been showing off. He wasn't wearing a helmet. Meanwhile, the stupid ski resort has a drug problem! I'm sure Daryl Winters or whatever his name was wouldn't like *that* on his social media feeds."

"What was the name of the detective who visited you?" Blake said. "I'll see if I can contact him."

Sandra pulled Detective Miller's business card from her pocket. "He left me this. I want to burn it."

Blake plucked it from her hand. "Don't worry, San. I'll take care of it."

"Really? That would make me feel better. Wait . . ." She took the card and snapped a photo of it with her phone. "Just in case I need to call him. You know, so I can *confess*." She rolled her eyes.

"You should go home and try to relax."

"I'm sick of being home, Blake," she said. "I've been home for two weeks. Staring at the walls. Unable to concentrate. Having marathon crying sessions with Pam. I can't do it anymore. Here. I brought my computer." She pointed to her briefcase. "Put me to work. Give me something to do."

"I think it's too soon, San . . ."

"Too soon nothing. I need to occupy my mind or else, I swear, I'll go crazy." She began to cry again. What was happening to her? Sandra was *not* a crier. Whenever she and Alex watched a tearjerker, Alex was the one sobbing into her shoulder. Like Chuck had been at the funeral with Beatrice. Alex and Chuck. Two crybabies. And now Sandra was one, too.

"All right, all right." Blake pulled her into his arms. "It'll be all right, San. We'll figure this out. Together. What do you want to do here?"

"I don't know." She pulled away. "I would volunteer to water the plants, but I think I just killed five peace lilies in my condo. I can't concentrate on anything. I can't write. I can't read. I am consumed with the fact that Alex is gone. And that I'll never see him again. Ever."

And then she saw him.

She picked up a photo frame from Blake's desk of the three of them on the Harry Potter ride at Universal Studios in Florida. She remembered that day vividly. Alex had been talking for years about visiting the Wizarding World of Harry Potter, and they had finally saved up enough money to go for an extended weekend. Alex loved rollercoasters. Both literal and figurative.

She placed the photo frame down. "What's this?" She picked up another frame she hadn't seen before. In it was a photo of Blake and Tara smiling together with an Elvis impersonator standing beside them. "You got married in Vegas?"

"No, city hall. That was taken at a show somewhere. I forgot where. Tara's a big Elvis fan."

Sandra placed the photo frame down. "How is . . . *Tara*?"

"She's okay. Why did you say her name like that?"

Sandra was tired of being polite. She had had a shitty couple of weeks. "Why wasn't she at the funeral, Blake?"

Blake took a deep breath and gave a long exhale. "I was wondering when you were going to ask me about that."

Sandra crossed her arms. "Well?"

"I begged her to go, San. I thought it was crazy for her not to attend the funeral services. She knows what Alex meant to me. But . . ." He shook his head. "She was adamant. She said funerals trigger her."

"Funerals trigger everybody."

"She implored me to try to understand. She said her parents were killed by a drunk driver when she was a kid, and she was forced to go to the funeral. She said it was so traumatizing that she has never gone to a funeral since."

An image of Tara as a sad, but fashionable, little girl popped into Sandra's head, and she shook it away. Sandra didn't want to understand. She wanted to be mad. "But she didn't even call, Blake."

"She told me to tell you how sorry she was. How sorry she *is*. I must have forgotten in all the craziness. I'm so sorry, San. Tara feels awful about Alex."

"Why are you defending her?"

Blake seemed affronted. "I'm not defending *anyone*, Sandra. I'm just telling you what happened. Tara is an innocent party here."

Sandra moved some neatly stacked paperwork from the chair in front of Blake's desk and sat down. "I'm sorry." She shook her head. "I'm not myself. And I don't know if I'll *ever* be." She picked up one of the papers beside her. "What's this?"

Blake glanced at the paperwork in her hands. "Oh. I really don't want to talk about that now." He tried to take it from her, but Sandra pulled her hand back.

"It looks like a contract for a wedding photographer," she said.

Blake sighed. "Well, I was going to tell you and Alex at dinner that night at the ski resort, but Tara wasn't there, so I figured I'd wait until the next night. But then . . ." He shook his head.

"Tell us what?"

"Tara and I had been planning a wedding reception for next month. It was Tara's idea, really. To get all our family and friends together to celebrate, since no one really got the chance to yet." He shook his head. "But with all that's happened, I think we should cancel."

Sandra stood up. "Blake, no. Don't cancel."

"But San—"

"We need something happy. All of us."

"Yeah, but how am I supposed to have a party when my best friend in the world is gone and can't be there?"

"He'll be there. In spirit."

Blake shook his head. "I don't know."

"C'mon, Blake. Alex would want you to have this party. You know that. He really liked Tara. And we both know he liked to party."

"He really liked Tara?"

"Yeah. *Really.* And he would want to celebrate your happiness." She hugged him, and for the first time in the past two weeks didn't feel like bursting into tears. Maybe it was because she had found a tiny way to move forward in this Alex-less world and still feel like she was honoring his memory.

Blake looked into her eyes. "I'll do whatever you say, San. If you think it's okay to move forward with this . . ."

"I do," she said.

"Well, if that's true . . ." He looked down at the floor and then back up at her. "Then I have something I would like to ask you."

"What is it?"

"Well, I was going to ask Alex to be my best man. But . . . I was wondering . . ."

"Are you asking me to be your second choice? Plan B? Sloppy second?" she asked.

Blake appeared mortified. "No!" His cheeks reddened.

"I'm just kidding." Sandra laughed out loud, surprising herself. That was something Alex might have said. "Of course, I'll be your best man. I would be honored." She hugged Blake hard, and they stood there for a moment before Sandra pulled away. "Okay, enough of this mushy stuff. What can I do? I need to keep busy. Please, give me a task."

"Sandra, you don't have to—"

"Please! Pretty please! Anything! I need to feel like I matter."

"Of course, you matter. Oh, all right . . ." Blake looked around the room and picked up a box that was on the shelving unit behind him. "I was supposed to bring these over to Chuck's."

"I'll do it!" Sandra reached for the box. "Geez, this is heavy. What's in here?"

"Chuck's band was profiled in *Newsday* since his gig at the Long Island Music and Entertainment Hall of Fame is one of the first concerts on the summer calendar. I got him a bunch of copies of the newspaper. And some additional flyers are in there for the gig."

"He was in *Newsday*? That's amazing!" Sandra said, and then began to cry again. Apparently, she was not yet done with crying.

"What's wrong?"

Through tears, she said, "Alex would have been so happy for him."

Blake reached for a tissue from a box on his desk. He wiped her nose. "Yes, he would have been. Alex was the one who found Chuck's band. And now he will go on and do great things and know it was all because of Alex."

Sandra nodded.

He tossed the tissue into a nearby garbage pail. "Okay. Please drive safely. And don't worry about the detective. I'll take care of it."

"Thanks, Blake. I don't know what I would do without you."

She walked out Blake's door and glanced over at Alex's office. The door was open, like it always was. The tray Pam had brought over with the oatmeal cookies was still on his desk, empty. She would have to go in there soon and help Blake clean it out.

But that was a job for another day.

She walked down the Napkin Marketing staircase to street level and hurried to her car, putting the box into the back seat. As she got into the driver's seat, her phone rang, and she fished it out of her purse.

Pam again.

Sandra let the call to go voicemail. She promised herself that she would call her mother-in-law back tomorrow, first thing. She had done enough crying today.

CHAPTER 16

Friday, April 4, 10:30 a.m.

Sandra was having second thoughts about making this delivery as she got closer to Chuck's house in Suffolk County. She remembered the first time she had been there.

With Alex.

For a music-themed Halloween party.

Alex had somehow gotten the idea they should go as '80s duo Hall & Oates. The mustache she had worn all night was itchy and felt like a fuzzy caterpillar on her lips, but Alex loved it. In fact, he made her keep it on when they got home that night and made love. She cry-smiled again, thinking about him singing Hall & Oates's smash hit "You Make My Dreams" in his drunken sex voice as she pulled in front of Chuck's split-level home.

She had to get used to this. Seeing the people and places she used to with Alex. She couldn't hide for the rest of her life, as much as she wanted to. Alex wouldn't have wanted that for her. And she really wanted to live her life as she would have with *him*. Wide open. He had taught her how. She just needed to remember. She retrieved the box from the back seat of her car, slammed the door with her foot, and made her way up the concrete path toward the front door, hoping the Christmas lights might cheer her up. *Alex loved Christmas.*

The door opened as she got there, and Chuck hurried outside to take the box from her hands.

"Hey there," he said. "I didn't expect to see *you* today."

"I volunteered." She shrugged. "Trying to keep busy."

"Come in, come in!" He hurried inside, placing the box on the floor beside the front door, and motioned for her to follow. "Bea, Sandra's here!" he called.

Beatrice appeared in the doorway to the kitchen; behind her, Sandra could see part of the refrigerator, which featured photos of her and Chuck, held in place by magnets in the shape of musical notes.

"Sandra, hi!" Beatrice ran toward her and wrapped her in a hug. Sandra hugged her back, reminding herself to *mean it*, which is what Alex would tell her when her hugs were lackluster. *Life's too short for limp hugs,* he would say.

Life's too short . . .

"Can I get you anything?" Beatrice asked. "Something to drink? Something to eat?"

"No, I'm fine, thank you."

"Please, come sit." She motioned toward the couch.

"Okay, but I can only stay for a few minutes." Yes, she had *so much* to do. Like stare at the walls of her apartment.

Sandra sat down on the couch, alone, and Beatrice and Chuck sat on the love seat, all of which seemed weirdly appropriate.

"How are you doing?" Chuck asked.

Sandra shrugged. "Okay, I guess."

"Really?" he asked with concern.

"No. Not really. I'm a mess, but I'm hoping I can find a way to move forward. Second by second. Minute by minute."

"I hear you. I'm trying to do the same thing, but I keep playing back in my mind what happened that morning at the ski resort," Chuck said with a shake of his head.

"Me too," Sandra said. "If you don't mind my asking, what exactly happened. I mean, right before the accident."

Chuck glanced at his wife, who shook her head. "Sandra," he said, "I don't know if that's a good—"

"Please," Sandra said. She wanted to know. For *her* sake. But also because she couldn't stop thinking about the detectives who had shown up at her door. Maybe Chuck would tell her something that would help her make sense of what they had said. Why Alex had possibly died of some kind of drug overdose. It didn't seem possible.

"Okay, I guess." He gave Beatrice a sideways glance and began talking before she could stop him. "We were up at the top of the slope. We had just gotten off the lift," Chuck said. "It was such a beautiful morning. Cold. Really cold, but sunny. We had been singing some song—I can't remember the name of it now—and just laughing."

"That sounds like Alex." Sandra gave a small smile.

"And because of the bracelets we were wearing, we didn't go immediately to the trail. The resort had this fancy-schmancy chalet at the top of the mountain that served coffee and other hot beverages, and because we were wearing that bracelet, we had an all-access pass to everything on the resort, including that chalet."

"There was a coffee station up there?"

"Yeah. You've never seen it?"

Sandra shook her head. She'd imagined the top of the mountain was just trees and snow. And maybe a few grizzly bears. "So, you and Alex went to get coffee at this fancy-schmancy coffee chalet?"

"Well, kinda. We were heading toward it because we wanted to see how, you know, the other half lives"—he was smiling at the memory—"when we heard a whistle. We turned and saw Blake waving at us. He was already at one of the outdoor tables. When we got there, Tara was bringing over two coffees."

"Only two?"

"Yeah, she and Blake had already drank theirs, so Tara went to get two for Alex and me. That was nice, right?"

Something inside Sandra tightened. Yes, it was nice, and she remembered Blake saying something about Tara getting coffee for the group, but now Sandra was feeling left out. *Tara* had been there in Alex's last moments. Not Sandra.

"Then what happened. Tara handed the coffee to you?"

Chuck furrowed his brow. "No, she put it on the table, and then she kind of . . . like, fell."

"She fell in the snow?" Sandra asked.

"It all happened so fast. One minute, I was reaching for my coffee on the table, and the next I was helping Alex help Tara up. You know Alex. He's always the first one to help someone in trouble."

Sandra nodded, mostly to keep from having tears drop from the corners of her eyes.

"Tara seemed so embarrassed," Chuck said, "but Alex told her not to worry about it. That he falls all the time."

"*I'm* actually the clumsy one," Sandra said, although that sounded like Alex. Pretending to be clumsy so Tara wouldn't feel bad.

"You can't be any clumsier than *this* guy," Beatrice said, poking her husband.

And it seemed like Beatrice was doing the same for Sandra.

"Then the rest is kind of a blur," Chuck said. "Alex and I drank our coffees—quickly because we wanted to beat the crowds—and then before I knew it, we were double-daring one another to see who could get down the expert trail first—"

"As grown men do." Beatrice smiled.

"Mostly, I remember just laughing. I can't remember the last time I laughed that much."

The tightness in Sandra's chest was lifting a bit. She knew talking about Alex would make her sad, but Sandra was happy to know that the last moments of Alex's life were filled with merriment. Bright sunshine and laughter. With a friend. Alex deserved that. She was glad Chuck had come along with them on the trip.

"Blake and Tara had already gone down, so Alex and I chugged our coffees and headed to the slope." Suddenly, Chuck's face filled with sadness, and his eyes met the floor. "I could hear him behind me. He was laughing, but I was so intent on beating him down the trail so that I could tease him about it for the rest of his life." He looked at Sandra. "I wish I would have turned back to get one last look at him, you know? I didn't know I wouldn't ever see him again." Tears filled his eyes.

"It's not your fault, baby," Beatrice said.

"Beatrice is right, Chuck," Sandra said. "It's not. But if it makes you feel any better, I'm feeling pretty guilty myself."

"You, guilty?" Chuck asked. "Why?"

"Guilty for not saying no to this stupid ski chalet trip. Guilty that I didn't learn to ski or else I would have been up there and maybe been able to help him—or keep this from happening." She sniffled and could feel the tears falling. So much for no more crying.

"It's not your fault either, Sandra," Beatrice said. She reached forward and handed her a tissue from a box on the coffee table. "This was a horrible accident that was no one's fault."

The detectives appeared in Sandra's mind's eye. Was it really an accident?

"Let's talk about something else," Chuck suggested, and Sandra saw Beatrice subtly nudge her husband. He shook his head.

"Wait," Sandra said. "One more thing, Chuck. Did you see anything weird up there? On the top of the slope?"

"Weird, how?"

"Like, were people doing drugs?"

Chuck shuddered slightly, prompting Beatrice to gently put her hand on his knee. He shook his head. "No, nothing like that. I swear," he said. "Why?"

Sandra was focused on the words *I swear*, which seemed weirdly defensive. Like Chuck had his hand on a stack of Bibles and was called to testify at a criminal trial. Or like he was a child trying to convince a parent. "No reason," she lied. She knew she wasn't the greatest liar, but she didn't want to say anything about the detectives' visit. She had a feeling she could trust Chuck, but the shudder and *I swear* made her unsure. "I'm just trying to picture the scene," she said.

"Just couples, mostly," he said. "And college kids, and families with young kids. All family-friendly stuff."

Sandra nodded and wiped the lingering tears on her cheeks with the tissue. "Thank you, Chuck. I guess I just needed to feel like I was there. And you helped me do that. So, thank you. I miss him."

"I do, too," Chuck said.

Beatrice nudged Chuck again. Chuck shook his head again.

"What's going on?" Sandra asked.

Nudge.

Shake.

Nudge.

Shake.

Finally, Beatrice cleared her throat.

"Sandra, it's so funny that you should stop by," she said. "Chuck and I were just talking about you." She reached for Chuck's hand.

"I don't think now's a good time," he whispered, squeezing her hand.

"I think it's the perfect time," Beatrice whispered back. "She's *here*. You should tell her. In person. That's the right thing to do."

"Tell me what?" Sandra asked.

"Let me grab us some snacks," Beatrice said. She kissed Chuck on the cheek, nodded, and disappeared into the kitchen.

"What's going on, Chuck?" Sandra asked again.

"Well... it's just that... well... I don't think that now's the right time... but you're here, like Bea said, and... I'm not sure how to say this... I think the band..." His skinny legs were fidgeting under him. "I've been talking with the guys, and I think the band and I... *we*... are going to work with another marketing firm moving forward."

"You mean, you're no longer going to work with Napkin Marketing?"

Chuck's eyes were pleading with her. "I hope you understand, Sandra. As much as I want to support Alex's company..." He moved forward on the love seat. "For me, *Alex* was Napkin Marketing. And now that he's not... well, now that he's not here, it's just not the same."

Sandra got that. *Nothing* was the same.

"Frankly," Chuck continued, "I think the feeling is mutual between me and Blake. Blake never seemed all that interested in me or the band, and he practically told me the other day that I should seek other marketing services."

"Seriously?"

"I mean, he didn't come out and say it, but I could feel it, you know?" Chuck shrugged.

"I don't know, Chuck. Blake seemed really pumped about your coverage in *Newsday* today."

"I'm sure he was! That bodes well for business. I talked up Napkin Marketing as much as I could in the interview, and there's a great mention of the company in the article. But, to be clear, I wouldn't have gotten that coverage if Alex hadn't been able to get us that gig at the Hall of Fame. Blake isn't really a music guy, and he pretty much told me that maybe Napkin Marketing might be moving in a different direction and may not be the right fit for us going forward."

"When did he say this? In the past two weeks?" She shook her head. "I've said things in the past two weeks that I'm not proud of." She thought about how she had exploded on the two detectives. "Grief makes you do crazy things."

"It was before that. Maybe a month ago."

"A month ago?"

Chuck nodded. "I thought about bringing it up with Alex, but we had the wedding preparations going on, and I didn't want to get in the middle of a work thing between him and

Blake. He mentioned something about Blake wanting to diversify recently, so I thought it was related to that."

Diversify. The word made Sandra think of Tara again, how Blake mentioned that Tara said it might be a good idea to diversify. "Yeah, but I didn't think that meant Blake wanted to divest the company of all the music acts they rep. There are a bunch. If they got rid of everyone, the company would fold."

"Maybe he won't get rid of them all. Maybe it's just us. I don't know. Like I said, he didn't come right out and say that I should find another marketing firm. But I got the impression he wanted me to, you know? And then when Alex told me that Blake got married, I thought maybe that had something to do with that."

Blake did mention Tara had some *interesting ideas* for the business. Was getting rid of Chuck one of them?

"Please tell me you understand," Chuck said.

"I think Alex would want you to do whatever was best for the band. He certainly wouldn't want you to stick around just for him."

"You really mean that, San?" His cheeks reddened. "Is it okay that I call you San?"

Sandra smiled. "Sure. And yes, I really mean that."

"Thank you. And I hope this doesn't mean we can't still see one another from time to time. I hope you think of us—me and Bea—as friends."

Sandra couldn't help but feel surprised. Somewhere, deep down, she always thought the people she knew through Alex would drift away if he weren't around, like she wasn't good enough to be friends with on her own, like she would repel them without Alex's internal magnet drawing everyone closer. "I'd love to stay friends."

"You look a bit shocked," he said.

She laughed. "Sorry. I don't mean to. I guess I figured I'd lose a lot of the friends I knew through Alex now that he's gone. We were so different."

"Yeah, you both have different styles, for sure, but anyone who has met you both can plainly see you have the same heart."

Sandra smiled. "That just might be the nicest thing anyone has ever said to me, Chuck."

"Great!" Chuck sprang up and came toward her. "I'm sorry. Another hug coming your way. I'm a hugger."

"Yeah, I figured that out. Another reason why you and Alex got along so well." She hugged him like she meant it.

"I'm so glad to have gotten that off my chest. Bea was right as usual." Chuck hurried over to the box Sandra had brought that he left on the floor. He opened it, lifted out a copy of *Newsday*, and flipped the pages, holding up the full-page article on Rockknot. "Alex was the one who made this happen. I don't know what he did. Maybe he's good friends with the entertainment editor or bombarded him with press releases, but *Newsday* came a-knocking for this little story." He smiled. "It's funny. I always thought if I were profiled in my hometown paper that it would be because I had been picked up for shoplifting or something."

"There's still time!" Bea said, entering the room. She was carrying a tray full of sandwiches and what looked like a bowl of hummus with crackers. She placed the food down on the coffee table. "I made us a little something. I know you said you weren't really hungry, Sandra, but I think we all need to eat."

"You really didn't have to go to any trouble," Sandra said.

"Yes, I did. And I insist that you join us for an early lunch."

Chuck put the newspaper down on the coffee table. "There's no use arguing, Sandra," he said with a smile. "Bea always gets her way. Trust me, I know." He held up the wedding ring on his finger.

"Okay, I'd love to," Sandra said. She could see why Alex really liked Chuck. There was a warmth about him. And Beatrice had it, too. In Sandra's experience, not many people did. Or maybe she just hadn't given them the chance to show it. She promised herself she would going forward.

"Great." Chuck reached for a sandwich.

"Plate, mister," Bea said, handing him a paper plate.

"Ha. You sound like me and Alex." Sandra reached for a sandwich. "Alex never met a finger food he didn't like."

"To Alex!" Chuck raised his sandwich.

"To Alex," Sandra said, and they clinked sandwiches.

"Remember when Alex convinced you to do that dance on TikTok to our wedding song?" Beatrice laughed, dipping a cracker in the hummus.

"I'm *still* getting likes and shares on that," Chuck said.

"Alex was a classic rock guy." Sandra took a bite of her sandwich. "He totally got your music."

"Classic rock rocks," Chuck said. "Beer, Sandra?"

"Sure, why not?" she said.

"None for you, babe." He planted a kiss on Beatrice's head. "I'll get you a bottle of water." He left the room.

Sandra dipped a cracker in the hummus and smiled. "I had a feeling," she said.

"Really?" Beatrice asked, her cheeks reddening.

"Yeah, you're glowing. Congratulations. How far along are you?"

"About six weeks. Thank God my wedding dress fit, or else my mother would have flipped."

"How is your mother feeling?" Sandra asked.

"So much better. Thank you." Beatrice wiped her mouth with a napkin. "I wasn't sure we should say anything. You know, about the baby. Alex mentioned to Chuck that you guys had had some trouble conceiving. I didn't want to look like a jerk."

"Don't be silly. I'm so happy for you and Chuck. Alex would be, too. You guys will make great parents."

As Sandra reached for another cracker, Beatrice began talking about how she found out she was pregnant, while Chuck returned with their beers. So much was swirling in Sandra's mind. Sadness mixed with happiness mixed with the fear and anger of what might have happened at the top of that Vermont mountain. Plus, everything that might have been if Alex had still been alive.

CHAPTER 17

Friday, April 4, 1:00 p.m.

"How did it go?" Blake asked when Sandra returned to Napkin Marketing.

"Good," she said, walking into his office.

He leaned back from his desk and crossed his arms.

"What?" she asked.

"Sandra Wilson, I've known you a long time, and I know that you answer *good* when things are *not good*. Did something happen at Chuck's?"

"Everything was *fine*, Blake. How's *fine* for a word?" she asked, rolling her eyes. "Does that pass the test?" She was in a bad mood—a mood that had manifested itself on the ride back from Suffolk County. She knew whatever she was feeling wasn't necessarily Blake's fault, but she couldn't get the edge out of her voice. The detectives and their insinuation. Chuck and his weird twitch when she mentioned drugs. Beatrice and her baby happiness. It was all too much. She picked up her briefcase, which was still on the floor in front of his desk. "If you've got any PR materials you need, I think I'll do them at home. I've had enough fresh air for one day."

"Now, what does *that* mean?" he asked, concerned.

"Nothing. Don't mind me. I'm in a shit mood. And I don't think you can blame me."

He stood up. "If it helps, I put in a call with that Detective Miller guy. Just waiting for a call back. Maybe I can get some more information from him."

Despite her reluctance, the tension in her shoulders eased a bit. "Not sure what that's going to do, but thank you. Yes, it does help." Sandra was about to turn and leave when she said, "Blake, can I ask you a question?"

"Sure. Anything."

"Did you tell Chuck that he should find another marketing firm?"

Silence. Never the best answer to a question. Especially for Blake. She had been in many meetings with Blake and Alex over the years, and when Blake didn't answer a question right away, she knew it was because he was thinking of a way to soften what was a difficult response. Finally, he said, "Well, no. I didn't tell him that, but I'm sure he got the hint."

"Why do you want to get rid of Chuck's band? Is this all part of the diversifying thing you were talking about with Alex? Because if you ask me—and I know you didn't—Chuck's band has the highest profile of all your clients, and that only bodes well for Napkin. Plus, you know how Alex felt about Chuck."

"Yes, all too well."

"What does *that* mean?"

"San, sit down."

"I don't want to sit down."

"Okay, fine. Don't sit down."

"Why are you managing me?"

"I'm not *managing* you. I'm just trying to talk to you."

"Well, *talk* then." The edge in her voice was getting edgier.

Blake exhaled. "Listen, there are some things you don't know."

"Like what?"

"I guess . . . what I'm trying to say . . . is that . . . well, I know you think that Alex told you everything."

"He did."

"Well, yes and no," Blake said.

"What does *that* mean?"

"It means that sometimes Alex kept things from you."

"Things? What exactly are you trying to say, Blake?" Sandra crossed her arms and glared at him. "Like an *affair*?"

Blake's eyes opened wide. "No, no, no! I'm not saying anything like that. You know Alex loved and adored you. That's not what I'm saying. He would never . . . you know." He paused. "What I'm saying is he could also be protective of you. And also of other people."

"Yeah. So?"

"So, there are some things about Chuck you may not know."

"Like what?"

Blake hesitated. "I feel weird telling you since Alex isn't here, and if *he* didn't tell you—"

"Exactly, Blake. Alex isn't here. So, just tell me."

Blake exhaled again. "Fine. About a year before Napkin Marketing signed with Chuck's band, Rockknot, to do their marketing, Chuck was in rehab."

Rehab? Was that all? Sandra was beginning to think that Blake was about to tell her that Chuck was a serial killer hiding from the police. "So? Why wouldn't Alex tell me that Chuck was in rehab?"

"Exactly. It's not a huge deal. And he probably felt there was no reason to," Blake said. "That this was all behind Chuck. And you know Alex. He accepts people for who they are. He roots for them and always likes to start off a relationship with a clean slate."

"Yeah, I know," Sandra said, but the more she thought about it, the more she felt a little hurt that Alex didn't confide in her. "Alex knows I wouldn't have held it against Chuck."

"Like I said, maybe he thought it wasn't even a big deal and was in the past. I don't know why he didn't tell you."

Suddenly, the hair on the back of Sandra's neck stood up. "Wait, what was Chuck in rehab for?"

"Drug addiction."

Sandra's heart began to pound. "What kind of drug? Blake, was it—"

"I know what you're going to say, San. I thought the same thing this morning when you mentioned the detectives and the fentanyl, but I'm sure it's just a coincidence."

"So, it *was* fentanyl?"

"Yes and no."

"What do you mean?"

"Are you sure you don't want to sit down?"

Sandra glared at him.

"Okay. Chuck was hooked on heroin, from what Alex said, and somehow—I don't know exactly what happened—snorted a bad batch or something. It was laced with fentanyl or however they say it. I don't know all that lingo like Tara does, but all I know is that Chuck OD'd and almost died. It took a long time for him to kick the habit, but he went to rehab and finally did. And he wanted to make a fresh start." He shrugged. "Alex loved Chuck's music, and loved *him*, and convinced me to give him a chance. Frankly, I don't think he wanted to tell me about Chuck's past, either, but since we were going into business together, he thought I should know. Full disclosure. I appreciated that. And, of course, Alex was right. Working with Chuck and his band turned out to be good business."

Sandra was half listening to what Blake was saying. She was remembering how Chuck and Beatrice had reacted when she asked if there had been any drug use up in Vermont. Chuck had gotten squirrelly. And Beatrice protective. "I asked Chuck if there were drugs passed around the morning that Alex died."

"You did?"

"He said no, but he acted weird for a minute."

"Weird how?"

"It was like a knee-jerk reaction. Visceral. His wife put her hand on him to steady him. Maybe I triggered him. Maybe he thought Alex told me about his past and that I was essentially accusing him of getting Alex mixed up with drugs and causing his death. I don't know."

"From what Alex mentioned, Chuck almost fell off the wagon again recently, but Chuck's wife gave him an ultimatum. Said she would leave him if he ever got caught up in all that again."

"Wow, I can't believe it. They seem so . . ."

"Seem so what?" he asked.

"I don't know. Calm and cool. *Together.*"

"Yeah, well, things aren't always what they seem," Blake said. "Listen, San, I don't want to start accusing people of things. But you brought up Chuck and why I thought it might be a good idea for us to part ways. I want to believe all that is in Chuck's past, but you just never know. And with what you told me about the detectives this morning..."

"Are you going to tell Detective Miller about Chuck when he calls you back?"

Blake shrugged. "I don't know. I don't know if I owe it to Alex to say something or owe it to him to *not* say something."

She nodded. "But, seriously, it just doesn't make sense. Why would Chuck want to kill Alex?"

"Who's to say he wanted to kill him? Maybe he had fallen off the wagon and thought Alex could use a good buzz. Maybe he spiked Alex's drink for fun. Maybe it was a complete accident. But think about it, if you were Chuck and your band was just starting to take off, and you had something to do with another person's death, wouldn't you try and cover it up? If you look at it that way, it's not surprising he wants to cut ties with Napkin Marketing. And the easiest way to do it is to blame *me* for the break."

Sandra was unable to comprehend everything Blake was saying. It was all too much. Blake must have sensed her confusion. He reached out and held her hand. "Listen, whether or not Napkin diversifies its client list, or whether or not Chuck's history has anything to do with what happened to Alex, I have to say, I agree with Chuck."

"Agree with what?" Sandra asked.

"That it's a good idea for us to go our separate ways."

Sandra nodded, although it seemed wrong. Logical, but wrong. But she figured she had to get used to that. The rest of her life was going to feel that way without Alex by her side.

CHAPTER 18

Friday, April 4, 9:00 p.m.

Since she had gotten back from the office, Sandra couldn't sit still. She had thrown out all the casseroles and lasagnas that had been sitting in her refrigerator, gathering mold. Had scrubbed the oven, swept the floor, vacuumed the carpeting, spritzed the windows, and straightened and re-straightened the pillows on the couch. She had an overwhelming desire to clean, to purge. And since Blake hadn't given her any writing to do, she decided that moving her body was the only way to quiet her overactive brain. She imagined what Alex might say if he saw her in one of these moods.

Yo, San, if you're hell-bent on cleaning, my sock drawer could use a little lovin'.

Hey, San, the last time I saw you move this fast, you were running away from a slug on the front pathway.

Sandra, relax. Whatever it is, it will be okay. I promise.

She stopped to take a breath and nearly fell over. She never realized how much Alex kept her balanced, kept her in check. How he had been a crutch she had leaned on for the past twenty-three years, a crutch that had been suddenly taken away, leaving her hopping around on one leg.

Chuck wasn't the *only* one with an addiction.

Alex had been her drug.

And she needed a hit.

Instead, here she was, in the throes of withdrawal, forced to go cold turkey from the one person who made her whole. She threw her dust rag on the coffee table. All this busy work was doing nothing to keep her from thinking about him.

But what else could she do? She checked her to-do list on the refrigerator that she had scrawled on a piece of paper over the past two weeks.

Call adoption families and tell them about Alex

Yes, she needed to do that. Even if Alex's uncle had taken care of that already, it was only right that she personally reach out to these families who had been kind enough to welcome her and Alex into their homes. She needed to let them know that their—well, *her*—circumstances had changed.

She pulled out her phone and a file from her briefcase, opening it on the coffee table. There were only two families left on the list that hadn't yet given Sandra and Alex a definitive no. The last one was the Burke family. Sandra had no desire to speak with Mrs. Burke. She decided to call Casey instead. She dialed, put the phone on speaker, and listened to the line ring as her eyes glanced at the time flashing at the corner of her phone screen. Oh no! She quickly hung up. It was after nine p.m. Sandra was sure Mrs. Burke wouldn't approve of her reaching out at such a late hour. She was mad at herself for not checking the time beforehand. And equally mad at herself for still worrying about what Mrs. Burke thought of her. Sandra sighed. She had no idea what she was going to say to Casey, anyway. Maybe she should have written a script. She put her phone into her pocket, since it was too late to call anyone, and walked back to the to-do list on the fridge.

Clean out Alex's closet

She took a deep breath and walked toward the bedroom, standing in front of the closed door with her hand on the doorknob. She had to go in there eventually. Now was as good a time as any. She had to face Alex's memory. The thousands of minutes they had slept side by side, crotch to butt, or *nipples to nipples*, as Alex liked to say. The thousands of happy moments they had spent in there. She needed to feel them now, to inhale them and hold them in her lungs. She turned the knob and opened the door.

She didn't know what she was expecting—maybe for Alex's spirit to float through her and snap her out of her funk—but the room looked just the way it had the morning they packed up for Vermont. It *looked* the same, even though it *felt* empty. The bed covers were flopped on Sandra's side, which was where Alex had thrown them. *There you go again, stealing all the blankets, San.* Alex's pajamas were lying on the floor near his side of the room. *What's the point of putting them in the hamper, San? I'm just going to wear them again tonight. They're not THAT dirty.* A paperclip, lip balm, tin of mints, portable charger, and some pocket change were lying on Alex's nightstand. *If I ever get picked for* Let's Make a Deal, *San, I'll be ready!* She glanced at the large empty spot on the wall above the bed where their wedding photo used to hang but was now buried beside Alex in the ground.

Alex was everywhere and nowhere. His words, his memories, overpowered her, and yet did nothing to nourish the hole inside of her. She lay down on the pile of blankets on her side of the bed and then rolled over to the other side, inhaling Alex's smell on his pillow. She could identify every aspect of it. His cologne. His mouthwash. His saliva. His general Alex scent. She pulled the blankets over her, hoping to keep it all contained.

High school sweethearts weren't supposed to last. How could they? How could two people who hadn't yet been fully formed create a life together? They were just learning about themselves and what they wanted. And yet she and Alex had defied the odds. She thought of the woman at Chuck's wedding reception who had asked how she and Alex managed to stay together after all these years. Sandra had said *luck*, and there was definitely a measure of luck in any success in life, but the truth was they were having too much fun together to realize that the years were flying by. Sandra had never believed in soulmates, something Alex had always teased her about. *How could a romance writer not believe in soulmates, San?* She had always thought it was silly to think there was only one person in the whole universe meant for another person. And yet, if the definition of a soulmate was a person with whom you could be your most authentic self, and also the person who would force you to grow in ways you never imagined, Alex *was* her soulmate. She wished she could tell him that. Tell him he was right. (He always loved that.) Tell him they had hit the jackpot.

But Alex was gone. And Sandra was a widow at forty years old. The word made her skin crawl. She imagined old ladies in black watching the world through windows or televisions.

Sandra's phone rang. She fished it out of her pocket.

Oh no. Casey.

Sandra sat up in bed. Casey was calling? She must have seen Sandra's number appear on her phone screen. Sandra cleared her throat. This wasn't going to be easy. She clicked the green button. "Hi, Casey."

"Hey, I saw you tried to call me. Or was it, like, a butt dial?"

Say "butt dial." Say "butt dial." "Yeah. I wanted to talk with you. I'm sorry. I hope I didn't call too late."

"No way. I was doing homework. What's up?"

"Well, I have something I need to tell you. I'm not sure if you've heard."

"Heard what?"

Sandra exhaled. Casey didn't know. Sandra wondered why Mrs. Burke hadn't been contacted by Alex's uncle or whether he had contacted anyone at all. Maybe Sandra should have put on her to-do list *Call Alex's uncle*. "Well, something's happened . . ."

"What is it? Your voice sounds funny."

"Well . . ." *Just say it.* "There was a terrible accident a couple of weeks ago. And . . . well, Alex was . . . killed."

"What?! Are you serious?"

"I wish I wasn't."

"Oh, Sandra. I'm so, so sorry." To Sandra's surprise, Casey began crying on the other end of the line. "I know how much in love you and Alex were. I know that we had only just met, but when I saw you guys, I thought to myself, *See? There is hope for love in this world.* You guys just fit. An eleven, right? Side by side, right?"

Sandra didn't know what to say. She was envisioning the number eleven in her mind and one of the ones skiing and then tumbling out of the picture, leaving a single one behind. A single, solitary, lonely, old, friendless, unlovable one.

"How did it happen?" Casey asked.

"A skiing accident."

"Oh my God, did it happen that day I saw you at the restaurant? The day you guys were heading to Vermont?"

"The next day," Sandra said, the tears welling in her eyes again. "I just thought you should know. And I wanted you to hear it from me, if possible. I also wanted you to know that Alex thought you were a special young lady and that he would have been honored to raise your little boy. We both would have been."

"Wait, I don't understand," Casey said. "You mean, you're not interested in adopting my baby anymore?"

Something got lodged in Sandra's throat, and her words wouldn't come out. Was it a wad of mucus? A wad of regret? How could Casey think her plans could just continue as if nothing had happened? She cleared her throat. "Casey, honestly, I can't even imagine my future, let alone guiding the future of a baby. This was something Alex and I were supposed to do *together*. We were supposed to be parents *together*. I'm not sure of anything anymore. Plus, your mom was pretty clear. She wants *two* parents to adopt your baby. And, to be honest, I can't say I blame her. I'm not even sure I can take care of myself at this point."

"This is so terrible. I'm so sorry. I wish I could have come to the funeral and pay my respects."

"Just you saying these nice things is enough, Casey. Alex knows you would have wanted to be there."

"Really, this is the saddest thing I've ever heard . . . in, like, forever."

Me too. "I wanted to also say that . . . well, I think you're quite a wonderful young woman, and I think you will do well in whatever you choose to do in your life. You have a great outlook and a great support system, and I send you great love and wish you nothing but happiness and success." That weird obstruction was working its way back into her throat, and Sandra hurried the rest of the words out. "I'm sure you're going to go and do some great things. And I'm sure you'll find just the right family to raise your little boy."

"Thank you, Sandra. That means a lot. And I'm sure you're going to go off and do great things, too. Please stay in touch."

"Goodbye, Casey." Sandra clicked off the call and swallowed, unable to imagine any great things coming her way. But that was the celebrated thing about youth, right? Idealism and hope, although right now idealism and hope seemed so silly and a waste of time, which corroborated Sandra's earlier thought that she was, indeed, old. She could definitely see more black clothing and bad television in her future.

She looked around the bedroom, at Alex's clothing and his closet. She had already closed one door to her past by speaking to Casey. She couldn't bring herself to start going through Alex's things and close any more. She grabbed her phone and quickly left the bedroom, this time leaving the door open. Baby steps. At this rate, she'd be sleeping in her old bed in maybe a few weeks, if not months. And maybe get to Alex's closet in a decade.

She opened her laptop on the coffee table and checked her email. Still nothing from Blake. Nothing from anyone. She thought about opening her work-in-progress romance novel to keep busy, but didn't dare. She had been working on that thing the day Alex died, and a piece of her was angry at the book for keeping her so busy that she wasn't around when her husband needed her. It was so much easier to blame the book, or the resort, or anything else for Sandra not being there. It helped alleviate some of the guilt she felt.

She needed some kind of diversion, to focus on something happy. What was something happy in her life?

Blake.

Blake was having a wedding reception soon. *That* was happy, wasn't it? Sure, he was marrying a woman who wanted nothing to do with Sandra, but Sandra was going to try to focus on the positive. She was going to channel Alex: stop focusing on herself and be happy for their best friend.

She opened a document on her computer and titled it "My Best Man's Speech." Shooing away thoughts that Alex was supposed to be the best man, should be writing this speech, and that she was a poor substitute, she began to write.

Hello, everyone. My name is Sandra. I am your best man for the evening.

This was so wrong. Alex should have been writing this. Or, more truthfully, she should have been writing it *for* him, which is probably what he would have asked her to do.

For those of you who may not know, my husband, Alex, was supposed to be the best man for Blake tonight, but . . .

But he died.

But he left me.

But he possibly died of a fentanyl overdose that may or may not have something to do with Chuck Landon, the lead singer of Rockknot, one of his clients.

And also one of Alex's friends.

One of his so-called friends.

A possible killer pretending to be one of his so-called friends.

But in his absence, I am honored to be here to support my best friend, Blake.

She leaned back. Tara. She should say something about Tara. But, for the life of her, she couldn't figure out anything to say.

Blake, we've been friends forever, and I'm so thrilled that you found someone who makes you as happy as you deserve to be. I know how important that is.

Sandra's breathing became labored.

I'm wishing you and Tara much love and happiness in the years to come.

She was beginning to hyperventilate. *That's good enough for now*, she thought, closing her laptop. Writing those few sentences had nearly killed her.

She looked around her apartment. How clean everything looked. Between that, opening her bedroom door, and penning the beginning of a best man's speech, she had made more progress today than she had in weeks. Progress on her new life. Her new existence.

Post Alex.

Post happiness.

The doorbell rang, and Sandra's thoughts turned to the detectives. Had Blake spoken to them? Had they come back to ask her more about Chuck and his drug past? Or had they taken the calcium tablets to a lab and discovered there *was* fentanyl in them and came to clasp handcuffs on her wrists and take her away? Had someone laced Alex's vitamins with fentanyl?

Had Chuck?

Her body froze. He certainly had the access while they were sharing a hotel suite in Vermont.

She shook her head. Chuck loved Alex. But could Blake be right and Chuck have poisoned Alex by accident?

The doorbell rang again.

Sandra pushed up her eyeglasses and hurried to the door, peeking through the peephole. She opened the door.

Her mother-in-law was standing there with a bottle of wine in her hand. "I don't know what to do," Pam said.

Sandra opened the door wider. "Good. Neither do I."

CHAPTER 19

Friday, April 4, 10:00 p.m.

Sandra pulled the wineglasses from the cabinet and set them on the table while Pam took a seat. Sandra had never seen her so disheveled, even during her cancer treatment. Her hair was unbrushed, she wore no makeup, revealing dark circles under her eyes, and she had on a pair of baggy slacks that resembled pajama bottoms, along with an oversized shirt. Sandra hadn't even been sure Pam *owned* any clothing not suitable for business. Pam sat in the same place she normally did, facing the front window. Sandra would have to get used to seeing her mother-in-law at her table without Alex seated beside her.

"Did you have a cleaning service come in?" Pam asked, looking around.

Sandra gave a small smile. "No. I just couldn't sit still. I had to do something, so I figured why not be productive?" She poured two glasses of wine and handed one to Pam.

"Alex would be in shock," Pam said with a giggle—or a noise that was trying hard to be a giggle.

"I know, right? We were a happily messy couple." Sandra raised her glass and clinked it with her mother-in-law's.

Pam took a sip of wine. "How are you doing?"

Sandra shrugged. "You know."

"Yeah, I *do* know." She took another sip of wine. "Is it me, or does everything seem so dreary now? I feel like it's been raining nonstop for weeks and weeks."

"Well, it *has*." Sandra pointed to the window. "You're absolutely right. I can't remember the last time I saw the sun. It's like Mother Nature knows Alex is gone and is in mourning, too."

They sat there, the weather talk behind them, and a sad silence settled upon them. Suddenly, Pam shifted in her chair and asked pointedly, "Have you been avoiding me, Sandra?"

"Avoiding you?"

"Yes, I've been trying to call the past day or so."

"No," Sandra said, but then admitted, "Well, yes, maybe a little, but I was planning on calling you tomorrow. I was just trying to keep busy and cut down on how much crying I do in a day. Not that it's helping."

"Well . . ." Pam put her wineglass down. "That's not very nice. I've already lost a son. I can't lose my daughter-in-law, too." She sniffled.

Sandra reached for her hand. "I'm so sorry, Pam. You're right. I was being selfish. You know I love you and am always here for you. I wasn't thinking."

Pam reached for a napkin on the table and dotted her eyes. "No, I'm sorry. I need to be mad at someone. Unfortunately, you invited me in."

"I know." She squeezed her mother-in-law's hand.

"Is that the only reason you weren't taking my calls?" Pam asked. "Because you didn't want to cry anymore?"

Sandra took another sip of wine. "Yeah, why?"

"Well, I thought there might be another reason."

"Like what?"

"Well," Pam hesitated, "I thought it might be because of the conversation I had with the detectives who came to see me."

Sandra quickly swallowed the wine before it could go down the wrong pipe. She placed her glass down. "You spoke to Detective Miller and his partner?"

Pam nodded. "They rang my bell the day before yesterday and started asking questions. It was weird."

"It *was*, right?"

"Detective Miller kept asking me questions about you and Alex. I asked him why he was here, and he said there were some things in Alex's toxicology screening that he was investigating, but he wouldn't say what."

That was strange. Detective Miller hadn't told Pam about the fentanyl? He had no problem blurting it out to Sandra. The security footage of her giving Alex his calcium tablets appeared in her mind. So did the accusatory look in the detective's eyes.

Pam took another sip of wine. "He kept asking me things about you and Alex, about your relationship, and . . . I have a confession to make, Sandra. I feel terrible."

"What confession?"

"I told the detectives about you and Alex trying to have a baby. And how difficult it was."

"That's okay. It wasn't a state secret."

"I know, but they were asking me about any conflicts or arguments that Alex may have had, and of course, I said I couldn't think of any. Everybody loved Alex. But before I said that, I paused. I mean, it was just for a second, but the cops *saw* that. And then they focused on it. Like I was covering something up. And I panicked. I didn't want to lie."

"You shouldn't lie, Pam. Whatever you said, I'm sure it's okay."

"Well, the reason I paused was because one fight *does* stick out in my mind." Her eyes looked at the floor as if she were embarrassed. "It was the one that you and Alex had. You know, about getting pregnant."

Sandra's eyes opened wide. She knew exactly what fight her mother-in-law was referring to. "Alex told you about that?"

"No"—Pam shook her head—"he never told me. He would never betray you like that. If he would have told me, you would have known about it. He told you everything."

Not everything, Sandra thought, at least when it came to Chuck.

"I'm... I'm so ashamed to admit this," Pam continued, "but that day when you and Alex were fighting, I had stopped by the condo to drop off some fresh fruit from the farmers' market. As I got closer, I heard you arguing. So... I eavesdropped."

Sandra's mind drifted back to that day, a day she would rather forget.

"You were arguing about having a baby," Pam said. "You were both so upset. I wanted to run inside and squeeze you both and tell you it would be okay, but I didn't dare. It wasn't my place. I was about to leave, and then... I heard what you said. About finding a man who had good sperm."

Sandra's heart twisted in her chest. "I feel terrible about that. Even after all these years. That was the worst thing I think I've ever said to anyone, Pam."

"I know, honey." Pam squeezed her hand. "We all say things we're not proud of when we're upset. Lord knows I've said all kinds of things—when Alex's dad died, when I was sick. And I'm sure Alex knew that."

"He said he forgave me."

"Then he did."

Sandra grabbed a napkin from the table and blew her nose. "I miss him so much, Pam. I can't ever imagine feeling better, like everything is going to be all right."

"I know. I can't either. But we just have to keep going, right?"

Sandra nodded. "Right."

Pam finished her glass of wine and placed it on the table. "Let's talk about something else, okay?"

"Good idea." Sandra started downing her wine as well. There was much more to drink, and they had a whole night to drink it.

"So," Pam said, "Blake got married, huh?"

Sandra nearly choked on the wine in her mouth, which dripped onto the table.

"I *knew* there was something weird going on." Pam mopped up Sandra's spill with a napkin. "Blake didn't look good to me when I saw him in the office. He looks a little off, doesn't he?"

Sandra wiped her mouth and nodded.

"I mean, how could he go off and get married to someone in secret and believe we wouldn't think it's strange? Is there something I don't know?" Pam inched her seat toward Sandra. "Tell me there's some kind of juicy gossip. Anything to get my mind off Alex."

Sandra set her glass down. "I don't know if I have any juicy gossip."

"But you don't like her, do you?"

"I don't know. It's complicated."

"Complicated how?"

"I just get weird vibes from her."

"What kind of vibes?"

"Just unfriendly. Like she's not interested in giving me a chance to be a friend. She didn't even come to Alex's funeral."

"Well"—Pam pursed her lips—"she didn't know him well."

"But she was *there*, Pam. At the ski resort. When he died. Even if she didn't know Alex well, shouldn't she show up and support Blake?"

"The older I get, the less I understand people, Sandra," Pam said. "What did Alex say about her?"

"Please, you know Alex. He likes just about everybody, and he seemed to really like Tara—despite the fact that I was trying to give him every reason not to. He kept telling me I should give her a chance."

"Sounds like my baby."

Pam's eyes began to water again, and Sandra was eager to change the subject. "Oh, Blake told me today that he and Tara are going to have a wedding reception for their quickie marriage next month."

"Why get married so quickly and then throw a reception a month later?" Pam shook her head.

"I don't know. But Blake was going to ask Alex to be the best man when we were all in Vermont together. He never got the chance to, so he asked me to fill in as a substitute. Honestly, the whole thing sounds—"

"Oh, that's a lovely idea!" Pam's face brightened. "Alex would have just *loved* that."

"I can't substitute for Alex, Pam. No one can."

"If anyone can, it's you, sweetheart."

"But I feel like such a fraud. Like my heart isn't really in it. I love Blake, and I would do anything to make him happy, and if he wants me to be his best man, I will, but I can't fake it, you know." *That's because you never had to with me, San.* Sandra wondered if she would ever stop hearing Alex's dirty jokes and snide comments in her mind. She hoped she wouldn't. They made her feel like he was still here.

"You'll have to do your best. For Blake. And Alex." Pam smiled. A genuine smile. It was nice to see. "Well, I'd better go. Before the two of us cry anymore."

"Really?" Sandra suddenly didn't want Pam to leave. Yes, she didn't want to cry anymore, but the last few minutes was the first bit of normalcy she'd felt since Alex was gone. There was so much Alex in his mother—warmth, sincerity, loyalty—and Sandra didn't want to let it go. "Why don't you stay,

Pam? I could use the company. The house is so quiet. Plus, you just had some wine. You probably shouldn't drive."

"What about the crying?"

"Well, if it happens, it happens. Maybe the key to this whole thing is to enjoy the grief, as weird as it sounds—really feel it and embrace it and know that you feel this way because you loved somebody so much. Something tells me I'm not going to feel this kind of emotion forever. People eventually move on, right? And I think I'll miss when I couldn't live for a single moment without missing Alex, hearing his voice in my head, smelling his smells, and hating that he's gone." She reached for Pam's hand again. "So, yes, let's cry our eyes out. And laugh. And cry again for the man we both loved to our core."

"Wise words for such a young woman," Pam said.

"Nah, I'm an old, miserable widow now."

"Welcome to the club." Pam giggled. A real giggle.

"I say we just sit on the couch, put on some stupid movie, and fall asleep," Sandra said.

"That's the best offer I've had in a long time." Pam reached out and cupped Sandra's cheek with her hand. "Okay, you talked me into it."

CHAPTER 20

Saturday, April 5, 9:00 a.m.

When Sandra woke up, Pam was already gone. Sandra felt on her face for her eyeglasses but then blurrily saw them folded neatly on the coffee table next to the remote. The bowls of late-night snacks and empty bottle of wine were all gone, probably washed and put away or tossed in recycling. The smell of coffee lingered in the air. She smiled. Pam was taking care of her. Like she used to take care of her and Alex. Another small piece of normalcy in this cold, Alex-less world.

Sandra got up and poured herself a cup of coffee. Beside the coffeepot was a note:

Loved our girls' night. Love you. Love, Me.

A warm feeling spread through her. She loved her mother-in-law, *really* loved her. Pam had been like a second mom to Sandra over the past twenty-three years. Spending time with her was just what she needed—the familiarity was comforting, and she liked having someone to chat with again. Maybe this was what moving through grief felt like. It was happening at a snail's pace, but in the right direction.

Her phone pinged, and she looked at the screen.

Daddy and I are thinking of you, baby. Dinner tonight? I'll make your favorite.

Sandra's heart swelled. Her parents had been touching base with her each day, tag-teaming their affection—giving Sandra space, but letting her know they were there. Another reminder that there was love all around Sandra if she bothered to look. She typed:

Sure. See you later.

She put her phone down and opened the refrigerator, gazing at the empty shelves. Good thing she was eating at her parents' house tonight. That was another thing she needed to do. Food shop. Unfortunately, that job fell under Alex's purview for the fifteen years of their marriage. She sighed. She was going to have to take it on unless she didn't expect to eat at home anytime soon.

Sandra pulled the week's circulars out of a pile of newspapers on the table. Usually, Alex would have already had them perused and circled, with a list of what sales were taking place at what stores. Even though Sandra had grown up in a home where saving money was more sacred than religion, she somehow had a knack for overpaying for everything—most of the time, unintentionally. If she needed a pair of jeans or a jar of tomato sauce, she could almost guarantee it would go on sale the day after she bought it.

She spread the circulars in front of her like she was playing a hand of poker and grabbed a pen and blank notepad from the counter. What did she need? She wrote on the notepad: *Everything.*

She had a feeling this wasn't Alex's method. She took another sip of coffee as she doodled a heart pierced by an arrow over the *g* in *Everything*. She stared at the chubby, lopsided doodle. In Roman mythology, Cupid used arrows to symbolize the sudden and uncontrollable nature of love. But now all Sandra could feel when she saw that arrow was the pain of its point.

She pushed the notepad away and picked up her phone. She downloaded the local supermarket app Alex had been badgering her to download for years and registered for an account. Then she threw the circulars into the recycle bin. She was going to have to figure out her own shopping strategy.

The doorbell rang, startling her. She was startled *every time* the doorbell rang these days. Ever since Detectives Miller and Menendez waltzed into her life. She expected them to come and take her away anytime now. At least she wouldn't have to food shop in prison.

She walked to the door, peered through the peephole, and open the door. "Hey, what are you doing here?" she asked.

Blake stood on her doorstep, the morning drizzle dotting his shoulders. He was holding her morning newspaper. "Newspaper delivery," he said with a smile.

He was wearing a pair of khakis and a sweater, his usual attire. Whether planning on a day at the office or a game of tennis, Blake essentially dressed the same—a trait she and Alex used to tease him about, saying Blake dressed more like Pam's son than Alex, who never met a faded T-shirt he didn't love. Blake looked nice, although he still had that off, gray look about him. But he was smiling and seemed happy. She opened the door wider.

"Wow, thank you, newspaper delivery boy! I didn't realize you offered such white-glove service."

"Yes, ma'am, we have to if we're going to compete with digital media." Blake stepped inside. "Still raining." He stamped his wet shoes on her welcome mat. "Sorry to come unannounced. I was just heading to the garage for an oil change and thought I'd stop by to check on you." He looked around. "Wow, you cleaned up. The place looks great."

"Yeah. It's part of my whole trying-to-keep-busy lie I've been feeding myself."

"Is it working?"

"Sometimes. Pam was here last night. She stayed over."

"That sounds like a good thing."

She nodded. "It was. Therapeutic. And fun." She studied his face. "Are you okay? You don't look too good."

"I'm great." Blake's smile widened.

"Blake, remember what you said about me with the word *good*? I could say the same for you with the word *great*. I don't buy it."

"San, you have enough on your mind without having me spill my problems onto you."

She closed the door. "Are you kidding? Spill away. I need something to get me out of my head. What's going on?" She glanced at the table near the front door. "Oh, and here." She picked up one of Alex's prayer cards from the funeral. "We just got these. I was about to mail them out, but since you're here, you get a special delivery, too."

Blake smiled and shoved the prayer card into his pocket.

"Tell me," Sandra said. "What's wrong?"

Blake shrugged. "Well . . ." He looked like he was having trouble putting the words together. "You're right. I haven't been feeling great, but . . ." He hesitated. "I'm sure I'm just tired. Grieving. Like you. Anyway, I would much rather talk about you. How *are* you?" He motioned toward the room.

"Other than trying to compete with Martha Stewart for cleanest living room."

"I'm okay. About to go food shopping."

Blake pretended to fall backward. "You? Food shopping?"

"Very funny." She punched him in the arm. "Yeah, yeah. I know. Hell hath frozen over. What can I say? I'm just trying to move forward, however I can."

"Good." He handed her the newspaper and then plucked a hair from her shirt. "Well, other than this idle hair, you look like you're okay here. That's good to see. I'll get going then. If I'm not at the garage at my appointment time, they'll give my slot to someone else. Bastards. And I have to meet Tara at the bank afterward. The bank rep forgot to have us sign some paperwork."

"Marriage stuff?" Sandra asked.

Blake nodded. "Yeah. Adding her to all the bank accounts. You know, this way if something happens to me—"

"Don't say that, Blake."

"San, if Alex's death has shown us anything, it's that shit happens, and can happen at any time. I want to make sure Tara is able to access all the home and business accounts."

"No, I get it. That's the smart thing to . . . wait. You put Tara on the business bank account?"

"Yeah. What's the problem? Did it a while ago."

"When?"

Blake furrowed his brows. "I don't know, San. I don't keep track of my everyday errands in my calendar. I did it when Alex was... here. I don't know. A month ago? Before Vermont. He said it was fine."

"He did?"

"Why wouldn't he? *You're* on the account."

"But that's different."

"How is it different?" Blake was looking at Sandra blankly.

"Because..." She shrugged her shoulders when she really wanted to say that it was different because she, Alex, and Blake had known each other for decades and knew they could trust one another. Putting a stranger on the business bank account left Napkin Marketing vulnerable. But she didn't say any of these things because of the puppy-dog, lovey-dovey look in Blake's eyes. Of course, Blake wouldn't have a problem with giving Tara legal access to the business's money, which, after he and Alex busted their butt for nearly a decade, totaled about a hundred thousand dollars. Blake was in love. And married. But from Sandra's perspective, Blake had just given a veritable stranger the keys to the castle.

"Because what?" he asked.

"I don't know. Forget it."

"San, seriously, when are you going to give Tara a break?"

"Seriously?" Sandra rolled her eyes.

"What?" Blake asked.

"Give *her* a break?"

"You haven't given her a chance."

"*I* haven't given *her* a chance?" Sandra could feel the resentment bubbling up. "I just lost my husband, and she hasn't reached out to me once. Not *once* in the past month, Blake."

"She just probably feels it's not her place. Have you tried reaching out to *her*?"

"You too? You sound just like Alex."

"Listen, Tara may not be grieving like you and me, but she's been there for me over the past few weeks. And she could be there for you, too. I don't know what I would have done without her. And she's got a lot on her mind. Things are weird at her school. They just had another big drug bust. A bunch of seniors were involved. Parents are calling up the school upset. There's a lot of finger-pointing. She's been in the principal's office a bunch of times trying to figure out if she's missed anything over the past few months or years with these kids. She feels responsible." He shook his head. "And she really hasn't been sleeping. A lot of late nights, researching online, reading up on these new drug variants popping up in her district and also how to find a way to get through to these kids to stay away from them."

"Yes, Tara is such a *saint*." The words tumbled out of Sandra's mouth, and she regretted them the moment they did.

"That's not very nice, San."

"I know. I'm sorry." She took a breath. "Don't mind me. I'm feeling very sorry for myself." She rubbed her temples. "I know bad things have happened to a lot of people. I know that in my *rational* brain. But . . . I look out the window and wonder how the world can still possibly go on when Alex isn't here."

"I know."

"You must think I'm a terrible person."

"Please, I know you better than anyone. And I *know* you're not a terrible person." He put his hand on her shoulder. "Just, you know, sad. I want you to feel like you can say anything to me. Our friendship is one of the things I value the most in my life."

"Me too." She wrapped her arms around Blake and was so happy when she felt him hug her back. She pulled away. "Okay, let me try that again." She exhaled. "It's really nice that Tara wants to help those kids and make a difference. Not everyone is like that. They're lucky kids to have someone who cares so much."

"Yeah, she really gives it her all. It's inspiring," Blake said. "In fact, she's been so scattered these days that . . ." He stopped talking.

"That what?"

"Nothing. I probably shouldn't say."

"Say what, Blake? You just gave me this speech that we can say anything to each other."

"I wouldn't call it a *speech*, San."

"That's not the point. You can tell me whatever it is. It's just me—the girl who crashed with you on your bicycle in high school."

"Oh, wow, I haven't thought about that in years." Blake laughed. "Well, it probably wasn't smart for me to let you sit on the handlebars."

"I told you you were going too fast."

"I couldn't help it. I lost control."

"Yeah, and I nearly lost my life."

"You're exaggerating," he said. "It was just a few scrapes."

"We were lucky."

"Yeah. Lucky."

"So, what's going on?" Sandra asked. "What were you going to say before?"

"No, it's just . . . Well, I don't want to get Tara in trouble."

"In trouble, how?"

"Even though I know it's not a big deal."

"What's not a big deal?"

Blake gave an exasperated sigh. "I was hanging up Tara's coat in the closet and there were some pills in the pocket. In a tiny little plastic bag."

"Pills?" Sandra's breathing hitched. "What kind of pills?"

"I don't know, San. I don't know anything about drugs. I asked her what they were, and when Tara saw them, she was mortified. Said she had completely forgotten she put them in her pocket. She said she found them on a ledge in one of the high school bathrooms, and when she called the principal to report it, some other kids came in and caused a disruption of some sort. I don't remember the details. She said she grabbed them, so they didn't get lost in the shuffle. And by the time they corralled the kids into the principal's office, she must have forgotten she had them."

Sandra's head was spinning. Tara's explanation sounded like a likely and plausible story, but Sandra couldn't unhear what Detective Miller had said about Alex's death—that fentanyl may have been involved. And fentanyl had been found at Tara's school. Tara had said so herself that morning at April's Café. Were these pills that Blake found fentanyl, too? "What did you do with the pills?" she asked.

"What do you think I did? I gave them back to Tara, so she could give them to whoever is supposed to get them."

"Blake . . . how much do you really know about Tara?" she asked gently.

"What do you mean? I know everything about Tara."

"How can you say that? You've just met."

"What are you getting at?"

"I don't know. Do you know if Tara has a history of drug use?"

Blake appeared astonished. "Are you crazy, San? Tara doesn't even drink. She's as straight as they come."

"I don't know. Call me crazy, but don't you think that's a weird coincidence?"

"What is?"

"Finding drugs in Alex's tox screen, and then you finding drugs in your wife's pocket?"

Blake's face went from astonished to angry. "What are you accusing Tara of, Sandra?"

Blake was using her full name. That wasn't good. She had stepped over a line. "I'm not accusing her of anything. I'm just saying it's a weird coincidence."

"What, am I supposed to talk to Detective Miller again and tell him I found drugs in my wife's pocket?"

"You spoke to Detective Miller?" she asked. "You didn't tell me."

"Yes, I told you I would. But there wasn't much to tell you."

"What did he say?"

"Nothing, really," he said. "Just what you told me. That Alex's tox screening showed there was fentanyl in his system."

"He just said it to you like it was nothing?"

"Yeah, why?"

"Because he didn't say anything to Pam."

Blake shrugged. "He probably didn't want her to know anything until he was sure."

"Okay, that's possible. Did you tell him about Chuck?"

Blake hesitated. "I did, San. I thought they should know."

She nodded, imagining Detectives Miller and Menendez showing up at Chuck's house in Suffolk County and asking questions about his past. She thought of Beatrice, pregnant and motherly. What would this do to their family? "So, do you think you should mention the pills in Tara's pocket, too?"

"What is your *thing* with Tara, Sandra?"

"I don't have a *thing*."

"Go ahead. You might as well say it. You think my wife killed Alex."

"No! I'm not saying that. All I'm saying is that it's *information*, Blake, the stuff about the pills in her pocket. Information that maybe the police should know."

"Well, I disagree, and I think I know my *wife* better than anyone." He shook his head. "I'm going to forgive you, Sandra, because I know you're grieving. You're not yourself. But the truth is, you've been cold to Tara from the moment I brought her to April's Café that day. And you've been sour on my marriage since the night of Chuck's wedding, when I called you and Alex on the phone. I could tell from the look on your face."

"I was *not*, Blake. I was just surprised. That's all. And I really have been trying with Tara."

He shook his head. "Listen, I'm gonna go." He opened the front door but then stopped. "Oh, I *did* want to tell you that—if it makes you feel any better—I got the feeling that the detectives don't really consider you as some kind of suspect in Alex's death."

"Really?"

"Yeah, which according to you, means now they can, full force, go and arrest my wife." Blake stormed down the pathway toward his car, parked on the street.

Sandra wanted to yell for him not to leave this way, but instead she watched him get into his car and speed away. She stood there long after he was gone.

This had been the first fight she and Blake had had in a long time. She couldn't remember the last time they had been cross with each other. And now, with Alex gone, for the first time in a long time, Sandra felt completely alone.

CHAPTER 21

Saturday, April 5, 11:00 a.m.

The supermarket parking lot was mobbed. Sandra was learning quickly that Saturday morning was the wrong time to go food shopping. No wonder Alex was always stopping at the stores on his way home from work.

She had gotten a later start than she intended. The fight with Blake had left her unsettled. She had tried calling him before and after she had taken a shower, but he hadn't picked up. She imagined him sitting at the garage, stewing while he waited for his oil change. She wanted to apologize, and he wasn't going to let her. She knew Blake well enough to know it would take a while for him to come around. He had a habit of letting things fester.

There was a sign for additional parking on the roof, and Sandra swerved her way to the upstairs lot, which was virtually empty. She couldn't understand all that honking and yelling downstairs when there was a perfectly usable parking lot upstairs. Lazy bastards.

She got out of the car and grabbed a shopping cart that someone had neglected to return to the corral. She pushed a button for the elevator and waited with a few other customers who were looking at their phones. Probably brushing up on the sales. Would they be able to tell she was a newbie? Did they know Alex? Was there a coupon-clipping group on Facebook she needed to join?

When the elevator arrived, Sandra squished herself inside with the others and descended. When the door opened, a *fooding* frenzy greeted her. People pulling donuts from racks. Ripping bananas from bunches. Sandra followed the other customers into the store and rolled up her sleeves, ready to join the fray.

She made it through the first aisle practically unscathed. So far, so good.

She continued shopping, proud of herself for stocking up on a few sale items. About halfway through the store, she turned into the frozen aisle, feeling triumphant, and stopped. A few feet in front of her, near the frozen vegetables, was Tara—standing there in a stylish camel-colored coat, cinched at the waist, inspecting the side of a box, as the freezer door beside her filled with condensation.

Questions pinballed across Sandra's mind. Was Tara shopping *before* meeting Blake at the bank? Had they already finished and she had decided to stop at the supermarket? Was Blake here, too? Had he told her about their argument? Was *that* the coat in which Blake had found the pills?

Sandra couldn't move, like her feet were trapped in hardening concrete. She had the urge to ease the shopping cart back and return to the previous aisle, forgetting all about her intense desire for rocky road ice cream, but there were already hordes of shoppers behind her, making her feel like a salmon trying to swim upstream.

"Excuse me!" shouted an old woman to Sandra. "You're blocking the waffles!"

Tara looked up at the sound of the old woman's voice, and her eyes met Sandra's, opening wide with recognition. Sandra could see the instant discomfort on her face—not the reaction of a woman who could be *there for Sandra*, as Blake had suggested. It was the look of someone who had just locked eyes with a vicious predator and wanted badly to escape but dared not move.

"Excuse me!" the old woman behind Sandra shouted again, and Sandra pushed her cart forward.

"Hi," she said to Tara as she wormed her way through the aisle.

"Hi," Tara said, and then looked away, putting the box of vegetables back in the freezer.

Sandra stopped her cart next to Tara's and waited a moment, wondering if Tara might say something. *Anything.* An *I'm sorry for the loss of your husband.* Or *How are you holding up?* Or *Blake told me what happened.* Any wisp of compassion, but Tara said nothing, letting the freezer door close and then cinching the belt of her stylish, possibly drug-riddled coat.

"Well, take care," Sandra said abruptly, pushing her cart to the end of the aisle before the old woman behind her called the supermarket police.

Sandra's head was pounding as she rounded the endcap. She wasn't used to being rude. She wasn't sure if she *had* been, if Tara wanted to chitchat or was hoping Sandra would leave anyway. She felt faint and disoriented. In an unfamiliar place, running from an unfamiliar person.

Sandra looked around. She was in the bread aisle. Would Tara be coming up right behind her? Was Sandra going to have to dodge her, aisle after aisle? Plus, Sandra needed ice cream—and lots of it—but the last thing she was going to do was go back into that frozen aisle and face that callous, awful Tara again.

Tara in the frozen aisle. How appropriate. The ice queen in her natural habitat.

An image of Blake telling her that she *wasn't being very nice* appeared in her mind. Followed by Alex—adorable, sweet Alex—who was looking at her with those dreamy eyes and saying, *Let it go. Give her a chance.*

Sandra tried to distract herself by reading the labels of the various brands of multigrain bread, but her mind was hurling back in time, all the recent events playing in a loop. Meeting standoffish Tara at April's Café. All the largely unanswered texts sent to Tara. Tara not joining Sandra for coffee up in Vermont. Tara not showing up at the funeral for Alex.

Anger coursed through her. She didn't want to be nice. She was tired of letting it go. Tired of taking the high road. Of being the bigger person.

She hurried through the rest of the store, yanking random items into her cart. So much for a shopping strategy. Then, without looking back, she made a beeline for the self-checkout, ran all her items across the scanner, handed the machine her credit card, packed her stuff, and sped toward the front of the store.

The elevator door was about to close, but Sandra managed to make it inside. As the elevator rose to the second level, Tara's image reappeared in Sandra's mind—standing there, in front of the frozen veggies, looking as fashionable as she had the day Sandra had met her. As if nothing had changed. Meanwhile,

Sandra's *whole world* had changed. Tara knew that. And for her not even to acknowledge that seemed cruel and awful.

Sandra exited the elevator and began pushing her cart toward her car, when she stopped. Tara was already in the parking lot, in the next aisle over from Sandra, hauling groceries into a gray Kona. She must have hurried out of the store, too.

Sandra wanted to turn around and wait by the elevator bank for Tara to drive away, but something came over her. She kept walking. She didn't know if it was because she missed Alex or was mad at Tara, but she marched toward her, the wheels spinning furiously in her mind and on her shopping cart. By the time Tara was about to bring her cart to the corral, she looked up at Sandra in surprise.

"How dare you!" Sandra shouted when she reached Tara's car.

"What?" Tara appeared aghast.

"How dare you disrespect Alex like that!"

Sandra was surprised those were the first words that chose to come out of her mouth. She hadn't realized how deeply Tara's absence from Alex's funeral had hurt her simply because Alex had done all he could to champion her. Tara could hurt Sandra all she wanted, but not Alex. He was too good and kind. "Alex did nothing but give you the benefit of the doubt. Nothing but try to welcome you into our friend group."

Tara's skin was ashen, matching her fashionable coat, as if Sandra has slapped her. "But . . . I—"

Sandra's mouth kept moving. "Listen, I don't know what kind of trauma you're dealing with, but if it really caused you not to be able to support your husband's best friends, maybe *you're* the one who should be in therapy."

The anger was pouring out, and Sandra couldn't stop it. "Or, maybe you could have at least sent a text to say how sorry you were, if you couldn't find it in your heart to do it in person. I'm tired of your bullshit."

"My bullshit?" Tara asked, her face all scrunched up, clearly offended.

"Yes, your *bullshit*. You have been a bitch since the day I met you. A total arrogant, elitist *bitch*."

Tara's mouth was agape, and as much as Alex would be appalled by Sandra's behavior, he wasn't here, would never be here, and if Sandra was destined to become a little old widow who dressed in black and binge-watched too much TV for the rest of her life, she was going to begin her new life with a bang. "I have been nothing but friendly toward you and tried to invite you for coffee or to hang out, mostly because of Alex's prodding. But you have made it clear from day one that you wanted nothing to do with me. And don't look so shocked. *Please*. I would think this little innocent act of yours would be beneath a trained psychologist. You must think I'm a fucking idiot."

Tara slammed the trunk of her car. "Wow, even if you *are* grieving, and, for Blake's sake, I'll give you the benefit of the doubt that you are, you *are* a bitch."

"*I'm* the bitch?" Sandra's skin was on fire. "Being a bitch is doing everything you can to not make friends with people who are trying to make friends with you. Seriously, the least you could do is fake it. Play nice with your husband's bitchy friend. Oh, and are we not even going to talk about how you and Blake got married after a few *months*. How ridiculous is that? Who does that? A mental patient? A gold digger?"

"How could you say that?" Tara asked, indignant.

"What do you mean, how can I say that? Any rational person would say that."

"Did you ever think that maybe there were other things going on that *you* didn't know about?" Tara crossed her arms. "You come across so high and mighty when maybe *you* should take a good look in the mirror, Sandra."

"What is *that* supposed to mean?"

"It means that if you can get past yourself, you'll realize that maybe the world doesn't revolve around you. And that you're not a very good friend. Blake is always saying how empathic you are. Always making excuses for you. You really have him snowed, don't you? You're, you're—"

"I'm what? Go ahead. Say it. You know you want to."

Tara ran her tongue over her front teeth, as if calming herself. "What I do with Blake is really none of your business," she said coolly.

"Blake is my best friend. I think *that's* my business. And I won't have you fucking him up. Or fucking up the business he and Alex invested years in."

"You really have to stop obsessing over Blake. It's pathetic," Tara said in a condescending voice, like Sandra was one of her high school students. "Let him live his life."

"Obsessing?!" Sandra screamed. "I'm *obsessed*? You came in and were looking to destroy what Blake and Alex built, *Yoko*, with all your talk about diversifying. Why don't you mind your own fucking business?"

"I don't have to listen to this." Tara moved toward the side of her car. "Sandra, I think you need some serious help."

Sandra moved with her. "Oh, I'm sure you do. That's what all you psychologist types think. That we're all sick and in need of therapy. This way, you all have a purpose for your pathetic existence." She crossed her arms. "Oh, and let us not forget about the pills. How they suddenly showed up. Right after you mentioned fentanyl at the restaurant. Don't you think that's a little strange? And coincidental?"

Tara pulled the driver's side door of her car open, looking at Sandra. "Don't you think I should be asking *you* about the fentanyl?"

"What are you talking about?" Sandra asked but feared she knew the answer. Had Blake told her about the detectives' visit and the footage of her handing Alex the calcium tablets? Was Tara implying that was fentanyl? But Blake also must have told Tara that he got the feeling that Miller and Menendez didn't consider Sandra a suspect.

"I think you know what I'm talking about," Tara said, looking satisfied with herself. "Yes, Blake told me about that. You should consider yourself lucky that I don't talk to the cops."

"*You* talk to the cops? Don't change the subject. *You're* the fentanyl expert. I barely knew what it was until you brought it up at the restaurant."

"How *coincidental*," Tara said.

They were starting to make a scene. People were watching them from their cars, as they carried children and groceries into front and back seats. Sandra looked up at the security cameras. Just what she needed. More footage of her doing suspicious things. "Just leave me the fuck alone," she said, turning around and marching toward her car.

"It would be my pleasure," Tara said, getting into the driver's seat of the Kona and slamming the car door.

By the time Sandra got to her car and put all her groceries in the back seat, she was dizzy and sweating. Then as Tara's gray Kona sped out of the parking lot, she slammed her door, put her key into the ignition, and burst into tears.

CHAPTER 22

Monday, April 7, 10:00 a.m.

Sandra didn't think life could get any worse after Alex's death. How wrong she had been. The last two days had been the worst of all. Staring at the four walls of her condo. All alone. Feeling not just sad, but awful and guilty. Blake still wasn't answering her calls, and Sandra wasn't surprised after everything that had transpired between her and Tara on Saturday. She imagined Tara showing up for their bank meeting in anger, and the two of them trying to think up ways to nudge Sandra out of the business. And out of their life.

She couldn't blame them. Sandra had said such despicable things. Yelling ugliness in the heat of anger was apparently nothing new for Sandra; she thought she would have learned her lesson after her big fight with Alex years ago. She sighed. She should have just turned her shopping cart around. She should have turned away. Taken a page from the Alex Connor handbook. But something inside her couldn't let it go.

Would the rest of her Alex-less life be filled with uncontrollable rage?

She sat on the couch and stared at the best man's speech that she had made no progress on. Would Blake even still want her to be his best man? Probably not. She looked at her watch. Thank God for Pam, who said she was going to play hooky this afternoon and come over again for another girls' night. Sandra didn't plan on telling her what happened, unless she already knew. If Blake had told his mom, she wouldn't waste any time calling Pam. What would Pam do? Cancel? Would she take Blake's side? Sandra had been looking forward to cooking a meal for her mother-in-law, like she used to, although she would have to use whatever she had in the house because there was no way Sandra was going back to the supermarket after her performance in the parking lot on Saturday. She imagined a sign on the wall with her photo and a line drawn through it. *No shoes. No shirt. No service. Oh, and no Sandra.*

She picked up the phone and tried calling Blake again, but unsurprisingly, her call went to voicemail. She still didn't know exactly what she was going to say anyway. Yes, she would apologize for the unfounded accusations she had made, because Blake was her best friend, but she still had her doubts about Tara's story. Was it really a coincidence for fentanyl to be an issue in Tara's school district and also have had something to do with Alex's death? Sandra had spent the last two days researching fentanyl online. Scary stuff. And what about Chuck and his own sordid drug past? Both Tara and Chuck were two of the last people on earth to see Alex. A dull pain caused Sandra to double over. She would never forgive herself for not being with him when he died.

She scrolled through the photos on her phone until she came to Detective Miller's business card. She knew in her heart that Blake would never tell him about Tara, about finding the pills in her coat pocket. He loved her, and when you loved someone, you saw them in a certain way. You were often too close to the truth.

A crack of thunder rattled the windows. It had been raining again, pouring all morning. This was the kind of day that she and Alex liked to spend in bed—call in sick from work, order takeout, and just enjoy each other. The simple things.

Alex . . .

She missed him more today than she did weeks ago. Her night with Pam made her think she was on her way to some kind of normalcy, but in the past two days, Sandra had fallen off the grief wagon. When would she ever begin to feel the slightest bit of longtime, sustained relief? She had a feeling she never would—especially not if she didn't get to the bottom of Alex's death.

Sandra picked up her phone and punched in Detective Miller's number before she changed her mind. He picked up on the second ring.

"Detective Miller."

"Um, hi, Detective Miller. This is Sandra Wilson. You came to see me last week about the death of my husband, Alex Connor?"

There was a pause and then, "Yes, how can I help you?" Detective Miller was all business.

Sandra took a breath. This was it. What Alex would call *the rubber meeting the road*. If Sandra went ahead with this, her lifelong friendship with Blake would essentially be over. This was a betrayal of the highest order. Blake had always called Sandra his ride or die, the person who would bring the shovel to help bury the bodies. And she would have. She just never thought that body would be Alex's.

SANDRA PUT DOWN THE phone. Her hand was shaking. Her heartbeat racing.

Detective Miller had listened quietly to what she had to say, that her friend Blake had found some pills in his wife's pocket, that she didn't know what kind of pills they were, and that she was sure it was just one big coincidence but thought he needed to know. A voice in Sandra's head kept telling her that making accusations against her best friend's wife would only bring more suspicion Sandra's way, but she did it anyway. She felt compelled to. For Alex. And when she was done, there was another pause before Detective Miller thanked her for contacting him and hung up. And that was it.

Did he believe her? Did he care? She wondered what would happen next. Was he going to follow up on her information? Was he on the phone right now with Blake or Tara? There was only one way Detective Miller would know about the pills in Tara's pocket if Blake hadn't told him. Through Sandra. Blake would know she was a rat. There was no denying it.

Deep down, she hoped he would understand why she did what she did. It wasn't about Tara. It really wasn't. It was about Alex.

Sandra closed her laptop as the doorbell rang, startling her. She looked at the time on her phone screen. Was Pam a couple of hours early? Maybe Pam was early because Blake *had* told his mother about what happened and she told Pam. Was Pam coming to chastise Sandra? Side with her? Hug her? She couldn't have her mother-in-law mad at her, too. There was only so much Sandra could take. Of all people, Pam should understand. Alex was *her* life, too.

Lightning lit up the windows, and there was another crack of thunder as Sandra walked toward the front door and pulled it open. The storm door was full of condensation, but through it, she could see the outline of a body. She opened the screen door and bowed.

"Welcome to the second meeting of the Old Widows' Club," she said lightly, hoping Pam would laugh, but when she straightened up, Alex's mom wasn't standing on her doorstep.

Tara was.

TARA

CHAPTER 23

Monday, January 13, 7:00 p.m.

Tara pulled into the library parking lot, surprised to see so many cars. This was the last place she wanted to be on a Monday night, and she figured others would feel the same, but perhaps she underestimated the allure of reading. After the long day she'd had at the high school, all she wanted to do was read a good book and take a hot bath, but she had committed to the Microsoft Excel class the library was offering. Her colleagues were counting on her not only to learn the program but teach them what she learned as well.

When she stepped inside the library and found the Excel classroom, she immediately felt intimidated. Everyone seated in the class looked so young. And so did the man at the front of the room, writing on the whiteboard, who was probably half her age. That was her teacher? Her grandfather had always said that you knew you were getting old when your doctors were younger than you were. He probably hadn't taken a continuing education class.

Tara sat way in the back, as if the teacher had cooties and she needed to maintain social distance. She folded her jacket across her lap and took out her laptop.

"We'll give everyone another few minutes," the teacher said with a boyish grin, pointing to the name Gavin on the board. "That's me. Gavin. Happy to help you learn Excel these next few weeks."

Tara nearly gasped. Now that she got a good look at him, Gavin looked a lot like Ted, the one person she had been trying to forget. Yes, Gavin was much younger, but he and Ted definitely had the same features. Large, almond-shaped blue eyes. Short dark hair. Great. Not only was she forced to sit here instead of taking a hot bath, but she would be forced to stare at a face that reminded her of the guy she had fallen in love with—and been ghosted by.

"Is this seat taken?" Someone was pointing to the desk next to Tara's.

"No, not at all," Tara said, glued to Gavin's Ted-ish face; she opened her laptop.

She was afraid Gavin's likeness to Ted would keep her from absorbing anything from this class, that she would spend the whole time daydreaming about the guy she thought she was destined to marry, but she was suddenly distracted by the cologne of the person sitting next to her. A citrus scent, Tara's favorite.

She glanced at him as he took out his laptop. He had short brown hair that was closely cropped on the sides and longer at the top. His hands were well manicured, and his skin looked silky smooth like it was regularly moisturized.

"I'm a bit nervous," the guy said to her, rolling up his shirt sleeves. "Everyone looks so much younger than me."

"I thought the same thing," Tara said.

"I'm Blake, by the way." He held out his hand.

"Tara." She shook it.

"Nice to meet you, Tara."

"Nice to meet you, too."

"So, what brings you to Microsoft Excel class?" he asked.

Tara hesitated. It had been a long time since an attractive guy who wasn't her colleague or the parent of a high schooler started talking to her—beyond *good morning* and *have a nice day*, the usual chitchat. "Well, I'm a high school psychologist."

"Impressive," Blake said.

"I guess." Her cheeks warmed. "At a recent school board meeting, my principal said we have to start using Microsoft Excel to keep track of our students and assessments."

"What had you been using before?"

Tara was embarrassed to say that she was using good old-fashioned notebook paper and manila folders—perhaps another function of her age. "Pen and paper," she said.

"Hey, it's worked for centuries, right?"

"That's true." She smiled. "My colleagues across the school district and I decided we should learn about Excel, and someone mentioned that this class was taking place, and so..."

"So, you drew the short straw," Blake said.

"Something like that." She laughed.

"Well, I guess that's lucky for me. I'll have someone to talk to."

Tara's body buzzed with excitement, surprising her. This rarely happened in her world—meeting a guy and striking up a conversation. She wasn't good in social situations that weren't clinical, where there wasn't a process she could cling to and follow. She rarely went to bars or coffee shops—where people typically met one another. Which was why she had turned to online dating, where she could hide behind words and pictures on a screen.

The instructor closed the classroom door. "Okay, everyone, it's go time. How y'all doin'?"

The twenty or so students in the room shrugged and looked at one another.

"That good, huh?" Gavin laughed. "Well, just in case you're in the wrong room, this is Microsoft Excel 101, a two-hour class that takes place tonight and next Monday that covers all the basics, so if you're a beginner, don't worry, you'll be fine." He smiled, looking even more like Ted. Tara's insides twisted. "I like to begin my classes with a round of introductions. It's always nice to see why people are here and what they expect from my class. I would ask for volunteers, but from experience, I'm assuming I'll get none." He looked around at the quiet and still bodies. "Okay, I'll start." He cleared his throat. "My name is Gavin Sayer. I work for Rockwell, an insurance company based on the North Shore. I've worked there for a few years, since I got my MBA at Adelphi University."

Ha, Tara was right. Gavin *was* just about half her age. Mid-twenties.

"Last year, I was approached by the Nassau County library system, which expressed some interest in teaching residents Excel, since your school district will be implementing it and has already begun rolling it out. I've been teaching it ever since. On a personal note, I live in the district with my wife, who is a teacher in another district, and our eight-month-old baby, a poodle named Ruby." Several students laughed. "Okay, anyone want to go next?"

If Tara could sink lower in her chair, she would have. She knew her body language was screaming *not me*, just like it had in high school; old habits died hard. Gavin looked in her direction, and just when she was sure he would call on her, Blake raised his hand.

"I guess I'll go," he said. "Hi, everyone. My name is Blake Townsend. I'm forty-two years old, I'm the cofounder of a marketing company called Napkin Marketing, and my official line is that I'm taking this class to get a refresher on Excel. But the truth is that I really don't have anything better to do on a Monday night."

The class laughed.

"Thank you, Blake," Gavin said. "Next victim?" A perky blonde in the front row raised her hand and began telling her story.

"Figured I'd start with a joke," Blake whispered to Tara. "Everyone in here looks so uptight."

"Nicely done," Tara whispered back.

When everyone else in the room had given their spiel, Gavin glanced at Tara. "And last, but not least," he said, motioning toward her. The class turned around and stared.

"Go on, you got this," Blake prodded, as if she were about to give the commencement address at a graduation.

Tara cleared her throat. "Hi, everyone, I'm Tara Hoffman. I'm a high school psychologist for the district high school and I'm here because, as Gavin said, we'll be implementing Microsoft Excel in our school and I . . . well, I thought I needed to learn it. I'm a complete newbie and kind of nervous."

"You'll do fine," Gavin said with a smile. "And now that that's done, let's get started."

Twenty minutes later, Tara was poking around an Excel spreadsheet, trying to remember some of the basic functions Gavin had outlined, but she was already having trouble.

"Can I help?" Blake asked.

"It's obvious I need it, right?" Tara said.

"Well, not so obvious. What are you looking to do?"

"I'm typing, but nothing's happening."

"Oh, you need to click on the box first." Blake reached over and showed her. Tara clicked, began to type, and the letters appeared on her screen.

"You must think I'm an idiot," Tara said with a roll of her eyes.

"Not at all. Everyone is a beginner at some point. Trust me, I'm no expert."

"You seem like you are. You seem very comfortable with the software."

"I'm good at faking it," he said with a smile.

"How are we doing back here?" Gavin said, standing over Blake and Tara and glancing at their computer screens.

"Great," Blake said. Tara was quiet.

"Terrific. Any questions, you know where I am," Gavin said.

As Gavin walked back to the front of the room, Blake whispered, "I have underwear older than that guy."

Tara giggled. "Me too."

By the time the class was over, Tara felt a little more relaxed. She still struggled with remembering the various functions, but she no longer considered Excel to be this scary monster she had made it out to be in her mind. Being familiar with Microsoft Word helped because the two programs worked in many of the same ways. It was just like she told her students: the unknown is scary because it's unknown, but more often than not, you'll find that whatever it is you're afraid of is not as bad as you think. She closed her laptop, stood up, and put on her coat.

"You did great," Blake said, standing up as well.

Tara had somehow missed how tall Blake was when he first arrived. He must have been at least six feet. And he was trim, his khakis fitting just so. He clearly cared about his appearance. "Getting there," she said.

"So, I guess same time next week?"

"I guess so."

Blake turned to leave but then stopped. "Um, I hope you don't think this is too forward, but there's this great new sweet shop down the block. Not far from here. They have all kinds of things—cookies, cakes, ice cream. I had been planning on stopping by to check it out after class. And I was just thinking that maybe you would like to join me."

"Are you talking about Isabel's?" she asked.

"Yeah, you've heard of it?"

She nodded. "I've been meaning to try it."

"Wow." Blake put his hands in his pockets. "I mean, would you want to check it out? With me?"

Tara didn't know what to say. She had promised herself after the whole Ted debacle that she would take a hiatus from men for the foreseeable future. But this—whatever this was with Blake Townsend, Microsoft Excel wizard—seemed to be off to a *normal* start. She wasn't typing on a screen. She wasn't agonizing over which photos to post on a dating site. She was talking to a real-life person in a real-life setting. And they had met not in some meat market, but in a normal, quiet place they had visited for a reason other than to meet someone. Their encounter was totally spontaneous—and with no pressure.

"Sure," she said, surprising herself. She cinched her coat.

As she and Blake got to the front of the classroom, Gavin was standing at the front door, saying goodbye to his students. When he saw Tara, he said, "Hey, it looks like you're getting the hang of it."

"Yeah," she said, walking out the door.

Tara had a feeling Gavin was talking about Microsoft Excel, but she felt like she was perhaps also getting the hang of this dating thing. At least for the moment.

CHAPTER 24

Monday, January 13, 9:15 p.m.

Isabel's turned out to be a quaint little place with hanging chalkboard menus in pastel colors and displays of mouth-watering pastries and desserts. Like the library parking lot, it was crowded for a Monday night, and Tara recognized a few students from the Excel class. She wondered if most of the patrons were spillover from the library.

"Can I help you?" asked a young man with braces from behind the counter.

Tara scanned the menu. "I think I'll try the peppermint chocolate cupcake."

"Oooh, that sounds good," said Blake, who was standing next to her.

The young man reached into the display case and grabbed Tara's cupcake. "Will that be all?"

"Yes," she said.

"I've got that." Blake reached into his pocket for his wallet.

"You don't have to," Tara said.

"Hey, it was my idea to come. And I'm old-fashioned, so if it's okay, I'd like to pay."

Tara was hesitant. Blake seemed nice, but she didn't want to owe anything to a relative stranger. Against her better judgment, she let him pay. After all, it was just a cupcake. And she wanted to loosen up a little when it came to dating. This might be a first step. "Okay, thank you so much."

"My pleasure." Blake turned his attention to the young man. "I'll take a piece of that blueberry pie."

After paying for their sweets, they walked off the line, and Tara found an empty table in the back next to a gaggle of high school girls who were alternating between giggling and looking at their phones.

"Let me get that for you." Blake pulled out her chair.

"Thank you," she said, sitting down.

"Can't wait to dig in," Blake said after he was seated. When he took a bite of his pie, his eyes lit up. "I don't think I've tasted anything this good in years."

Tara sampled her peppermint chocolate cupcake. "Wow."

"Right? I might just have to move in here."

"This used to be a bar." Tara motioned around the room. "One of those old-timey Long Island taverns with old men drinking scotch in the afternoon and complaining about their wives."

"Sounds miserable."

"I would walk by all the time, glance at the dark windows, and wonder if there was anyone in here. When it closed last year, I guess I got my answer."

"Yeah, I've never been down this street before. I live in the next town over." Blake pointed east. "My district library didn't have much in the way of business classes. Lots of financial planning and Pilates, but no business."

"Yeah, you don't look like you need Pilates," Tara said but then wanted to kick herself. She had just given away that she was admiring Blake's body.

He smiled and graciously ignored her comment. "I thought about taking a continuing education class at one of the local universities, but they're so pricy. Didn't want to spend the money. I guess that makes me cheap."

"I'd say, for a small-business owner, that makes you smart and savvy. Why spend the money if you don't have to? Especially if all you need to do is brush up on a few things."

"That's kind of you to say." Blake took another bite of his pie. "So, that must be cool—being a psychologist."

"It *can* be when I'm not buried in paperwork." Tara ripped off another piece of cupcake and plopped it into her mouth. "Sometimes I feel like a bit of a fraud, talking to parents about their children when I don't have any children of my own."

"On the contrary, I think that can make you an asset to them. You can offer an objective opinion about their child and not get swept up in the emotion of being a parent." He shrugged. "Or maybe I just feel that way because I don't have children either." He laughed.

"Never married?" she asked, surprised at herself for posing such a personal question.

"No. You?"

"No. Never seemed to find the right person, I guess."

"Yeah, same."

They both bit into their desserts.

"I don't know where the time went," Tara said. "I just celebrated my forty-eighth birthday a few months ago." Okay, now she was *really* going off-script. Telling a man her *real* age the day they met? She either didn't care at all about this guy or, even worse—was beginning to like him a whole lot.

"Happy birthday!" Blake said, and she found herself relieved he hadn't said one of the usual guy lines: *You don't look forty-eight at all!* Or: *Baby, you make forty-eight look good.* "Overall, I think people put too much emphasis on age. It really doesn't mean all that much. It's about how you use the years you have."

"Totally agree. You know what's funny?" Tara took another bite of cupcake. "I find the people who are the most stressed about their age are young people. I work with kids who are sixteen, seventeen, eighteen years old, and they're freaking out because they haven't already figured out what they want to do for the rest of their lives. I'm, like, *you're eighteen*."

"Kids have so much more pressure on them these days," Blake said with a nod. "I feel lucky to have grown up in the time we did."

Tara agreed, and as they continued to talk about their lives, she was pleasantly surprised to see Blake listening to what she had to say. She didn't know many people who were that attentive. Most individuals she met, at work or elsewhere, liked to do most of the talking, and she let them. She figured they either needed to vent or liked the sound of their own voice. But Blake was different. Their discussion was a balance of voices and opinions, without one judgmental tone. So much better than the disjointed conversations people had these days typing onto a screen and then waiting for someone else to type back. Tara felt like she was experiencing a real connection, and it both scared and excited her.

When they were done with their desserts, Blake said, "Meeting you was such a nice surprise. I don't really get out too often. The business keeps me busy, and I'm not really one for places with loud noises."

"Me either," Tara said. "I'm sort of a homebody."

"Me too. Some of my clients are musicians, and they're pretty outgoing."

"Wow, you work with musicians? Anyone I may have heard of?"

"I don't know. Do you know Chuck Landon of Rockknot?"

She shook her head. "Can't say I do."

"They're up and coming. Really good. Classic rock, if you like that kind of thing. I kind of don't." He chuckled. "Rockknot has all these concerts and performances that I really should attend—to be supportive and all—and it's such a relief that my business partner, Alex, goes to them. He's the outgoing one. I'm somewhat embarrassed to say I'm more of a yacht rock guy and much more comfortable just hanging out at home, which is probably why I haven't had very many dates in the past year or so."

"I know what you mean," Tara said.

Blake nodded. "So, you're not seeing anybody?"

She shook her head. "No. I kind of was for about six months, but I'm beginning to think that it wasn't really anything."

"What do you mean?"

She hesitated. She wasn't used to talking about her private life so readily, but she felt surprisingly chatty. Perhaps she was on a sugar high from the cupcake. "I decided to dip my toe into online dating last year. I had been putting it off because . . . well, it just all seemed so icky."

"Yeah, I don't really do online dating for that reason. Maybe if I did, I'd have more dates." He chuckled again.

"Well, I met someone on YourPerfectMatch.com. This guy Ted. Ted Baker. He seemed to be really sweet, and we hit it off. After about a month, we moved from the dating site to texting and then to phone conversations. We would have these long talks into the night, telling each other our hopes and dreams." She searched Blake's face for ridicule or judgment, but there was none. "I know it sounds dumb."

"Not at all. It sounds great. So, what happened? Did you eventually progress to FaceTime?"

Tara shook her head. "No, he didn't want to. He said that he had put on a few pounds and was embarrassed."

"So, you never got to *see* him?" Blake raised his eyebrows.

"I know, I know. Possible catfish, right? I thought the same thing. He promised he wasn't catfishing me." She laughed, remembering the plea in Ted's voice. "The photo he had on his dating profile looked fine, but he said the photo was taken a few years ago and that he looked a little different."

"That's not uncommon from what I hear," Blake said. "People posting old photos of themselves from a time when they think they looked younger or more in shape."

"The truth is, Blake, I didn't care what he looked like. He seemed like such a wonderful person. Down to earth. Caring.

I really felt like I had made a friend. *More* than a friend. And then one day, Ted just . . . disappeared."

"He ghosted you? After how long?"

"About six months." Tara shrugged. "I mean, sometimes I think perhaps he just *died* suddenly and that's why I haven't heard from him, but I don't think so. The timing was a bit suspect."

"How?"

"It was after we decided to take the relationship offline. Sometimes, I think I was being too pushy or he thought I was treating him like one of my patients."

"Pushy? If you ask me, it sounds like you were being very *patient* with him. Maybe *too* patient."

"I was really hurt by the whole thing. When he disappeared, I didn't realize how much my life revolved around Ted. We had scheduled times to chat at the end of each day, and I would think about him as I worked, excited to talk to him and tell him about my day." She looked down at the table. Why was she telling Blake this? "I'm ashamed to say I searched for him often online—on social media sites—but I couldn't find him. And I must have read and reread our text messages over and over after he disappeared, to make sure I didn't say anything that insulted him or turned him off."

"I can't imagine you did." Blake looked like he wanted to reach for Tara's hand but was refraining. "I'm so sorry this happened to you. If it makes you feel any better, I think Ted's a jerk."

She laughed. "That *does* make me feel a little better." She crumbled the napkin that was on the table. "And would you believe that Gavin guy, the guy teaching our class, looks like him?"

"No way."

"Yeah. I mean, I'm 99 percent sure it's not him—the voice is higher pitched, and he's much younger than the photo I have." Tara dug out her phone, found the one photo of Ted she kept, and held up her phone screen for Blake to see. He studied it. "Is it creepy that I still have it on my phone?"

"No, it's not, and yes, you're right. I can see a slight resemblance around the eyes," Blake said.

"Yeah, that's what I thought, too, which was enough to get my attention." She put her phone on the table. "Let's just say talking to you during class was a nice distraction from obsessing about the face of my instructor."

"Well, if it's okay with you, I'm wondering if I can continue to be a distraction," Blake said. "Would it be okay if I saw you again?"

"Well, you'll see me next Monday." She smiled coyly.

He laughed. "Yeah, that's true. But I was thinking more along the lines of this weekend."

Tara looked across the table at Blake Townsend's intent eyes and shy expression. For the first time in months, she didn't feel an uncontrollable angst. The emptiness was a little less—hope once again rearing its beautiful head. Hope that she wasn't going to be alone for the rest of her life. Hope that she'd have somebody to share meals, bathroom mirrors, blankets with. To think, she had been dreading this Excel class for weeks, never realizing she might stumble onto something more than a few business hacks.

"Yes," she said, picking up her phone, clicking on the photo of Ted, and deleting it once and for all. "I'd like that very much."

CHAPTER 25

Saturday, January 18, 9:30 p.m.

"That was such a great movie," Blake said as he and Tara exited the theater. "I love black-and-white films."

They began walking down the street toward the parking lot, their arms swinging dangerously close to one another, slightly brushing. Tara wondered if Blake would reach for her hand. She wanted him to. She also wondered if she should reach for his first. Online or in person, this dating thing was mentally exhausting.

"I love black-and-white films, too," she said, "but I think we're the only ones. There was hardly anyone in the audience."

"I'm telling you, kids these days are not only riddled with stress, but they don't know what's good." He stopped walking. "Look at me. I sound like an old man." He pulled a lock of his dark hair. "Do you see any gray?"

"Ha, you're *far* from old," Tara said as Blake continued walking next to her. "I should know. You're younger than I am."

"Yeah, well, these days I tend to feel like an old man."

"Why?"

He hesitated, as if lost in thought, but then quickly smiled. "Just tired, I guess. I've been working so much. I thought the first few years of building my own business would be the toughest, but it never seems to get easy. That's probably another reason I haven't dated much. Working so much has left no time for fun."

"Work-life balance is so important," Tara said as they reached the parking lot. "When the school day finishes, I try to leave my work problems at the office. It's hard, though."

"Tell me about it. I'm usually working way into the night."

"What about your business partner?" Tara asked.

"Alex? Alex is great. We've been friends since we were kids."

"Does he share some of the burden? I know you mentioned he was the one who went to most of your clients' concerts."

"He does more than that. He'll go to clubs and restaurants all over the Island to check out local bands and see if they've got anyone taking care of their socials and marketing. Alex really has a way with people. You have to meet him. You'll love him."

"You have a way with people, too, Blake," Tara said as they reached Tara's car. She wasn't sure what to do. Get out her keys? Shake his hand? Wait for a kiss? Lean in and make it happen? She was forty-eight years old and felt like a loser for not having gotten any of this down pat.

"I would have totally picked you up." Blake motioned to her car. "We didn't have to meet at the restaurant."

"I know." She shrugged. "I guess I just want to take it a little slow." The sensible girl in her wanted to take it slow, but the lonely woman was eager to see where their connection would lead, sooner rather than later. She dug out her keys and popped open the back door, placing her handbag on top of some sports equipment.

"You play baseball?" Blake asked, eyeing the baseball bat lying in the well of the back seat.

"Is it that surprising?" Tara laughed. "Nah. This stuff belongs to one of my kids. Rachel Sanberg. Her dad doesn't know she was kicked off the high school team, and Rachel doesn't have the heart to tell him. I told her I'd keep her mitt, cleats, and bat until she works up the nerve. I've been counseling her each week."

"That's nice of you."

"Even though I lost my parents when I was about her age, I know how hard it can be to navigate that parent-child bond. I remember it well."

"I still find it hard to navigate," Blake said with a nod. "And I'm so sorry to hear about your parents."

They stood there awkwardly until he pointed to the other side of the lot. "Well, I'm parked all the way over there. Sandra's always making fun of me because I park in the spot farthest from wherever it is I want to go. She says I'm avoiding people, when really, I'm avoiding getting pock marks on my car."

"Sandra?"

"Yeah, Sandra's married to Alex. I've known Sandra nearly as long as I've known Alex. They're my best friends. Really amazing people."

"Well, I would expect nothing less," Tara said.

"Why is that?"

"Because you're a pretty amazing guy."

Tara inwardly cringed because that was a corny thing to say, and she didn't know if it was because of her age, her bad experiences with men and online dating, or her ticking biological clock, but she found herself pushing the dating boundaries more than she ever had before. Would Blake find it endearing? Or would he find it desperate and quickly say good night?

Blake took a step toward her, and when he brushed the hair away from her eyes, she tilted her head up as he planted a soft kiss on her lips. Tara's body hummed with electricity, and in that one, single moment, she didn't feel old or inexperienced. She suddenly felt plugged into the world and knew for certain that her self-declared hiatus from men had officially come to an end.

CHAPTER 26

Thursday, February 27, 6:00 a.m.

Blake rolled over and kissed Tara on the lips. "Good morning," he said before flinging off the covers and getting out of bed.

"Good morning."

She watched his naked form head to the bathroom and hop into the shower, feeling warm and content. She loved the nights she spent at Blake's place, which offered an even quicker ride to her high school than her own apartment—just a few turns to the parkway and then a few turns off. She likened the commute to their burgeoning relationship—smooth and seamless. Since the start, they had fallen into a comfortable routine. Making dinner together at his place or hers. Watching Netflix. Making love on the sofa and sometimes in bed. Blake was an attentive, intuitive lover, and all of Tara's insecurities vanished when she was in his arms.

The water turned off, and Blake stepped out of the shower.

"That was fast," she said with a smile, but Blake didn't answer. Water dribbled down his body from his hair as his hands pressed against the sink. He dropped his head, and before Tara could ask if everything was okay, Blake quickly flipped up the toilet lid and vomited into the bowl. Tara jumped out of bed, grabbing her T-shirt and sweats, which were tossed on the floor.

"Blake! Are you okay?!" She ran to the bathroom door.

"Yeah, fine." He flushed the toilet, stood up slowly, and took a deep breath. "Just a little lightheaded."

"Are you feeling under the weather?" She took a really good look at him. "You know, now that I look at you in the fluorescent light, you do look a little off."

"Everybody looks a little off in fluorescent light."

"I'm serious, Blake." She put the back of her hand on his forehead, which was wet but cool to the touch. "You don't have a temperature, but maybe you're coming down with something. I hope you didn't get it from me. The high school is like a petri dish of germs."

"I'm fine," he said with a wave of his hand.

"You don't look fine. Let me make you some tea."

"You really don't need to."

She wondered if he was trying to act tough for her sake, and she wanted to tell him that she thought the toughest men were the ones who were the most vulnerable—something else her male high school students failed to understand, which is why they often grew into men who didn't know how to express themselves and kept all their fears and feelings bottled up inside. "Are you sure?" she asked.

Blake leaned back on his heels and rubbed his temples. She wrapped her arms around his wet body. "I can take care of you. Just tell Alex you're not coming in today. And I'll spend the whole day pampering you. I'll call in sick."

"That's not really going to help."

"What do you mean?"

"You're going to need more than a day." Blake looked in the mirror. "I thought I could just forget about it for a little while."

"Forget about what?"

"But I'm realizing that doing that isn't fair to you." He looked at Tara through the mirror.

"What isn't fair to me?"

Blake exhaled and took her hand. He led her into the bedroom, and they sat on the bed. "I have to tell you something, something I haven't told anyone. Not my mom. Not Alex or Sandra. I thought I could shield you from it, at least for a little while because . . . you have been the best thing to happen to me this year, probably ever."

She squeezed his hand. "I feel the same way."

"I have to do the right thing. You deserve that. The truth." He hesitated. "There really is no way to say this, so I might as well just come out with it. I have Ewing's sarcoma."

The words hovered in the air in front of her, and Tara tried to make sense of them. "Ewing's sarcoma? Is that—?"

"Yes, it's cancer."

Her pulse quickened. Cancer? She stared at his face, which suddenly looked tired and gaunt and gray. "Oh, Blake."

"I've known for about six months. Got the diagnosis last year when I went to the doctor for a headache and they told me it would go away. When it didn't, they ran a bunch of tests and . . ." He shook his head. "That's when I found out."

"And you haven't told anyone?"

"No, probably because I'm still trying to accept it myself."

"But . . . aren't you undergoing treatment?"

He shook his head again. "No."

"Why not?" she asked, alarmed.

"I didn't want to, Tara. It would have been brutal. The cancer was too far gone. The doctor said so himself."

"Did you get a second opinion?"

He nodded. "Yes. Took the scans to two other doctors. They told me the same." He grabbed his phone, scrolled, and held up a scanned image for her to see. He pointed to a large, white, egg-shaped image on the gray photo. "That's the bad boy," he said. "It would be beautiful if it wasn't so . . ."

Tara searched the image and then Blake's face. "So, you're just going to . . ."

"Ride it out the best I can, yes." He put his phone down. "Until I can't anymore."

She searched his eyes. "What does that mean? Are the symptoms getting worse?"

"They're starting to. A bit. I have a feeling Alex and Sandra might sense something is up, although Alex—great guy—is not as perceptive. I've kinda been avoiding Sandra, who *is* perceptive."

Tara squeezed Blake's hand. The doctor in her wanted to tell Blake to go into treatment immediately, and yet the psychologist in her understood his choice—the denial of sickness because you were afraid and perhaps feeling well in the moment, followed by the desire to make the best of the time you have left and not spend it in a hospital. She knew treatment was the better option—there was no telling how well Blake's body would react to chemotherapy or radiation—and deep down, she knew that there were medical miracles out there, if only Blake were willing to give science a try.

"I've made my decision," he said as if sensing her thoughts. "And I know it was the right one."

"Not getting treatment? How do you know?"

"Because if I were undergoing treatment in the hospital they wanted me to go to, which was out of state, I wouldn't have been at the Microsoft Excel class last month. I wouldn't have met *you*." He pulled her toward him. "Since meeting you last month . . . I've felt *reborn*. I've felt so good these last weeks that, if I'm honest, I've also rationalized to myself that maybe the doctors had gotten my diagnosis wrong. Stupid, right?"

"Not at all."

"Well, it *was* stupid of me to keep this from you." He leaned his forehead against Tara's till their noses touched. "*Wrong* of me to do that to you. You deserve so much more."

"Blake, if you had gotten treatment, the odds of it going into remission—"

"The survival rate isn't great for adults and isn't great when it's not diagnosed early. The tumor is in my head, Tara. It's big and aggressive. Ewing's sarcoma is usually found in children. I'm a rarity. Lucky me, right?" He gave a small smile. "I've made my peace with what's happening. I'm not going to lie. There were a lot of nights I spent here, alone, feeling sorry for myself, but then I really thought about it. Not everyone gets to reach the age of forty-two. Not everyone is blessed with a loving family and really good friends. Like George Bailey, from my favorite movie of all time, I've lived a wonderful life."

"*It's a Wonderful Life* is your favorite movie?"

He nodded. "Wait . . . don't tell me it's your favorite movie, too?"

"One of them, yes." Tears filled Tara's eyes. "One of the many things we have in common."

"And then you came along." He caressed the side of her face before pulling away. "That said, though, now that you know what's going on, maybe it's not a good idea we see each other anymore."

Tara's breathing hitched. "What do you mean?"

"C'mon, Tara. You didn't sign up for this. It's my fault. I blame myself for asking you to go to Isabel's that very first day. I knew it was a bad idea, but I just thought you were so . . . so . . ." He wiped the corner of his eye. "Well, I thought you were great, and I think I convinced myself that meeting you was some sort of, I don't know, divine intervention. Jesus, I sound like one of the sappy romance books Sandra writes."

"Sandra writes romance books?"

"Yeah, it's a hobby she has."

"Well . . . she might be onto something." Tara stood up. "Perhaps it *was* divine intervention."

"Tara . . ."

"No, really, Blake. Who's to say?" She reached for his hand. "I want to be with you. For as long as we can." What she really wanted to say was that she had never met a man like him and how cruel the universe was to take him away from her—take Blake away from the world.

"What are you saying?" he asked.

"I'm saying I don't want to end things."

"But, Tara, there's no future."

"What is the future but the seconds, minutes, hours, and days in front of us? And there are still a lot of them. Let's spend them together."

"But I'm only going to get gradually sicker. Eventually, I'll have to be hospitalized."

"We'll cross that bridge when we get to it." She reached for her phone on the nightstand and pulled up her calendar. "Let's go somewhere."

"What?"

"You're feeling good now, right?"

"Yeah, but . . ."

"Let's go away for a weekend. Road trip. Air travel. Whatever you want. Is there any place you've always wanted to go?"

Blake smiled. "Well, I *have* wanted to go to the Poconos—you know, in Pennsylvania?—and stay in one of those corny hotels with the heart-shaped bathtubs."

"Let's go!"

"Really?"

"Sure, why not? I've never been there either."

"Okay. Let me check what weekend is slow for the business."

He smiled before reaching for his phone, and Tara thought it was the most beautiful thing she ever saw.

Like a rainbow between storm clouds.

CHAPTER 27

Sunday, March 9, 3:30 p.m.

Traffic snarled as they inched off the George Washington Bridge.

"It's always fun going on vacation," Blake said, changing lanes. "Not so much fun traveling back to Long Island. Every highway is like a parking lot." He looked up at the sky through the windshield and clasped his hands together. "Please, please don't let me die on the Cross Bronx Expressway."

"Please don't joke like that," Tara said.

He reached for her hand. "I'm sorry."

The weekend had been wonderfully kitschy and corny. Everything Tara hoped it would be. Although it had mostly rained, she and Blake made the best of their time—soaking in the heart-shaped tub, dining on empty- and high-calorie food, and making love in a round bed in a gaudy bedroom with mirrors on the ceiling. The time away from home was like a cross between *Dirty Dancing* and an old Bob Hope/Bing Crosby film, and they had spent most of it just laughing.

As far as she could tell, Blake had only gotten sick Saturday morning. After vomiting, he was otherwise okay. Tara had been trying not to obsess about Blake's condition, but she had been reading up on Ewing's sarcoma and secretly monitoring his symptoms since the day he told her he was sick. She was still hoping he would consider treatment, if it wasn't too late, but vowed to herself she would respect Blake's decision.

"I actually don't mind so much going home and getting back into my routine," Blake said. "One of the perks of running your own business is I can set my own schedule—choose where and when I work, although usually it's *all the time*." He laughed. "Before Alex and I started Napkin Marketing, I was working for this idiot of a boss who thought I was hired to be his personal slave. I was supposed to be doing the business bookkeeping, but before I knew it, I was paying his personal electric and phone bills."

"Yuck."

"One of my happiest days was telling that guy I quit—well, right after he fired me. Turned out for the best. Alex and I decided to go into business together a short time later."

"See? Things always work out." Tara immediately wanted to retract the words. Things *didn't* always work out. Blake was sick. And nothing would change that. Luckily, Blake appeared lost in a memory and didn't seem to hear her comment.

"It was hard the first few years," Blake said. "We were both freelancing to make ends meet, but we finally have enough clients to sustain a solid income between us—and that's saying something when you live on pricy Long Island." He laughed. "Napkin Marketing gives me a sense of purpose, too. I feel such pride in what Alex and I have been able to build, although I do worry that we're putting our eggs all in one basket."

"What do you mean?"

"Well, let's face it, I don't know how much longer I have."

"Blake—"

"The doctors have given me a year, and that was six months ago, and I want to make sure Napkin Marketing is set up for the future, long after I'm gone."

"Do you think the business is focusing too much on one type of client? Like, musicians?"

Blake shrugged. "Maybe."

"I can see your point. Diversification definitely reduces risk and can increase revenue by opening you up to new markets."

"You think?"

"Well, I'm no entrepreneur, but it seems like it would be the smart move, giving Alex a more competitive advantage and allowing him to take the business in different directions as needed. A bigger playing field."

"I think you're right," Blake said. "I worry about Alex and Sandra."

"Worry how?"

"Our little business has been able to sustain them so far, but they're looking to adopt, and even though they're having trouble, I *know* it's going to happen for them, so the business has to do well. With Long Island being so damn expensive, I need to make sure they're okay."

"You're a good friend, Blake."

"I try to be, but I'd be lying if I didn't admit that sometimes it all gets to me."

Tara thought she heard Blake crying one morning while he was in the bathroom and thought she was sleeping. She wanted to burst in there and tell him everything would be all right, but she knew it wouldn't be, and it broke her heart. "Let's focus on the positive."

"I usually do, but there's so much I won't get to see and do. Like spend more time with you. Or see Alex and Sandra's baby or what becomes of Napkin Marketing. Or take care of my mom as she gets older."

"I'd like to meet her, you know. Your mom."

"And I'd like you to, honey. But . . ."

"But?"

"I know what she's going to say. When she finds out I'm sick, she's going to tell me it's irresponsible for me to start a new relationship."

"But that's not her decision to make," Tara said. "It's ours. We're both going into this fully cognizant of the situation."

"Ha, you've never met my mother."

The traffic eased once they crossed onto the Whitestone Bridge—or at least Tara *thought* it was the Whitestone Bridge. There were so many bridges in this tiny, congested area of New York state that she often had trouble telling them apart. But, within moments, the cars in front of them returned to a dead stop.

"Great, more traffic," Blake said. "I was hoping we'd get lucky."

"You know what? Let's make the best of it." Tara pointed to the next exit. "Let's pull off here and wait it out somewhere."

"Good idea." Blake put on his turn signal. "I know a great spot." He followed signs to Francis Lewis Park.

"Francis Lewis Park? I've never been there before."

"It's a hidden gem."

As they found a parking spot, the rain stopped, and the sun poked out its head, shining brightly in the western sky and casting a gorgeous light against the Whitestone Bridge.

"Let's get out and get a better look," Blake said.

As they left the car, Blake reached for Tara's hand, and they walked toward the water, gazing at the landscape.

"All this was owned by Francis Lewis, a Welsh-born merchant," Blake said. "The British granted him this land for his service in the French and Indian War. The property changed hands a few times after that before it was bought by the parks department in the early 1900s."

"How do you know all this?" Tara asked as they began walking down one of the paths.

"My mom used to work nearby and took me here when I was a kid. It's so funny how we can drive back and forth on all these highways and bridges and never take the time to stop to see what's around us."

Tara leaned against him as a cold wind whipped up near the shoreline. She didn't know if it was the beauty around them or the afterglow from the wonderful weekend, but she was feeling alive and in the moment. "I love you, Blake."

The words came so easily, without fear of not hearing them back. This was the first time she had told a man she loved him. She hadn't even told Ted. Blake tilted her face toward him.

"You do?" he asked.

She nodded. "Yes. I love you. All of you. The well parts. The sick parts. Everything that makes you you."

"I love you, too, Tara." He leaned down and kissed her as the wind blew their hair into their faces. "You are the best thing that has ever happened to me. I want to spend every moment I can as close to you as possible." He stared into her eyes, and suddenly his face burst into a smile. "Call me crazy, but . . ." He bent down on one knee.

"Blake!"

"Will you make me the happiest man in the world, Tara Hoffman? Maybe it's selfish of me to ask you, considering all that's going on, but the thought of having you by my side fills me with so much love and gratitude. I used to wonder if that kind of love would ever come my way, the kind of love that Alex and Sandra share, and then you stepped into my life, making it bigger and brighter than I ever could have imagined. Will you be by my side for however long we have? Will you marry me?"

The words rushed to Tara's lips as tears spilled down her cheeks. She didn't need time to decide, time to think about it. This was the surest of anything she had ever been.

"Yes," she said, wrapping her arms around Blake's thin frame. "Yes, I will marry you."

CHAPTER 28

Sunday, March 16, 10:52 a.m.

"Please don't tell them." Blake was standing nervously at the bar at April's Café, squeezing the Bloody Mary he had just ordered for Alex.

"Blake, I really think you should," Tara said. "They're your friends. They deserve to know you're sick." She sipped her drink. "And I think it would be good for you, too, to widen your circle. It'll help you feel more supported."

"What?" Blake asked. "I can't hear you."

The noise level at April's was high. It was a nice restaurant but hard to have a meaningful conversation when you were talking over dozens of people. She spoke a little louder. "I said that I think it would be good for you to tell them!"

"I'm just not ready, honey."

She left it at that. Blake seemed tense, and she didn't want to make him even more so. She understood his reticence. He had already shared the news with Alex and Sandra that morning that they had gotten married. That was probably a lot to take in. Tara felt a little let down that she hadn't been there when he told them.

"I thought we were going to wait," she had said after she had taken a shower.

"I'm sorry. I couldn't help myself. I was waiting for you and just found myself calling them and telling them. I was bursting inside to share good news, *any* good news—it's probably the *only* good news I'll be sharing with them for the rest of my life."

She glanced at the beautiful—and expensive—engagement ring on her finger. She would have settled for a piece of string, but Blake said he wanted to spend his money while he still could. He relented when she had pushed for a modest ceremony at city hall, which turned out to be surprisingly intimate and perfect, but Blake had been hinting he wanted to throw a big reception in a few weeks. As hesitant as she was to overspend, she was happy he was bringing her more into his world and social circles.

"Do I look okay?" he asked her.

"Yes, Blake. As handsome as ever. Don't worry. It will go fine. I think they'll like me."

"Are you kidding? They're going to *love* you." He kissed her cheek before nervously checking his phone. "I know you think it's the right thing for me to tell them now—about the cancer. But it's just—"

"They're your friends, Blake. If they really care for you, they'll want to know."

"It's not just that. It's that . . . Sandra can be kind of . . ."

"Kind of what?"

He sighed. "She's my best friend, but . . ."

"But what?"

Blake hesitated, the way students who came to her office often did when they were about to tattle on a fellow classmate. "Sandra and I have kind of a history. Before she got together with Alex."

"You guys dated?"

"Well, yes and no. We were *young*. But we have different ideas of what that relationship was—and what it is now. I see us as best friends."

"And how does *she* see you?"

"She refers to me as her best friend, but she can be kind of . . . possessive. She's been this way since we were kids."

"I don't understand."

"She's told me over the years that she was the best thing to happen to me, and she didn't think any other woman would measure up. She makes it sound like a joke, but I know she doesn't mean it that way. She's always super-critical of the women I've dated, and I think that's why."

"You're saying she's in love with you?"

"I know. It's weird to say when Sandra adores Alex, but I don't know any other way to explain the things she says and does. I've told her I don't feel *that way* about her, but I don't think she hears me."

"Is that part of the reason you've kept me a secret from her?"

Blake looked down. The lack of eye contact was telling. And now it made more sense why he was so nervous.

"Maybe," he said finally. "You know, when we were teenagers, Sandra insisted we lose our virginity together."

"Insisted?"

"Yeah, she said it would be good for both of us."

What a strange thing to say. "Was it?"

"Not really. And ever since that day, she's been kind of *controlling*. And like I said, opinionated. She's had something to say not only about every woman I've ever dated, but something to say about how I dress, how I look. If I tell Sandra about the cancer, I *know* her. She'll tell me what to do without asking me what I want. She's going to want me to get treatment."

"You'll just have to politely tell her to butt out."

"It's always been hard for me to tell her no. As forceful as she appears, I also know that she can be very fragile."

"What do you mean *fragile*?"

"Oh, there they are!" Blake was already looking past her and waving.

Tara suddenly couldn't move. This was all too much to absorb. She had been looking forward to finally meeting Blake's best friends, but it was impossible to wrap her head around everything Blake had just said. *Sandra was controlling? Fragile?* An image appeared in Tara's mind of a glass statue holding a marionette. When she finally willed her body to turn around, to put on a happy face and greet the two people who would become a part of her new world, a dark-haired woman with brown eyes was wrapping her in a hug.

"So nice to meet you," Sandra gushed.

Tara stiffened. She didn't mean to; it just happened. *Controlling? Fragile?* She tried to override her body's knee-jerk reaction as best she could. "Nice to meet you, too," she said, worrying her reply sounded half-hearted. This new friendship wasn't off to the best start.

"I'm Alex," said the man beside Sandra. He came in for a hug, and this time, she found herself prepared and ready.

"It's so good to see you all together," Blake said with a smile. "The people I care about the most in this world, all in one place." He put his hand on Sandra's shoulder, and Tara couldn't help thinking it was like he needed to pacify her, to tell her everything would be okay with this new person intruding on their group. "C'mon, our table is ready. John, we're going to head to our table." He picked up the Bloody Mary on the bar and handed it to Alex. "For you, my friend."

He reached for Tara's hand, and she and Blake led the way into the restaurant.

As they walked, Blake said, "I'm so afraid she's going to grill you with questions."

"Don't worry. I'll be okay," Tara whispered into Blake's ear.

"I know," Blake whispered. "I was just hoping to spare you. Maybe you should sit across from her. This way, you'll be out of the direct firing line."

By the time they reached the table, Tara decided Blake was right. If Sandra had complete sidebar access to her, who knew what she might ask? What if she noticed Blake wasn't well? What if she asked Tara point-blank about Blake's coloring? Or why he was so thin? Tara waited for Sandra to choose a seat and then sat directly across from her, smiling as they took their seats. Only Sandra wasn't smiling back. She seemed agitated, like she was chomping at the bit, and Tara was so happy she had taken Blake's advice.

"So, how did you guys meet?" Sandra asked before Blake and Alex were even seated.

"I know, this must seem so sudden," Blake said.

"Not at all," Sandra said in a voice dripping with sarcasm.

As Blake relayed the story about the Excel class at the library, Tara sat back and listened to the exchange. Sandra definitely seemed bothered about something, and yet Alex appeared laidback and fine.

"Don't mind my wife," Alex said to Tara. "She's thinking about enrolling in detective school."

Tara smiled, wondering if he was making excuses for Sandra. Like Blake.

"So, why were you taking Excel, Tara?" Sandra asked. "What do you do?"

"I'm a high school psychologist," Tara said, barely recognizing her own voice, which sounded strangely standoffish. "My school district just implemented Excel, and I was trying to figure it out. It wasn't going well."

"You were doing fine," Blake said.

Alex again said something to lighten the mood, and Tara appreciated it, but Sandra didn't look like she was in the mood for laughs.

"That must be fun, working with kids," Alex said to Tara.

"Well, yes and no," Tara said. "We had a fentanyl overdose last week."

Tara began telling the story of what happened and, strangely, was happy to. Although she didn't like talking about work, the subject was objective and, hopefully, not triggering to anyone at the table—especially the woman who was glaring at her from the other side.

At some point, there was a lull in the conversation. Tara didn't want Blake to feel like he had to carry her, so she decided to initiate a dialogue with Sandra. "So, what do you do, Sandra?"

"I'm a writer."

"No, I mean for your job. You know, your profession."

Sandra's face dropped. "I'm sorry? That *is* my profession."

"Oh." Tara's cheeks warmed, and she turned toward Blake. "Blake said it was a hobby."

"A hobby, Blake?" Sandra said.

As Blake tried to assuage Sandra's anger, Tara felt like, at any moment, a giant hook was going to poke into the restaurant and haul her away. How had an innocent question ignited a firestorm?

"She does well," Alex finally said to Tara as Sandra continued glowering at Blake.

What? Blake mouthed to Sandra.

Alex began defending his wife again, and Tara wondered if this was a regular thing—everyone tiptoeing around Sandra. It must have been exhausting being married to or friends with someone who constantly needed to be handled with kid gloves. Tara hoped Blake didn't expect her to play along. She would do anything for him, but this wasn't the way to deal with a narcissist, which is what Sandra seemed to be. Tara needed to set and communicate clear boundaries, avoid engaging in any manipulative practices, and prioritize her own self-care. It had always been surprising to Tara how often she had to teach high school girls these kinds of strategies; social media had turned a whole generation of kids into self-obsessed ego-trippers.

For now, though, she was going to plow through this brunch, answering Sandra's probing questions with tact and poise.

She would try to make this work.

Because Blake loved Sandra.

And Tara loved Blake.

And that's what you did for the people you loved.

CHAPTER 29

Saturday, March 22, 8:00 a.m.

"I still can't believe you didn't say anything to Alex and Sandra at dinner," Tara said, placing down her fork with the last of her eggs.

She had spent most of the previous night pacing in the Vermont resort's hotel suite—unable to read, unable to focus—waiting to hear how they had taken the news of Blake's diagnosis. Tara thought having Chuck present might prove a good distraction so that the dinner didn't become too heavy or emotional. It wasn't until she woke up this morning that Blake told her he had chickened out. Again.

"I just couldn't." Blake pulled on his ski bib. "It's like my mouth wouldn't work. Sandra kept looking at me like something was wrong."

"But isn't that all the more reason to tell her? Something *is* wrong."

"I know you said having Chuck there might help keep things from getting too down, but I just felt awkward. I kept wishing you hadn't given up your seat to him. Maybe it would have been easier."

Tara hadn't meant to ruin Blake's plan, but she felt bad for Chuck and didn't want to see him have to eat alone on his first night at the resort. "I'm sorry," she said.

"There's nothing to be sorry about. I'm the one who couldn't go through with it." He let out a long breath. "I'll tell Alex and Sandra at dinner tonight. Even if Chuck is there. I promise. As long as you're there with me."

"I'll be there." She smiled. "Keep reminding yourself that telling them is one of the reasons you wanted to go away with them for the weekend." She knew another reason was that Blake was hoping she and Sandra would bond. That had yet to happen.

"Yeah, I know, but now that we're here, I feel like I don't want to ruin the party, you know?"

"I get that." She wrapped her arms around Blake, who looked so cute in his bib. "But I don't think of it as ruining the party. I think of it as having meaningful time with your friends and telling them what's going on in your life."

He kissed her lips. "You always know the right way to phrase things. You're right. Okay, tonight. I promise." Blake ran his hands up and down her pink ski bib. "Don't you look adorable. My little pastel ski bunny."

She playfully pushed him away. "What's Sandra going to be doing while we're skiing?"

"Knowing Sandra, she'll find a nice little cozy corner to do some writing."

"Won't she feel left out?" Tara asked. "Maybe I should forgo skiing and spend some time with her."

"Awww!" Blake planted a kiss on Tara's lip-balmed mouth. "You're such a sweetheart. But Sandra's fine. In fact, she enjoys her alone time. Especially when she's writing."

"Okay, I guess." Tara shrugged, glancing at the last of her breakfast. "Did I thank you for ordering room service for me and serving me breakfast in bed?"

"No, you haven't." He kissed her again. "But you can thank me later."

She giggled. "Are we meeting Alex and Chuck at the rental place?"

"No, Alex can lollygag, so I texted him that we'd meet him up at the ski-up coffee shack at the top of the slope. Before we go, though, I want to walk through the buffet, first. You have to see the amount of food. It's unbelievable. We'll eat there tomorrow morning, so you can get the full experience."

"Sounds like a plan."

Blake wasn't kidding.

The resort buffet was the kind of spread Tara associated with King Arthur's court—abundant, only instead of oversized turkey legs and gallon-sized goblets of ale, there were giant breakfast burritos and supersized milkshakes. As they walked through, Blake was pointing out the many different types of macarons when suddenly someone called, "Blake!"

Tara turned and saw Alex waving from one of the booth seats.

Blake waved back.

"Chuck's not with them, Blake," she said. "Maybe now's the time to tell them?"

"I thought you said Chuck could be a distraction."

"He *could*. But why not take advantage of the moment?"

"Now? I'm not ready. I figured I'd give myself time before dinner to mentally prepare. But I should go over and say hi. Look at Sandra's face. She wants me to."

Tara wanted to tell Blake he didn't need to do whatever Sandra wanted—just because she was needy or because they were childhood friends. But, instead, she walked beside him as he headed toward their booth.

"Hey there!" Alex said when they got there. "I thought you guys didn't want breakfast."

"We don't, really," Blake said. "Just passing through. Where's Chuck?"

"He wanted to check out the hotel and grounds. You want to join us?"

Tara gave Blake a nudge. She knew she was pushing it, but this really was a good opportunity to tell them about his cancer. The mood in the restaurant was light and bustling, everyone about to begin their day. Plus, they didn't have to sit and linger, because they were eager to hit the slopes.

"No," Blake said. "Thanks anyway. We're going to head over that way. Check things out, too. I'll see you in a bit."

Blake and Tara kept walking, and Tara couldn't help but feel disappointed. "Didn't feel right?" she asked.

"No."

"That's okay." She patted his hand. "We have plenty of time."

THE COFFEEHOUSE, MOUNT BREW, at the top of the ski slope was impressive with an array of coffee, tea, and hot chocolate flavors that put Tara's local Starbucks to shame. After she and Blake stood at one of the stand-up high-top tables and finished their coffees, Blake looked at his watch.

"That Alex. He's always late," he said, a nervous tone in his voice.

"Don't worry. It's still early," Tara said. "We'll have plenty of time to ski."

"Yeah, but I'm sure Chuck and Alex will want coffee, and the line is only going to get longer the more we wait."

"I'll tell you what. Maybe I'll save time and go get Chuck and Alex some coffees so that when they get here, we can skedaddle."

"You're so thoughtful." He kissed her cheek. "I'll go. You wait here."

"And impede on your bro time? Not a chance." Tara smiled. "What does Alex drink?"

"If I know Alex, he'll drink anything. And I'm pretty sure Chuck will have whatever Alex is having. The guy adores him."

"Okay, I'll use my judgment."

"Are you *sure* you don't want me to go instead? It's the gentlemanly thing to do." He winked.

"No, Sir Lancelot. You wait here and flag them over when you see them."

By the time Tara was heading back with the tray of coffees, she was happy to see Chuck and Alex had made it. They were chatting with Blake, all of them laughing at something. It was good to see Blake laugh. She wanted him to laugh as much as he could for as long as he had left.

"Here you go, gentlemen," Tara said, holding up the coffee tray. "I hope you both like mocha."

"How thoughtful of you," Alex said. "I like anything."

"Told you," Blake said with a smile.

As Tara put the tray on the table, her ski got caught on Blake's, and she lost her balance, landing in the snow, her skis folding beneath her.

"Are you okay?" Alex said, rushing toward her. He was standing over her, his face shadowed by the sun behind him.

Tara inwardly chastised herself. She was happy to have the awful banter at April's Café behind her, but nearly spilling coffee on her new friends was a second impression she didn't need. "I'm fine. Just a little embarrassed. I'm usually not this clumsy on skis."

Chuck appeared beside Alex, who reached for Tara's hand.

"Here, I'll take your other hand," Chuck said.

Tara was hesitant. Chuck was so thin, his body like a ski, that she worried he wouldn't have the strength to hold her. She was relieved when Blake came into view.

"I've got you, honey," he said.

She grabbed onto him as Alex and Chuck helped to lift her up.

"Are you okay?" Alex asked.

"I'm fine, everyone. Please, continue your conversation, and hopefully we can all forget how clumsy I am."

"Can't be clumsier than me," Alex offered. "I fall all the time."

"It's my fault," Blake said. "I shouldn't have been standing that way."

"It's no one's fault," Tara said. "What were you guys talking about?"

"Oh, Blake, here, was giving us the lay of the land," Chuck said, pointing into the distance.

As he and Blake continued their conversation, Alex turned to Tara. "So, what do you think of this place? Nice, right?"

"*Really* nice." She glanced at Chuck. Part of her was hoping she could keep Chuck occupied, freeing Blake up to have a moment with Alex. Maybe without Chuck or Sandra hovering nearby, Blake would be able to talk to Alex about what was going on. But Chuck seemed invested in whatever he and Blake were talking about, and she didn't want to interfere. Another missed opportunity.

"It's so nice to see Blake happy," Alex said, taking a sip of his coffee. "I hope the two of you will be as happy as Sandra and me."

"Thanks, Alex. That means a lot."

"I don't know, with you here, it's like I feel a missing piece of the puzzle has been put into place."

Tara stared into Alex's blue eyes, which squinted from the sun. She found it odd that he would say such a thing. He didn't really know her at all. She searched his eyes for meaning but only saw clearness and assurance. "That's maybe one of the nicest things anyone ever said to me."

"I mean it," Alex said. "I just want to say that I know you've only met us, but all we want is Blake's happiness."

Tara's insides twinged. She felt terrible knowing something about Blake that Alex didn't.

"Are you okay?" he asked.

"Yeah," she lied. "Just thinking about how fast this all must seem to you."

"You mean your marriage to Blake? As I told Sandra, when you know you know." Alex took another sip of his coffee. "Speaking of Sandra . . . she really means well. She's a special person. I don't know what I would do without her. She's got a big heart."

Tara wondered if he meant *ego*.

"I know you don't really know her, and maybe this is kind of forward, but it might be nice if you texted her."

Tara was confused. Had she made promises to Sandra that she couldn't remember? "Did I do something wrong?"

"No, not at all. I know everyone has different texting etiquettes, but I really think you and she should get to know one another. I think that you could be really good friends."

Tara had gotten the impression that Sandra didn't like her and wanted nothing to do with her. But Alex's words were so heartfelt. Not only did he appear to be Sandra's defender but also her wingman. She found herself not wanting to disappoint him. "Okay, I will. I'll text her."

"Great." Alex smiled wide.

"C'mon, honey," Blake called, pulling on his sunglasses. "I see a bunch of children coming this way, and I'd like to make it down the mountain before we get bombarded with kids."

"Blake has no tolerance for children," Alex said with a laugh as he, too, placed his sunglasses over his eyes.

"Well, I work with children—teens—all day," Tara said, pulling down her own goggles. "And I can say I'm with Blake on this one." She looked at Alex. "See you on the other side."

"See you on the other side," Alex said as she and Blake skied toward the slope and Chuck and Alex downed their coffees and began singing a silly song, laughing.

CHAPTER 30

Wednesday, March 26, 7:00 a.m.

Tara buttoned the top button of Blake's white shirt. The neck was loose, his tie sagging. He had lost more weight. She could feel his bones as she ran her hands along his hips.

"Do you really have to go to work today?" she asked. "Maybe it's better if you stay home."

He had been sobbing for days since they had gotten back from Vermont. They both were. What happened to Alex seemed impossible to endure. A beloved friend. A bright spirit. Gone. On top of everything Blake had been going through, he now had to grieve his best friend.

And then there was Sandra. Tara would never forget the look on her face at the resort when she realized Alex was dead. It was one of the most horrible scenes she had ever witnessed, and what made it worse was knowing that after losing a husband, Sandra would also be losing a best friend. She would lose Blake, too. And she didn't even know.

"I can't stay home," Blake said. "All I'll do is think about him."

"I still can't believe it. It doesn't seem real." She shook her head. "Alex was... such a nice person. I'm so sorry I didn't get to know him better."

Blake's body tensed beneath her hands. "I know." He turned away.

"Blake?"

When he turned around, there were tears in his eyes.

"We'll get through this together, okay?" She reached for his hand.

"Okay." He squeezed it. "Poor Sandra."

"I know. I can't stop thinking about her, how she must feel. I know we're not the best of friends, but I want to help. I want to do something." She suddenly remembered what Alex had asked of her. To reach out. Make an effort. With everything that had happened, she had forgotten. "Do you think you can give me Sandra's phone number? I'd love to reach out to her and let her know I'm here for her, too."

Blake's face softened. "That would be nice. Where's your phone?" She handed it to him, and he punched in the number.

Tara stepped out of the bedroom to let Blake finish getting dressed; she dialed Sandra's number. The line rang and rang, and Tara disconnected the call before it went to voicemail. She didn't want to intrude. Sandra must have had dozens of people reaching out. She decided to send a text message instead, which seemed impersonal but maybe was better because Sandra could respond in her own time.

> Hi, Sandra. It's Tara. I just wanted to say how sorry I am about what happened. I didn't know Alex well, but we talked a little bit at the top of the mountain, and he had such a kind way about him. Genuine. Real. If you ever need anything, please don't hesitate to reach out to me. I would like us to be friends. Sincerely, Tara

"I'll see you later, honey." Blake kissed Tara's forehead. "I'll be home at the usual time."

"Are you really sure it's a good idea to go into the office?"

"Yeah." He caressed her cheek. "It'll help keep me busy to focus on paperwork. Oh, which reminds me. The bank guy we met with called. We forgot to fill out a form. I told him we'd stop by when we can."

"Okay." She hugged him and didn't want to let him go. Catastrophe could befall a person at any moment. On a ski slope. On the way to work. She wanted to cherish every second she was alive, that she and Blake were together. "I love you, Blake."

"I love you too, honey. Don't worry. I'll be okay. I'll see you later."

She nodded and watched him go, feeling both terrified and grateful that Blake Townsend had stumbled into her life.

CHAPTER 31

Saturday, April 5, 7:00 a.m.

Tara watched Blake as he lay in bed, staring at the ceiling. Something was definitely on his mind. She didn't know what. Alex? The cancer? Sandra? Something that had happened at the office? He had been quiet for the past few days. She didn't want to pry and hoped he would open up to her, but since Alex's death, he had become more and more reserved and isolated. She wanted to be understanding but was feeling left out and emotionally abandoned. On top of that, she felt *guilty* for feeling left out and emotionally abandoned. This wasn't about her. This was about Blake. But she couldn't help feeling alone. Everything was coming to an end. Alex. Blake. Napkin Marketing. Her happiness. And there was nothing she could do about it.

"You okay?" she asked.

"Yeah." He nodded. "I'm just thinking about Sandra."

Well, that answered her question.

She had to admit, that bothered her a little—Blake thinking about Sandra in their bed. But the guilt washed over Tara again. This wasn't about *her*. Sandra had lost her husband. *Of course* he was thinking about her. Tara wondered how she was doing. Sandra had never responded to her text. Tara was trying not to read into that, but it was difficult.

"Are we still meeting at the bank later?" she asked Blake.

"Yes, after my oil change. Does that work?"

"Sure." She smiled. "I'll stop at the supermarket beforehand. Pick up a few things. Make you a nice dinner."

"Okay." Blake continued staring at the ceiling. "There's something I need to tell you."

A chill ran through Tara's body. Blake's tone was strangely ominous. She sat up in bed. "What is it?"

He shook his head. "I don't know what to make of it."

"What do you mean?"

"A detective came to visit Sandra this week."

"Detective?"

"Yes. From Vermont. One of the detectives at the resort."

There had been a few detectives at the Vermont resort, but Tara couldn't conjure up any of their faces. "That's weird. What did he want?"

"He said there are suspicious circumstances surrounding Alex's death."

Another chill went through her. "What kind of suspicious circumstances?"

"I have to be honest, Tara. I thought Sandra was overreacting when she first told me. I told you, she can be . . . fragile. I offered to call the detective myself. I figured I'd get the real story. She gave me his business card." He reached over to his nightstand, pulled the business card from his wallet, and showed it to her. He placed it on the nightstand.

"Did you?" Tara asked. "Talk to him?"

Blake nodded.

"What did he say?"

"He didn't really say anything about Sandra. But he told me that there was fentanyl in Alex's toxicology screening."

Tara gasped. "How is that possible? Was Alex a recreational drug user?"

"No!" Blake sat up. "That's what's so strange. Yes, Alex drank. *A lot* sometimes. But drugs? No way."

"So, what do they think happened? Do they think he accidentally overdosed? Or . . ." Tara didn't want to think about the *or*.

"The detective wouldn't say. I only know what Sandra told me."

"What did she tell you?"

Blake hesitated. "She showed up at the office last week. Really distraught. She said the detectives showed her security footage from the resort of her handing Alex a bottle of calcium tablets at the buffet."

Tara's eyes opened wide. "You mean the morning we saw them?"

"Yes, but don't look so shocked. They were just calcium tablets."

Tara knew what she wanted to say. *How could you know for sure?* But she held her tongue. Would Sandra want to kill her husband? It seemed absurd. Then she had a thought. "Did he take one of the tablets at breakfast?"

"Why?"

"I've done some research on fentanyl since the drug bust at the school. It's pretty fast acting. He would start feeling the effects quickly. If Alex had popped a pill into his mouth at breakfast, he would have felt the effects way before he got to the top of the mountain. But when I saw him that morning, he was clear-eyed." There. She had exonerated Sandra.

She thought this would make Blake relieved, but his face went white. "What's the matter?" she asked.

"Alex didn't take his calcium supplement at breakfast."

"How do you know?"

Blake looked her in the eye. "Because he popped one into his mouth at the top of the ski slope just before you came with the two coffees."

CHAPTER 32

Saturday, April 5, 12:00 p.m.

Tara stormed into the apartment, dropped her shopping bags on the floor, and shut the door. Who the hell did Sandra Wilson think she was?

"Tara, is that you?"

"Blake, you're home?" She thought they were supposed to meet at the bank.

"Hey, honey." He walked toward her and stopped. He looked like he had something on his mind, but his brows furrowed when he saw her. "What's the matter?"

She wanted to tell him how much of a bitch his best friend was. How Sandra had made a scene in the supermarket parking lot—saying terrible things. But she couldn't get the words out. "Oh, Blake." She ran into his arms.

"Tell me. What's wrong?"

She hugged him tight. "I ran into Sandra at the supermarket. She was crazy. Wild-eyed and accusatory." She looked at him.

"She was asking me about the fentanyl like *I* knew something about it. What the hell?" She paused. "The whole thing was weird and unsettling. I basically said I should be asking *her* about it." Tara dropped her head into her hands. She hadn't handled that situation well at all. She should have been more professional, more understanding. Sandra had lost *a husband*. She was angry. She may have even killed her husband with pseudo-calcium tablets. Who knew? But Tara had never been attacked like that. She reacted emotionally, not clinically.

"Come, sit down." Blake brought her to the living room couch and sat next to her. "Tell me exactly what happened."

As Tara relayed the events, he listened attentively. And when she was done, he sat there quietly.

"It doesn't surprise me after what happened," he said finally.

"What happened?"

"I stopped at Sandra's this morning before getting the oil change."

"You did?"

"Yeah, I thought I should check on her. After what the detective said. After what we," he hesitated, "were talking about this morning. I had to look her in the eye. I know it can't possibly be true. Sandra could not have had *anything* to do with Alex's death."

If Tara had had any inkling that morning that it could be true, that Sandra was capable of killing Alex, she was even surer about it now. She had witnessed Sandra's anger firsthand. The fire in her eyes. The clenched fists. Heavy breathing. Fixed stare. Tara shuddered to think what would have happened if they hadn't been in a public place.

"But it didn't go well," Blake continued. "We ended up arguing."

"Why?"

He shrugged. "Listen, I get it. When you're being accused of something, the easy thing is to point fingers at someone else."

Tara shook her head. "I don't understand."

"I didn't like the things Sandra was saying about you."

"About me?? What was she saying?"

"That you . . ." Blake struggled with the words. "That you might have . . ."

"Wait, she thinks *I* killed Alex? Is that why she mentioned the fentanyl?"

"I don't know."

"Blake, what is her problem with me? I have done nothing but try to befriend her. Since the day I met her, it's like she never even gave me a chance."

Blake pulled her close. "Maybe she's . . . what's the psychological term? Projecting?"

Tara nodded. "I thought the same thing when I got into the car after seeing her. When I cooled down. That maybe it was psychological projection. That Sandra was angry with me to avoid dealing with the difficult emotions surrounding Alex's death. But I never thought she would think that *I* had anything to do with Alex's death." Tara could feel tears welling in her eyes.

"You didn't do anything wrong, honey."

Tara knew that but somehow felt like she had. She should have been able to keep her wits about her. Be rational. Even if Sandra was lashing out. Even if Sandra was having delusions. "Do you think I should call and apologize?"

"Apologize?? For what? She attacked *you*!"

"Apologize maybe for the way I handled myself? I don't know." Not that Tara thought that would do any good. Sandra had yet to respond to her text. It was clear she didn't want to be friends.

Blake squeezed her hand. "You know, I can't believe I'm going to say this, but no. I don't think you should call and apologize."

"No?"

"All my life, I feel like I've always been worried about what Sandra Wilson did or had to say. This may sound cruel, but I'm so tired of thinking about her all the time. It's driving me crazy."

Tara nodded. "I totally get that. But I think she needs our help, Blake."

He smiled and planted a kiss on Tara's lips. "You're so kind. We *will* help her. But, maybe just for this weekend, let's take some time off from Sandra Wilson." He looked at the shopping bags. "Oooh, what did you get?"

That was one of Tara's favorite things about Blake, his wide-eyed joy over simple things. Like flavored seltzer. Or a family-sized cereal box. She felt her anxiety ebb a little. "What would you like for dinner tonight?" she asked.

"What do you have?" Blake peeked into one of the bags.

Not much. Seeing Sandra in the frozen aisle had triggered Tara, and she left the supermarket before she had finished shopping—never realizing the main event would take place in the parking lot. "How about we bring home some takeout after we go to the bank?"

"Sounds good to me."

TARA WAS FEELING SO much better. After meeting with the bank rep, she and Blake had taken a long walk in Eisenhower Park despite the drizzling rain. Holding hands. Stepping in puddles. It was just the therapy she needed. On the way home, they stopped off to get Tara's favorite Thai food, and she had practically wiped her plate clean at dinner.

She was cleaning off the kitchen table when she heard a thud from the bathroom.

Blake?!

She ran toward the sound, and when she got there, Blake was on the floor, holding his head.

"Oh my God, what is it?" she asked, running toward him.

"I'm fine. I'm fine."

"You don't look fine." She looked in the toilet bowl to see if he had vomited, but it was clean. "Tell me. How can I help?"

He shook his head. "I just got this shooting pain. A blinding pain on the side of my head."

She nodded as fear coursed through her. This was the first time Blake had complained of a headache. She tried to help him up, but he was having trouble balancing.

"I think we should call your doctor, Blake."

"No, it's fine."

"Blake, it's *not* fine."

"It will pass. It always does."

He reached forward and tried to kiss her on the lips, but he missed and kissed her cheek. Was he having vision problems, too?

Tara's heart raced. It was happening, wasn't it? The symptoms were getting worse. She wasn't sure what to do. Up till now, she had let Blake dictate how he wanted to live the rest of his days. But at some point, he was going to have to realize it was time to seek medical help. She watched him stagger toward the toilet bowl and sit on the lid. "Maybe you should lie down," she offered.

He nodded, and Tara walked him to their bed. She helped him put on his pajamas and get under the covers.

"What would I do without you?" he said.

She kissed his forehead. "I don't know." She laughed.

"I mean it, Tara. You coming into my life changed everything."

"Close your eyes now, Loverboy. I'm going to straighten up a little bit and I'll join you and we'll watch some crappy Netflix movie in bed."

"Sounds perfect."

Tara hurried out of the bedroom and finished cleaning the dinner plates from the kitchen table. She quickly washed them and then popped into the bedroom to check on Blake, who was fast asleep. He seemed peaceful. Calm. She sighed in relief and softly closed the bedroom door.

In the bathroom, she picked up Blake's clothing, which was bunched on the floor. She was about to place it all in the laundry hamper, when something fell out of one of Blake's pockets onto the tiled floor. Something plastic.

Tara's first thought was that it was a credit card, but it was too rectangular. She picked it up and read the words at the top.

Alexander Connor

She scanned the rest of the writing and flipped it around. The front showed a picture of Jesus Christ.

Tara leaned back against the cold tile wall, confused.

This wasn't a credit card. It was a prayer card. For Alex's funeral.

A funeral Tara thought never happened.

CHAPTER 33

Sunday, April 6, 7:00 a.m.

Tara hardly slept. Why did Blake have a prayer card in his pocket? Had Sandra given him one yesterday? For a funeral that didn't take place? She was sure she was making a much bigger deal out of this than it was, but she needed Blake to explain.

She felt his arms wrap around her from behind. "Good morning, Florence Nightingale." He kissed her cheek. "Thank you for taking care of me last night. I'm sorry I fell asleep. I guess I didn't realize how tired I was."

Why was there a prayer card in your pocket? The words wouldn't leave her brain and go to her mouth. "How are you feeling?" she said instead.

"Much better." He got up before she could say anything else and went into the bathroom. She heard the shower run.

Tara sat up in bed, fingering the prayer card in her hands. She had held on to it all night between her palms, like she had been praying. She was trying to relax, trying not to sound accusatory, trying to learn from her experience with Sandra. When Blake came out of the shower, his towel around him, she turned toward him calmly.

"Blake?"

"Yeah. You know, I feel much better this morning."

"That's great." She held up the prayer card. "What's this?"

Blake looked at it. "That's a prayer card. For Alex."

"But I assumed there weren't any funeral services because you didn't mention anything. There was a funeral?"

"Yes."

"Did you go?"

"Tara, really?"

"Well . . ."

"No, I didn't go. It was a small, little thing for Alex's immediate family."

"Yeah, but you're practically family, Blake."

"It doesn't matter, Tara. It's not important."

"It's important to me. Why didn't you go?"

"Listen, Sandra only wanted family there, okay? So, I skipped it."

"Wait . . ." Tara placed her feet on the floor. "You're saying she only wanted family there—and *not me*."

Blake was quiet, and Tara couldn't believe how hurt she was, even though she knew Sandra didn't like her. "Blake, you could have told me. You could have gone without me."

He stepped toward her. "I wasn't going *anywhere* without you."

"I don't understand. Why is Sandra being so cruel? Why is she making you choose her or me? This should be about Alex."

"Honey, I don't need to go to a funeral service to grieve my best friend. It's fine." He began getting dressed.

"Are you going somewhere?" she asked.

"I thought I'd stop by the office and finish up the taxes. With all that's been going on, I didn't get the chance. I don't need the IRS breathing down my neck, too."

"The office?" Blake rarely went to the office on Sunday. "Do you think that's a good idea after what happened last night? Do you think you should drive?"

Blake pounded his chest with his hand. "Me, Blake. Feel fine." He smiled. "Really. You're such a worrywart. What do you plan on doing today?"

Tara wanted to say she planned on spending the day with him relaxing, making sure what happened last night in the bathroom didn't happen again. She didn't know he was expecting to go into the office. Perhaps she would go with him, read while he finished up his taxes, and then they could do something together. She waited for an invitation, but it didn't come. "I guess I'll just putter around the house," she said finally. "Do laundry. Catch up on some reading for my book club."

"Sounds like a perfectly relaxing Sunday." He kissed her on the mouth. "I'll see you later."

Tara watched him go. She held up the prayer card. It had been a long time since she spent a Sunday morning with Jesus. And for some reason, today, she didn't want to let him go.

CHAPTER 34

Monday, April 7, 7:00 a.m.

Blake slapped his alarm clock while Tara stared at the wall.

Another sleepless night.

She had waited for Blake to come home yesterday, but he never did, texting her that the taxes had taken longer than expected. She stared at Alex's prayer card, which she had placed on the nightstand. Crazy thoughts swirled through her brain. She had this weird feeling that Blake hadn't gone to Napkin Marketing yesterday. That Blake had lied to her. All day long, her anxiety had decided that Blake was cheating on her. That Blake spent the day having sex with Sandra, who had killed her husband by disguising fentanyl as calcium tablets so she could be with Blake, her first love. Tara had been playing that scenario over and over in her head ever since.

"Good morning." Blake wrapped his arms around her; she turned toward him. "Sorry I was gone all day yesterday," he said. "When I'm mired in paperwork, I forget the time. And I'm still not done. Lots more to do today. I hope you can forgive me."

"Do I feel warm?" she asked, changing the subject.

"Warm?" He felt her forehead with the back of his hand. "It doesn't feel like you have a fever." He looked into her eyes. "Yeah, you're right. You don't look too good."

"Just feeling under the weather." Tara hadn't lied about being sick since she was in high school. "Maybe I'll stay home today. One of the students on Friday was complaining of a stomachache. I might have caught something."

"Do you want me to stay home with you?"

"No, that's okay. I'm fine. And I don't want you to get it."

Tara reached for her cell phone on the nightstand and called her principal as Blake put on his socks—one of the many pairs she had spent all day yesterday washing. Tara never used any of her sick days, so she had lots to spare. She always figured the kids depended on her, and she liked to be there for them.

"It's funny to hear you calling in absent." Blake buttoned his shirt. "Will you need a doctor's note to hand to the teacher? Wait, I forgot. You *are* the doctor." He laughed.

She smiled. Was it possible to tell whether a person was cheating just by looking at him? Blake didn't seem nervous. He wasn't stuttering. He certainly didn't look sorry. But people did crazy things when they were dying, didn't they? Like screwing their best friend/first love while their wife was puttering around their apartment waiting for them? Still, something didn't connect. Tara didn't know Sandra and Alex well, but she could tell they were *tight*. That there was a strong love there. But then why was Sandra so angry with Tara for marrying Blake? An image of Blake and Sandra fucking on Blake's desk at the office appeared in Tara's mind. If Blake *had* done something deceitful, while he was sick, *because* he was sick, could Tara find it in her heart to forgive him?

"Okay, I'm off." Blake grabbed his keys and opened his nightstand drawer, pulling out a small umbrella. "I think it's supposed to thunderstorm later this morning." He looked at her concerned. "If you need *anything*..."

He started to come toward her, but she put up her hand. "You shouldn't kiss me anymore. If I'm sick, you don't want to get it. Especially in your condition. You need to stay healthy."

"Okay, Typhoid Tara." He smiled. "I'll see you later. Text me what you want for dinner, and I'll bring something home."

The front door closed, and Tara hurried to the window. She watched Blake get into his car, pull out of his parking spot, and drive away.

She dashed into Blake's office and stood there. She had no idea what she was looking for. She was beginning to worry about herself for spinning out of control simply because she had found a prayer card in Blake's pocket. But then what was with the disappearing act all day yesterday? She couldn't unthink that something was up. That something wasn't right. But what did she expect to find in Blake's office? A notation in his desk calendar that read *Lie to Tara today*?

She went to his desk and sat in his chair. She rummaged around, but didn't see anything incriminating. Maybe the place to start was Blake's computer. If there was something suspicious going on, that would be the place to find evidence. She turned on the unit. The monitor warmed, and Blake's lock screen popped up.

Roadblock No. 1. She didn't know Blake's password.

Should she have? Was that something married couples shared with one another? Tara would have been happy to. She had no secrets when it came to Blake.

She opened a few drawers, but there was nothing handwritten anywhere. She knew the password had six characters. She could hear Blake tap them onto the keyboard every time he went into his office. She took a chance and tried his birthday.

No luck.

She didn't know any of his relatives' birthdays, but no one in his family seemed particularly special to Blake, even his mother. She had a thought. She ran into the bedroom and grabbed Alex's prayer card. She returned to Blake's computer and punched in the six numbers of Alex's birthday.

Still locked.

She tried the six numbers of the day Alex died.

Locked.

She tried their wedding day. Maybe Blake had changed his password to honor the special occasion he shared with Tara.

Locked.

She didn't know how many more tries she had before Blake's computer locked her out completely.

Think, Tara, think. What did Blake talk about the most?

Suddenly, a small gasp escaped from her mouth.

She placed her hands on the keyboard and typed:

S-A-N-D-R-A

The screen unlocked.

Tara could barely see the screen because she could barely breathe. She leaned back in Blake's chair.

SANDRA was Blake's password?

What did that mean? An image of the two of them having sex on Blake's desk at Napkin Marketing reappeared in her mind, and she wiped it away. She breathed in deeply and tried to talk herself down. *It doesn't mean anything. Blake and Sandra and Alex have been friends for a long time.*

When she was able to see clearly, her eyes scanned the icons on the monitor's home screen. She took in all the shortcuts and their file names.

Documents.

Client list.

Proposals.

They looked innocent enough. She clicked on one that read *Media*.

A word document popped up with lyrics to a song called "The Girl Next Door." She clicked on it.

My forever love
You and me
Finally together
Just you see

What was this?

They say good things come to those who wait
The sweeter the reward
I would wait forever for the touch of your hand
Then, sweet San, our future toward.

Sweet San? Was this a love song? For *Sandra*?

Tara's mind was reeling. Had Sandra done away with Alex so she could be with Blake? Is that why the detectives had been poking around? Tara's heartbeat started to thump as she continued scrolling. There was love song after love song.

She closed the document. It was too much to bear.

Another shortcut caught her eye. *Scans.*

Blake's cancer scans? Wait, was it possible he had gone to the doctor yesterday or the hospital and didn't want to tell Tara because he didn't want her to worry? Her pulse slowed a bit. That made sense. Perfect sense. Maybe what happened Saturday night had spooked Blake and he decided to go to the doctor but didn't want to alarm Tara.

Her breathing steadied, and she clicked on the shortcut.

A PDF file opened with several scan images. The first was the one Blake had shown her—with the white egg-shaped mass protruding into his brain—only this image was more zoomed out and showed some patient info at the top in teeny-tiny type. Her eyes welled with tears. The tumor was large and hard to miss. She imagined there were going to be more nights like Saturday, more headaches in the days and weeks to come. And if Tara was scared, Blake must have been terrified. Had he run to Sandra? Someone safe? Tara reasoned he might be experiencing chaotic thinking, and if he was, she would help him through it. She would try to be understanding.

She zoomed in to the image and looked closer at the mass, wondering what it felt like to have such a destructive force inside you, working against you. She was about to close the file, but her eyes caught something in the top left corner of the page.

PATIENT NAME: AARON KRAFT

Aaron Kraft? Who was Aaron Kraft?

She scanned some more and found a birthdate.

013010

That wasn't Blake's birthday.

She stared at the screen, confused. What did this mean? Was this someone else's scan? Why would Blake have someone else's scan on his computer? Someone with the same deadly cancer? In the exact same spot?

She sat back. There had to be an explanation. Perhaps Blake's doctor had shared a scan of another patient who had the same tumor. But wouldn't that violate HIPAA laws? Would Aaron Kraft want his scans circulating to strangers?

She gasped for air when another possibility came to mind and nearly knocked her off Blake's desk chair.

This wasn't Blake's scan.

Someone *else* had cancer.

Blake didn't have months to live.

Some poor teenager named Aaron did.

Blake pretended to be sick.

Blake *lied*.

He lied, lied, lied, lied, lied.

PAIN FLICKERED THROUGH TARA's temples, and she rubbed the sides of her head. Could it be? She thought of the day Blake had told her about his cancer. How sad he was. How he had held on to her for dear life.

Why would he lie about such a thing? Why would anyone pretend to be dying? Was it so Tara would have sympathy for him? Marry him? But wouldn't he have to fess up eventually? When he *didn't* die? Nothing was making sense.

Tara closed the PDF and was about to shut down the computer, but something else caught her eye. An icon in the bottom-left corner of the screen. An icon she had seen before. Many, many times. Two hearts holding hands.

The YourPerfectMatch.com logo.

Why did Blake have a YourPerfectMatch shortcut on his computer? Hadn't he told her the very first day they met that he didn't really *do* online dating? She clicked on the dating app.

The shortcut opened, and the air suddenly left the room when Tara saw the name on the dating profile.

It wasn't Blake Townsend.

It was Ted Baker.

TARA STARED AT TED Baker's profile picture—the one that resembled Gavin, the teacher of her Excel class.

But Gavin wasn't Ted Baker.

Blake was.

How? Blake didn't sound anything like the Ted Baker she had spoken to. For hours a night, seven days a week.

Had he disguised his voice?

Then it hit her. The voice-changing app. The one she'd heard him using for Napkin Marketing's clients. He could give himself any accent, any dialect. British. Australian. *Ted Baker.*

Tara's heart hammered, and she began to sweat, her body trembling. She hadn't had a panic attack in years, since her parents died, and she willed herself to relax. She scrolled through the dozens and dozens of text messages she had exchanged with "Ted Baker," texts that Tara had practically memorized when he disappeared last year and she was looking for answers. But the truth was, it had been *Blake* who found answers. All the ones he needed.

Her fondness for citrus scents.

For black-and-white films.

Her love of sweets.

Her mention of wanting to try a new sweet shop in town called Isabel's.

Her adoration for *It's a Wonderful Life*.

Her description of herself as a homebody.

The list went on and on.

And in the very last text exchange was the smoking gun: Tara mentioning that she was thinking about taking a Microsoft

Excel class at her library in the new year because her school district had implemented the program.

Tara had shared everything about herself, and Blake knew. He *knew*. That's why they had so many things in common. He knew exactly what to say.

But why? Why had he done this to her? Tricked her into marrying him. Tricked her into *falling in love* with him. Her body began trembling again as anger and sadness consumed her.

She shut down the computer and ran out of the room. She got dressed, grabbed her car keys, and hurried out the door. As she started the car, she decided she was going to confront Blake and demand the truth. No more texting, this time. No more on-screen communication. But as she pulled the car into the street and began driving toward Blake's office, she thought again of Alex's prayer card, of Blake's disappearance yesterday, of his computer password, and Tara found herself making a detour.

SANDRA

CHAPTER 35

Monday, April 7, 10:00 a.m.

"What do *you* want?" Sandra asked.

Tara was just standing there on her doorstep. Like a statue. Her hands clenched in tight fists. Rain dripping from the ends of her blond hair. For a moment, Sandra thought she was in for a fistfight, the final showdown following the incident at the supermarket, but then Tara's breathing started getting uneven. Her body trembled in a way that was familiar, and whatever ice had built up inside Sandra's veins began to thaw.

"What's wrong?" Sandra asked. "Are you okay?"

Tara looked at her absently, like her mind was somewhere else.

"Is it Blake?" Sandra asked, panicked. "Is something wrong with Blake?"

The mention of Blake seemed to snap Tara out of whatever daze she was in, and she glared at Sandra.

"It's . . . tr . . . tr . . . true, isn't it?" she said between short breaths.

"What's true?"

"That you . . . you . . ." Tara swallowed. "That you . . ."

"Oh my God, this is ridiculous." Sandra opened the door wider. "Tara, come inside. Dry off. We'll get to the bottom of whatever this is."

"I will not . . . not . . . come . . ." Tara bent forward.

"What's going on?" Sandra hurried outside, the rain pelting her cheeks, and took hold of Tara's arms, which hung limply at her sides. "Are you on any medication?"

Tara shook her head. "Need . . . sit . . ."

Sandra held Tara firmly, guided her inside the condo, and sat her at the kitchen table. "I'll make you some tea. Maybe that will help."

Tara was heaving now, having trouble catching her breath. She bent over and put her head between her knees. "Pan . . . pan . . ."

"Are you having a panic attack?" Sandra asked, and Tara's head bobbed up and down vigorously.

"Okay." Sandra turned on the burner and hurried to Tara's side. "My mom used to get them," she said gently. "Don't worry. I'm here. And I'm not going to leave you." She rubbed circles across Tara's back. "The attack won't last long. It'll be over before you know it. Concentrate on your breathing. C'mon, breathe with me. In . . ."

Tara lifted her head, and Sandra crouched down so that she was in Tara's eyeline. "That's it. Now we're going to breathe out. Nice and calmly. You're in a safe place."

Tara's eyes opened wide. She shook her head.

"Breathe, Tara. Just breathe."

After a few minutes, the tea kettle started to whistle, the sound slicing through the room like a knife, and Sandra hurried to turn off the flame. Tara seemed better, her breathing regulated. Sandra poured water into a mug, plopped a teabag into it, and placed it in front of Tara, who cupped her hands around it as if she were in the middle of the Arctic and the cup of tea was her only source of warmth. Her complexion was regaining its color as Tara continued breathing in and out, and it was clear to Sandra this wasn't Tara's first panic attack. She seemed to know what to do.

Tara stared down at her cup as Sandra sat across from her. "Do you want something to eat? I don't have much. I . . . well, cut my trip to the supermarket short on Saturday."

"I'm not hungry."

"Are you sure?" Sandra asked. "I do have some eggs, and I can—"

"Why are you being so nice?" Tara said abruptly.

Sandra crossed her arms. "Because I *am* nice. Not that *you* would know."

Tara squeezed her teacup. "Where were you yesterday?" she asked.

"Excuse me?"

"Yesterday? Where were you?"

"Not that it's any of your business, but I was here," Sandra said. "Where else would I be? My life is over."

"Were you with anyone?"

"Is this the Spanish Inquisition?"

"Were you?!" Tara was watching her closely.

"No, I was not. I was alone, which is what I'll be for the rest of my life, if you really want to know. What the hell is going on? Why are you here?"

Tara glanced again at her cup. *Why isn't she drinking?* "I came over here to tell you that you can fucking have him."

Tara's bitchy voice from the supermarket parking lot had returned. And with it, so had Sandra's anger. "Fucking have who?" Sandra asked.

"Don't play stupid."

"I have no fucking idea what you're talking about," Sandra said. "Who do you want me to have?"

"How did Blake get the prayer card?"

Sandra nearly got whiplash from the quick change in topic. "What?! What prayer card?"

Tara rolled her eyes and gestured toward the stack of prayer cards on the kitchen counter.

"You mean Alex's prayer card?" Sandra asked.

Tara nodded.

"I gave him one when he was here on Saturday."

"Why give him one when you could have just invited him to the funeral?"

"Tara, I think something is seriously wrong with you. You don't invite people to funerals. They just *show up*. Except *you*, of course. *You* stayed home."

"You didn't want me there."

"Oh, *please*. You sure as hell could have come. What are you talking about?"

"You're a liar." Tara tried to get up, but she looked queasy and sat back down.

"Really?" Sandra folded her arms. "And why exactly am I a liar, pray tell?"

Tara suddenly seemed confused. She squeezed the mug of tea in front of her. "But you only wanted family there."

"And who stupidly told you that?"

Tara looked into Sandra's eyes. "Blake."

"Nice try. Blaming your husband. Real nice. Listen, Blake apologized for you not being there, but you really should have come."

"Blake apologized?"

"Yes."

"Blake was *there*?"

"Yes!" Sandra threw up her hands. "What are you not understanding? Alex fucking died. Left me here all alone. Completely by myself. We had a funeral. People came. It was sad. End of story." The tears returned to Sandra's eyes, and she let them fall. "And you know what? I don't know what the fuck to do. I feel... I feel... Like half of a person. The wrong half. The bad half. And the good half is gone. *Forever*." She stood up and turned around, wiping her eyes. "Why am I fucking telling you this?" She turned back around and faced Tara. "Like you give a shit about me. You made it clear from day one. You *don't*. You didn't respond to one single text I sent you. *Not one*." She paused. "Well, yes, *one*. To tell me you would rather snowmobile—*alone*—than spend time with me."

"Snowmobile?" Tara's breathing started picking up again, and Sandra could tell she was trying really hard to steady herself. "You... texted me?" Tara asked.

"Yes, several times. You *know* that."

Tara searched Sandra's eyes as she took her hand away from her teacup. "I think I made a terrible mistake," she said finally.

"You think? Is that some kind of apology for not coming to Alex's funeral? If so, I'll take it. It's better than I expected I'd ever get."

Tara was beginning to shake again. *Shit.*

"Listen, I'm sorry," Sandra said. "Forget what I said. It's over. In the past. Let's just move on. Don't worry about it." She looked at Tara's cup. "You haven't touched your tea."

Tara pushed the mug toward Sandra. "No, thank you." She put her hand on her chest as if to calm her racing heart. "Can I ask you a question?"

"I don't know." Sandra sat back down. "Is it going to piss me off?"

"I don't know."

"Well, what do we have to lose?" Sandra folded her arms.

"Do you love Blake?"

"Yes."

"You do?"

"Yes. He's my best friend."

"When you say he's your 'best friend,'" Tara said, using air quotes, "you mean . . . ?"

"I mean *best friend*."

"And when did you see him? Like, last?"

"Saturday morning. What's going on, Tara? What's with the twenty questions again? Do you want to know my Social Security number, too?"

Sandra waited for Tara to say something, but she didn't. She just kept staring at her.

"Why do you need to know when I last saw Blake?" Sandra asked.

Tara kept staring.

"Hello? Tara, are you there?"

Sandra feared Tara might have another panic attack, or was suffering from something worse like catatonia, but she seemed to be breathing steadily. Then Sandra remembered the fentanyl Blake had found in her pocket. Was she on drugs? Had Detective Miller told her that Sandra had called him over the weekend about it? Was Tara here to seek revenge? She looked into her eyes. That didn't seem right. "What's going on?" Sandra asked.

Tara looked down and shook her head. "When I was a teenager, my mother and father were killed in an automobile accident. Drunk driver."

"I know. Blake mentioned that. I'm so sorry."

"I think that's why I've always been guarded. Why I never got close to people. Why I never married. And I don't really have many close friends. Perhaps that's why I devote myself to my work." She looked Sandra in the eye. "It won't hurt me back, you know? It won't leave me like a person does. And then I met Blake. And somehow . . ." She looked away, toward Alex and Sandra's wedding photo on the wall. "It felt so right. It felt like we had a connection."

"Well, that's good, right?"

Tara ran her fingers through her hair.

"Why are you telling me this?" Sandra asked.

"I want to believe what you're saying."

"About the prayer card? And when I last saw Blake?"

Tara nodded.

"I don't see why you shouldn't."

"What if I told you that Blake intimated that you didn't want me at the funeral?"

"What? That's ridiculous. He knew that I did."

"Would you believe me if I said that?" Tara asked.

"No."

"But what if it was the truth?"

Sandra stood up. "Listen, Tara, I don't know what's going on. I think you need to see someone."

"But why would Blake imply that? That you didn't want me there."

"He wouldn't. That's why he didn't. You really expect me to believe you?"

"I have to tell you something."

"Now what?"

"I think Blake duped me."

"Duped you? How did he—?"

"And I think he's in love with *you*."

"Me? Don't be ridiculous."

Tara stood up, and Sandra wasn't sure what to do. Would Tara come at her? Try to attack her? But instead she just stood there.

"Listen, I don't expect you to believe me," Tara said, "but I thought you should know."

"Why would you think all those things?" Sandra said.

"Your name is his computer password."

"My name is his what? His password??" Sandra *did* think that was weird. "But who cares? It's a stupid password."

"There's more . . . There's a reason I think Blake proposed to me so quickly."

"Aha! So, you agree it was quick, right?" Sandra asked, feeling vindicated. "At the supermarket you made it seem like it was the most perfectly natural thing in the world for two people to rush into marriage without hardly knowing each other. I mean, I understand not everyone has to know each other for eight years like Alex and—"

"Blake told me he was dying of cancer."

"What?"

"He said he only had months to live. I believed him."

This was getting insane. It was clear Tara was having some sort of an episode. Sandra was about to calmly get her phone and call Blake, but then his skinny body came to mind. And his gray face. She remembered how he didn't look well for the past few weeks. Even Pam noticed. "Tara, wait, are you saying that—"

"And then there's Alex . . ."

Something twitched inside Sandra. "What about Alex?"

"I'm not sure yet. But I think that . . ." Tara trailed off and put her purse strap on her shoulders.

"You think that what?"

Tara hurried toward the door and stepped outside, raindrops marking the tops of her shoulders. "I think that Blake may have hurt Alex."

"Tara, I think you're not well." Sandra followed her to the door. "I wish you would come back and sit. Get out of the rain. Why would Blake want to hurt Alex?"

Tara looked at Sandra, exasperated. "To be with *you*," she said.

"Tara, Blake loves *you*. Come back inside. I'll call Blake and—"

"Listen . . ." Tears were in Tara's eyes, mixing with raindrops as they slid down her cheeks. "You and I never had a chance. I'm beginning to feel sorry about that. All I can say is, be careful."

"Why should I be careful?" Sandra asked.

"You said you were a nice person. I am, too," Tara said. "I am. I would never have done anything mean or terrible to your husband, to Alex. He seemed so kind, so *genuine*."

The tears began to fall from Sandra's eyes again.

"He was caring and considerate," Tara continued, "and, Jesus, it was clear to anyone who had eyes that he loved you so very much."

"Stop!" Sandra cried. "Just stop!"

"And I've been a psychologist for a very long time, and I always thought I had a sense about people, but I think my loneliness might have kept me from seeing Blake clearly. But I could see you and Alex very clearly. There was true love there. And I didn't know if I believed in it before I met Blake. Not really. Maybe I did while I was with him, and I shouldn't believe in it anymore after what he did, but I do. You and Alex had it. And I'm so very sorry I didn't come to the funeral. Goodbye, Sandra." Tara turned to walk away.

"Tara, wait..."

Tara turned back around. "I know you just met me. And I don't even think you like me. And that's okay. I'm not even sure *I* like me. But, Sandra, if the detectives believe Alex's death was suspicious. And I know I didn't have anything to do with it, and I'm pretty sure you had absolutely nothing to do with it, then who does that leave?"

The hair on the back of Sandra's neck stood up. "What are you saying?"

"I'm saying that I don't know what's going on, but I can't stick around for it. And, frankly, I'm not sure you should either."

TARA

CHAPTER 36

Monday, April 7, 11:00 a.m.

"Blake? Are you here?"

Tara entered the apartment, Rachel Sandberg's baseball bat in her hands. She had never really held a bat before and didn't think she could use it if she had to, but she felt better with it in her possession. She hurried into the bedroom and picked up Detective Miller's business card from Blake's nightstand.

She hadn't known what to expect when she went to Sandra's house, but everything was so clear to her now. Blake had killed Alex. She was sure of it. She didn't know how, but everything in her body told her he did it. To be with Sandra. She began punching numbers into her phone, when a dark feeling came over her. She needed to get out of the apartment right away.

She put her phone down, ripped open her closet door, leaned the bat inside, and pulled out a small piece of luggage. She opened it on the bed and began throwing in some clothes, anything just to get her by. She didn't know where she was going. Her old apartment had new tenants. She had no friends to count on, other than a few book clubbers who hardly even showed up for meetings anymore.

Then she had a thought.

The high school.

Somewhere familiar, safe, where she was surrounded by colleagues. And where there was a security guard. Yes, that seemed like a good plan. And she would call Detective Miller on the way.

She zipped up her luggage and pulled it to the floor, but when she walked toward the bedroom door, she gasped.

Blake was standing there.

She tried to let out a scream, but he was suddenly on her, his large hand covering her mouth. He glanced down at the bag in her hand.

"You're packing your stuff?" He smiled. "I don't think so. You're not going anywhere."

SANDRA

CHAPTER 37

Monday, April 7, 11:00 a.m.

Sandra lay on the couch, rubbing her temples. What had just happened?

It was clear Tara wasn't well, and Sandra wondered what was going on. Mental illness? Lack of sleep? Was Tara really a drug addict? Although Blake had found pills in her coat pocket, he didn't seem inclined to believe she was. But love blinded you. Kept you from seeing what was right in front of your face. And if he didn't see it, if Tara was really on something and was unstable, unhinged, Blake would be in danger.

She picked up her phone to call him, when her phone rang in her hand. She swiped. "Hi, Pam."

"Hi, sweetie. Is it okay if we push back our girl's night to tomorrow? I have to attend a work thingy tonight, unfortunately."

"Sure, that's fine."

Pam paused. "Is something the matter?"

Typical, intuitive Pam. She could tell from a three-word sentence that something was wrong. "I'm not sure. Blake's wife, Tara, was here."

"Oh?"

"She seemed a little . . . off."

"What do you mean *off*?"

A junkie looking for her next hit? "I'm not exactly sure."

"Well, that might be why Blake didn't mention his marriage to his mother. Can you believe that?"

"He didn't tell Mrs. Townsend he was married?"

"Nope, which is why I completely put my foot in my mouth when I spoke to Wallace yesterday. I thought she knew already. Maybe Blake was just waiting for the right time to tell her? You know how weird Wallace can be sometimes about stuff. Don't get me wrong—I love her to death—but she can be so critical and opinionated."

Sandra nodded. She knew Blake and his mother weren't really close, but to not tell her he got married? That seemed strange, although he hadn't told Sandra and Alex either until after the fact. And with the way Tara was behaving today, maybe there was a reason for that.

"So, raincheck, sweetie?" Pam asked.

"Sure, that would be fine. See you tomorrow, Pam."

As soon as she was off the line with Pam, Sandra tried calling Blake, but he wasn't picking up. He was probably busy with work. She left a message for him to call her. At this point, she wasn't even sure Blake was talking to her. He might still be mad from Saturday, but if Tara was struggling with *something*, and judging by her behavior today she was, and she was one of the last people to see Alex alive, then wasn't it possible she had something to do with Alex's death?

But then what about all those things Tara had said about Alex? Those nice things? Was she trying to throw Sandra off her trail? Should Sandra call Detective Miller back? She squeezed her eyes shut, trying to conjure up answers, when Alex's words came to her: *Promise me you'll give her a chance*. She opened her eyes. That was one of the last things Alex had said to her. To give Tara a chance.

Her phone rang, the words *Detective Miller* appearing on the screen, and Sandra dropped the phone onto the couch. What the hell?

Sandra had been thinking about calling Detective Miller, and then he suddenly rang her phone? Was this fate? Proof of Tara's guilt? She answered. "Hello?"

"Ms. Wilson?" Detective Miller was all business, as usual.

"Yes. Hi, Detective Miller."

"Hello, Ms. Wilson. I wanted to get back to you about your phone call this weekend."

"Yes. As I said, I just thought you should know what Blake said he found in Tara's pockets."

"I am back in Vermont this week for another case, but I appreciate you keeping me up to date. I must say, I am perplexed as to why Mr. Townsend wouldn't have mentioned that occurrence himself."

So am I, Sandra thought. "I don't know."

"Do you by any chance know where Tara Hoffman is?"

"Right now?"

"Yes."

"No, I don't," Sandra said.

"I've tried to reach her this morning at her place of employment, but I was told she called in sick today."

"She did?" Tara definitely *looked* sick.

"Apparently so. I was put through to her voicemail, which provided Dr. Hoffman's cell phone number. I tried that one as well but have been unable to reach her."

"You just missed her. She was here."

A pause.

"Tara Hoffman was in your home?" Detective Miller asked with a hint of surprise.

"Yes."

"The woman who, you told me on Saturday, may have had fentanyl in her pocket—the same drug that was found in your late husband's tox screen?"

Sandra exhaled. Hearing the course of events come from Detective Miller's mouth sounded strange. And incriminating. "Yes, she just showed up at my door out of the blue. She didn't seem well, Detective. It looked like she was having some kind of episode."

"An episode?"

"Yes, I don't know what was happening. But she left not long after she arrived."

Detective Miller cleared his throat. "Ms. Wilson, you said you and your husband had been bickering, yes?"

Sandra squeezed the phone in her hand. "No, Detective, *you* said Alex and I had been bickering."

"Yes, but as I said—"

"That argument was a long time ago, Detective."

"Be that as it may, Ms. Wilson, but our investigation showed that your husband met up with a woman at a work outing that matches the description of Dr. Hoffman."

Sandra tried to make sense of the detective's words. "Work outing? What do you mean?"

"I'm afraid I can't give specifics. But a witness saw a woman matching Tara Hoffman's description speaking to your husband. Would Tara Hoffman have any reason to speak with your husband not in your presence?"

Alex had spoken to Tara? No way. They had just met her a week before Alex died. But then Sandra thought of all those nice things Tara said about Alex. Had she gotten to know him elsewhere? *Separately?* Was it possible? If it was true that Alex hadn't told Sandra about Chuck's drug past, was there more lying by omission when it came to Tara? *Is that why Alex was so hell-bent on having Sandra give Tara a chance?*

"Ms. Wilson?"

"No, Detective. There wouldn't be any reason for Tara to speak to Alex that I can think of. But that person speaking to Alex could have been anyone. When was this?"

"The week before you arrived in Vermont. The witness could see them talking, but at a distance, and couldn't get an accurate ID on the woman. We were told, quote"—Sandra could hear a shuffling of paperwork in the background—"'I got the feeling they were friendly,' end quote."

"Alex was friendly with everyone, Detective."

"Ms. Wilson, we've seen this before with couples who have been together for a long time."

"Seen what?"

"Oftentimes, well, . . . er, boredom sets in, and a spouse may go looking . . . elsewhere."

"Boredom?" she asked, incensed. "With all due respect, Detective Miller, you didn't know Alex. You didn't know *us*."

"With all due respect, Ms. Wilson, isn't it possible that you didn't know *your husband*?"

SANDRA SAT ON THE couch after she ended the call with the detective, the phone still in her hands. What was Detective Miller trying to do? Mess with her love for Alex? Mess with his memory? Why? Did he really expect her to believe Alex was meeting with Tara behind her back? Did he still believe Sandra could have something to do with Alex's death?

Against Sandra's better judgment, she tried calling Tara. Sandra was *sure* Alex would have told her if they happened to run into each other, but she dialed the number anyway. The line rang and rang, but there was no answer. And Sandra could still see her unanswered "cup of coffee" texts leering at her from the phone screen, followed by Tara's "snowmobiling" text that essentially blew her off.

Why had Tara been so surprised Sandra had texted her? The evidence was right there.

She opened her laptop and did an online search for Tara's high school. She scrolled through the website until she found Tara's headshot along with her bio. She dialed the number underneath it, which looked like an office line, since the exchange was the same as all the other numbers for the school administrators, faculty, and staff.

No answer, but a voicemail played.

"Hi, you've reached Dr. Tara Hoffman. I am unable to come to the phone at this time. If this is an emergency, please dial 9-1-1. If it is after school hours and you need to reach me for a non-emergency, please contact me at . . ."

Sandra wrote down the number and stared at it. It was different from the one she had for Tara. Maybe Tara had a separate number for her work? Sandra tried the new number, but it also went to voicemail after a bunch of rings.

The doorbell rang, startling her.

Maybe it was Tara again? Or Blake?

Sandra put on her eyeglasses and hurried to the front door, peering through the side window. Chuck was standing on her doorstep. She opened the door. "Chuck?"

"Hi, Sandra." He ran his hands through his shaggy hair. "Sorry to just stop by like this. I wanted to talk to you in person."

"Is everything okay?"

"Yeah, it's just . . . May I come in?"

Sandra was about to say *sure*, but then she realized she *wasn't* sure. She liked Chuck, and so did Alex, but all the talk about drugs and mental illness and tox screens was making Sandra leery of everything. "I was just heading out," she lied. "Can we talk outside?"

"Okay."

Sandra quickly put on shoes and grabbed her purse, keys, and jacket. She rushed to the front door and closed it, gathering herself. "What's going on, Chuck?"

He shrugged, his thin frame stretching. "Something has been on my mind since you came to the house on Friday."

They began to walk down the front path. There was a chill in the air, and Sandra buttoned her jacket. "What is it?"

Chuck was wearing only a short-sleeved T-shirt, and Sandra thought of Alex, who had dressed the same in any weather. She didn't think Alex owned any long-sleeved shirts or sweaters. She had always teased him that he had an internal fire keeping him warm. She never realized the fire had been keeping her warm, too.

"Listen, there's no way to say this without just coming out with it, so"—Chuck struggled visibly—"I was a drug addict."

There it was. Chuck *was* a drug addict. Blake was telling the truth, which meant Alex had kept the information from her. "Chuck, um . . ." Sandra didn't know what to say.

Chuck studied her face. "Did you know already?"

"Kinda. Blake mentioned something."

"Yeah, well, I thought you should know. And hear it from me. I begged Alex not to say anything to anyone when we first decided to work together. I know a drug past isn't all that surprising for a rock and roll musician, but I really wanted to put that part of my life behind me. But I feel terrible about asking Alex to keep that from you. He told me you guys shared *everything*. I'm so sorry." He shook his head. "Is that why you asked me if there were any drugs on top of the ski slope in Vermont? Because you knew?"

"No, actually. I didn't find out from Blake until after that."

"Then why did you ask?"

Sandra didn't know what to say. Should she mention the fentanyl in Alex's toxicology report? She searched Chuck's close-set brown eyes. They seemed sincere. "Supposedly, they did some screening on Alex's blood after he died, and it showed there were drugs in his system."

"What? That's impossible."

"That's what *I* said."

"Sandra, I was with him until the end. I'm telling you, we had nothing to drink but coffee."

Coffee . . . That's right. Chuck said Tara had brought them coffees. Was that where she put the drugs? Was Tara really guilty?

"What are you thinking?" he asked.

"Honestly, I don't know anymore. My head is spinning."

"Wait, is that why some detective contacted me?" Chuck asked.

"You spoke to Detective Miller?"

"Yeah, that's the guy. He came to the house. He said he had seen me in Vermont, but I didn't remember. I made him show me his badge, like, six times because I thought it was a prank. He said he was doing some kind of routine inquiry about Alex's death, standard stuff, and was asking me all kinds of questions about my background, although he seemed to know already. He asked me if I saw anyone I didn't know around Alex, and all I could think of was the week before we went to Vermont."

"What do you mean?"

"Alex had stopped by when I was at the Long Island Music and Entertainment Hall of Fame earlier in the week. I walked him to the front door, and when he was walking to his car, he ran into some girl in the parking lot."

Chuck had been the witness Detective Miller was referencing? "A girl?"

"Yeah, it didn't seem like a big deal. They seemed to know each other. Friendly. The interaction lasted for all of fifteen seconds."

"What did the girl look like?"

He shook his head. "They were far away. And I was barely paying attention. Short blond hair. Tall. That's all I got."

That matched Tara's description. "Was it Tara? Blake's wife?"

Chuck's brows furrowed. "Hmmm... maybe? Why? Is that a big deal?"

"Nah," Sandra lied. "Don't worry about it."

"So, anyway, if I was acting a little weird when you came over on Friday, it's because the mention of drugs just kind of triggered me. It was a terrible time in my life. If I hadn't gone to rehab..." He shook his head. "I don't want to think about it. But now my life is really going well. The band. Bea. The baby. I can't believe I almost lost it all to some stupid white powder."

"That's amazing, Chuck."

"It's not easy, though. Yeah, I got my life together, but sometimes it's a struggle." He looked at her with sad eyes. "I'm so sorry if I caused some kind of wedge between you and Alex because I asked him not to say anything."

Sandra put her hand on his arm. "Not at all, Chuck. Alex was many things, but most of all, he was a good friend. There was no need for me to know about your past, and Alex knew that. That was an easy ask for him. Please don't feel guilty."

"Thank you, Sandra." Chuck gave a small smile. "Well, I'll let you get to wherever you have to go. Thanks for chatting."

"Say hi to Bea and Baby Landon," Sandra said as he walked back to his car, some kind of vintage sports car, which was parked on the street.

"Will do."

"Great car, by the way."

"Thanks. I just got it back from the shop." He got inside, started the car, and rolled down the window. "And all that stuff about Alex and the drugs?" he said. "Don't worry. There's got to be some kind of mistake."

Sandra nodded and waved as Chuck drove away. "I hope so," she muttered under her breath. But *something* was going on, and she needed to find out what.

TARA

CHAPTER 38

Monday, April 7, 1:00 p.m.

Tara tried to keep calm, but she could barely breathe.

She lay on the bed—the bed where she and Blake had made love countless times—and pulled at the binds around her hands and feet. The duct tape Blake had placed on her mouth was tight, pulling on her lips and cheeks. The more she struggled, the more she panicked and her nasal passages became congested; soon she wouldn't be able to breathe at all. She had to try to keep it together.

"Your clothing is so boring," Blake said, holding up a white silk sleeveless shirt. "Lots of expensive designer labels, but no real personality, you know? It's like you're relying on designers' tastes instead of having your own." He glanced at her with disdain.

"Blake," Tara said calmly, although through the duct tape it came out nonsensically, sounding like *blrg*. She needed to get him to take off the gag so she could tell him there was another way out of this, although for the life of her, she couldn't come up with one. She knew what Blake had done, and he knew she knew. What did he plan to do with her? Tara shuddered at the thought. But if she could talk down angry and compulsive high school students, perhaps she could get through to Blake somehow.

He placed the white shirt she had thrown into her suitcase tidily back into her dresser drawer and closed it. He looked up at her, studying her face. "Let me guess. You want me to *talk* to you, right?"

She slowly nodded up and down.

"I'm sure you do. All this talking. Talk, talk, talking. Does it really serve any purpose? Other than to enable people like you to have a job?" He closed the empty suitcase, taking his time zipping it up. He placed the suitcase on the floor and came toward her, sitting on the bed. Tara tried to move away as he placed his hand on her leg, making her flinch.

"What? You don't like me touching you anymore?" He squeezed her leg hard until she yelped beneath the gag. "I can't say I ever liked it, either, so I guess we're even there."

"Why?" she moaned, tears falling down her cheeks.

Blake snickered. "I have no idea what you said. Was it *why*? I'm sure you're thinking this is the part where the evil villain details his devious plan."

Tara shook her head no vigorously.

"You're right. It's not. I'm not that stupid. Or evil. Just setting things right." He looked around the room. "Although, I *do* have to say that you were onto something with doing this here. I set everything up at the office yesterday to have the grand finale take place there, but this is definitely neater, more sensible. More *believable*." He looked at her with his grayish face and thinning frame and smiled. "Thank you for that." He wiped a tear from her eye, and she turned her face away. "I knew something wasn't right this morning. You never call in sick. As usual, my gut instinct was correct."

Blake's phone rang, thankfully diverting his attention from her. How she had loved the way Blake used to gaze into her eyes. Now, she worried he might steal her soul.

He pulled the phone from his pocket, looked at the screen, and rolled his eyes. "Fucking bitch." He swiped the screen. "Hi, Mom." Pause. "Yes, Mom, I got married. You've been telling me for *years* I should find someone and settle down." Blake stood up and began to pace next to the bed. "There's a reason I . . . Yes, you shouldn't have heard it from Pam . . . But, the thing is, Mom . . ." Blake looked at Tara. "I think I've made a big mistake." Pause. "Something isn't right."

Tara watched Blake's face turn from sinister to kind, the face she knew, in an instant, as if a switch had been toggled.

"I've been feeling off for weeks," he said, "and . . . what? . . . Pam said I didn't look well?" Blake smiled with satisfaction. "She's right. I haven't been feeling well . . . Yes, it just *might* be something I ate."

Tara banged against the headboard and let out a muffled scream as Blake covered the phone with his hand.

"Listen, Mom, I have to go," he said, releasing his hand. "I'm on my way home. Tara didn't . . . Yes, Tara's her name. Tara didn't look too well this morning. I think she may have some kind of problem . . . I don't know, maybe drugs? . . . I know, I know . . . You're always right, Mom. Always." Blake smiled. "I'll call you later." He ended the call and tossed the phone on the bed, sighing as if exhaling a cleansing breath. "Okay, let's get this over with."

Blake left the room, and Tara struggled with her binds. She tried banging against the headboard, but she couldn't move well, even with her arms in front of her, because they were bound so tight—the duct tape ran practically up her forearms. Just when she thought she could scooch toward the side of the bed, Blake returned, carrying a cup of coffee. He sat down.

"You know, they seem to be going back and forth on whether or not coffee is good for you," he said. "Healthy? Not healthy? I wish they would make up their mind, although in the case of you and Alex, I think the vote is in."

Tara looked at the coffee in Blake's hands and flashed back to the top of the Vermont ski slope. She had brought coffee to Alex and Chuck. *She* carried the cups. *She* placed them on the small table. Was there fentanyl in them? She imagined the ski resort's cameras watching her, the way they had watched Sandra give Alex his calcium tablets. How could the coffee have been poisoned? Was the barista in on it?

Or . . . wait.

She remembered her fall. Right after she placed the coffee on the small tabletop. She thought she had tripped over Blake's ski, but . . . had *he* tripped *her*? She remembered lying in the snow, the sky clear and blue above her, and Alex's and Chuck's concerned faces asking if she was okay. Blake wasn't there at first. Had Blake put something in Alex's coffee then?

"You're finally putting it all together, aren't you? It really wasn't all that hard." He smiled. "There weren't any cameras. I checked, by the way." He held the coffee up in front of her. "Now, you're going to be a good girl and drink this."

Tara shook her head.

"Oh, yes, you will, *honey*."

Tara struggled as Blake pinched her nose and she couldn't breathe. When he took off the duct tape, she gasped for air as he began pouring the bitter, clumpy liquid into her mouth.

She tried to spit it out, but she began choking and some of it got into her throat. Blake closed her mouth and unpinched her nose, and Tara pulled precious air through her nose and, try as she might to reverse gravity, felt the liquid go down her throat.

Blake pinched her nose again. "A little more, honey, should do the trick."

Tara pushed against him, and as Blake tried to force his way on top of her, she whipped her duct-taped arms like a bat, knocking the coffee to the floor. Blake slapped her.

"You bitch," he seethed under his breath, covering Tara's mouth with the duct tape before she could scream. She wanted to vomit what she drank, but she couldn't. She was beginning to panic again and willed her body to relax, but she couldn't catch her breath.

Blake picked up the cup from the floor. "I'm going to get another cup. This time, I'll be *sure* you won't be able to move." He turned to walk out of the bedroom, when the doorbell rang, followed by a loud knock on the apartment's front door.

SANDRA

CHAPTER 39

Monday, April 7, 1:30 p.m.

Blake opened the door. "Sandra? What are you doing here?"

Sandra let out an annoyed exhale. "Blake, what took you so long? I was standing out here for, like, five minutes." She was lucky it wasn't raining anymore or else she would have been soaked.

"Um, I was just straightening up."

No surprise. Blake was *always* straightening up. A nervous tic Sandra was familiar with; Blake wasn't happy until everything was in its place. "Well, you could have yelled something to me." She pointed to his car. "I saw you were home. Is Tara home, too? Her car's here."

"No, she's not here." Blake stood at the threshold to his apartment. Why wasn't he letting her in? She took a good look at him. "What's wrong? You don't look too good."

He glanced at Tara's car. "Tara's gone," he said.

"Gone? What do you mean *gone*?"

"I just don't know where she is. Her car's here, but she's not."

"That's weird."

They stood there, looking at each other.

"Um, are you gonna let me in?" she asked. Maybe Blake was still mad at her from Saturday.

"Oh, right." Blake opened the door wider. "I wasn't thinking. Sorry."

Sandra could have argued he hadn't been thinking for months, which is why he had been so absent in her and Alex's lives. And also why he seemed to have married Tara on the fly. "Okay, what do you mean Tara's gone?" She placed her purse on the entryway table as the aroma of coffee hit her. "Are you making coffee? I'd love a cup."

As Sandra headed toward Blake's kitchen, he doubled over and let out a wail. "Oh, Sandra."

She stopped and ran to him. "What is it?"

He pulled at his hair, which looked weirdly thin. "Something is wrong. I know it. Tara didn't feel well this morning and called in sick to work. I offered to stay home with her, but she said I should go. I didn't feel right about it, I really didn't." He buried his face in his hands.

Sandra patted his back and led him to one of the dining room chairs. She had never seen Blake so broken up about *anything*. Not even Alex.

"I came back with some chicken soup from one of her favorite takeout places." Blake pointed to the brown paper bag on the table. "But she wasn't here. I'm worried, Sandra. I think something is very wrong."

"Yeah, me too."

He furrowed his brows. "What do you mean?"

"She came by my place about an hour ago. She didn't look too good."

Blake stared at Sandra as if she was speaking another language. Then he quickly snapped out of whatever daze he was in. "She came by?"

"Yeah, and she was talking nonsense, Blake. Crazy shit."

"What did she say?"

"Insane things!" Sandra threw up her hands. "That you told her she shouldn't come to Alex's funeral."

"What?"

"Yeah. And that you were . . . you were . . . in love with *me*."

"She said that?"

"Yes. And that your computer password was *my* name. Is that true?"

Blake glanced at his office. "Well, yes."

"It is?" she asked, surprised.

"Yes, I rotate it every six weeks or so. They say to do that with passwords. Right now, it's your name. Last month, it was my mom's."

Aha. That made sense. Sandra knew there was a reasonable explanation.

"I'm really worried about her, San. She's not answering my calls or my texts."

"Mine either. By the way, does Tara have two phones? One for business and one for personal use?"

Blake was looking at her strangely again.

"Hello? Blake?"

"I'm sorry," he said. "I'm just trying to make sense of all this. Did she say where she was going when she left your place?"

Sandra shook her head. "No, and Detective Miller is trying to reach her, too."

"Detective Miller?"

"Yeah, he called me because I . . ." How could she say this? "You might be mad when I tell you this."

"Tell me what?"

Sandra let out a long exhale. "On Saturday, I called Detective Miller and told him what you told me about finding the pills in Tara's jacket pocket."

Blake's eyes left Sandra and stared at the floor.

"Are you mad?" she asked.

He shook his head. "No. I'm not mad. You did the right thing, Sandra. I think I was just too close to see it all."

Sandra put her hand on Blake's shoulder. "It's going to be okay."

"She's been acting so strangely ever since Alex died."

The mention of Alex made Sandra stiffen. "How so?" she asked.

"She's just not herself."

"Blake . . ." Sandra bent down on her knees. He looked at her. "I know this is a strange question, but do you know if Tara ran into Alex the week after Alex and I met her at April's?"

"No, why?"

"I don't know. Chuck thought he saw them together."

"Chuck Landon?" Blake shook his head. "Seriously, San, do you really think you can trust a guy like Chuck?"

Sandra stood up. "I don't know, Blake. He seems like a good guy."

"C'mon, San. Once a junkie, always a junkie."

"Don't you think that's a little harsh?"

"So, what are you saying?" He looked at her angrily. "That Alex and Tara were having an affair?"

"No! I'm not saying that at all. I'm just . . . I don't know. I'm all turned around."

"Where did this happen? This supposed meeting between Alex and Tara?"

"Blake, let's not talk about—"

"Please, San. Tell me."

"It happened in front of the Long Island Music and Entertainment Hall of Fame."

"And you think Tara went there to see Alex?"

"Am I crazy?"

"Maybe, because I'm wondering if Tara was there to see *Chuck*."

"Chuck?" Sandra asked, shocked. "You think Tara and Chuck are having an affair?"

"No, San. But . . . what if I told you I think Tara might be a drug addict?"

Something inside Sandra shifted. "A drug addict?"

He nodded. "I think I was ignoring all the signs. The strange behavior. The pills I found in her pocket. I knew Tara was prone to panic attacks, although she hadn't had one in a while, so I thought the pills might be related to that, but what if I'm wrong?"

That tracked. Tara's anxiety. Her paranoia. Tara said she was having a panic attack at Sandra's house, but maybe that was just a cover?

"And . . ." Tears began to slide down Blake's cheeks. Now Sandra was *really* alarmed. She couldn't remember the last time she had seen him cry like that. If ever.

"What is it?" she asked, cradling his head in her hands.

"It's just . . ." He pulled away and pointed to himself. "*I* haven't been feeling well."

"Blake, you said you were fine when I asked you."

"I know. I didn't want to worry you. But I've been feeling bad. *Really* bad. I joked with Tara that it might be because of her cooking, but—"

"Tara said you were dying of cancer," Sandra said.

"What?"

"I know. It's all so crazy."

"San, I think I need to call Detective Miller," Blake said finally. "What if . . . what if . . . Tara was trying to poison me?"

"What?" Sandra knew she had been wildly speculating over the past weeks about Tara, but did Blake really think she was capable of that? And if she was capable of that, then couldn't she have hurt Alex? Could this all be true? "But why would she do that?"

"I don't know," Blake said. "Maybe to get access to the business's money? You know, feed her drug habit?" He looked up at her, his eyes pleading. "Do you think that's possible?"

Sandra looked into Blake's wide eyes and shrugged. "I guess anything is possible."

He grabbed her hand. "I'm so sorry. I don't know why I gave Tara access to the business finances. I was . . . I was . . ."

"In love, Blake." Sandra knew what that felt like, to believe so much in the person you've decided to share your life with, to never imagine anything coming between you. Love was special. And sacred. But it left you totally vulnerable in the wrong hands.

"I have to ask you something," she said.

"What?" He stood up. "What, San?"

"Do you think that . . . Tara . . . Alex . . ." She choked on the words.

Blake's eyes opened wide. "You think Tara could have hurt Alex, too?" he asked.

"I don't know."

"That's it. I need to call Detective Miller." Blake reached for his phone.

"Yes. Good idea. Do you still have his business card?"

Blake hesitated, glancing toward the bedroom. "I don't need it. I have the number in my phone."

"Great." She looked at him expectantly as he stood there with the phone in his hand. "What's wrong. Why aren't you calling?"

Blake looked at her. "Maybe it's better if I call him alone."

"But why?"

"Wouldn't it seem weird that you're here?"

"Why would it seem weird?"

"My wife going missing and my best friend here? My *female* best friend?" he asked.

Sandra didn't think that was weird at all, but Detective Miller was already questioning her choices. "He doesn't have to know. I'll be quiet." Then she rethought it. "Okay, maybe you're right. Maybe I should go. Maybe I'll try to find Tara. Does she have any usual haunts?"

Blake thought about it. "The library maybe?"

"Okay, I'll start there."

Blake opened the door, and Sandra hugged him one more time. "Let me know how it goes with Detective Miller."

"Okay."

"I'm here if you need anything, Blake. You know that, right?"

"I've always known that," he said with a smile.

She nodded. Then she grabbed her purse and stepped out the door.

TARA

CHAPTER 40

Monday, April 7, 2:00 p.m.

Tara lay at the bottom of the bedroom closet, unable to move, her empty luggage piled on top of her. She could hear faint voices coming from somewhere. Blake's and a woman's. Sandra?

Was it possible Sandra could be in on all this? And wanted to get rid of Alex so that she and Blake could be together? Tara remembered how Sandra had reacted to the things she had said at her place. About the funeral. And the password. She had seemed as surprised as Tara had been to find out the truth. Was it all an act? Or was Sandra really innocent in all this? If so, why was she here when Blake was supposed to be at work?

The blackness of the closet shifted colors as Tara began seeing things she knew weren't there, like spiders dangling from webs and fingers crawling toward her in the dark. Her breathing had slowed so much she wondered if she were even breathing at all. She was lightheaded, her thinking cloudy. Her tongue and throat felt numb. She didn't know how much fentanyl had gotten into her system, but it was probably enough to do permanent damage. She didn't have much time. She would pass out soon. Tara could no longer focus on the future, on what would happen in the hours and days to come. She only had the now. Twenty seconds? Maybe ten before she was unconscious?

Her foot was touching something at the edge of the closet. She nudged it. Rachel Sanberg's bat. She slowly reached out her hands to try to grab it, but while she could touch it, feel the smooth wood against her skin, her fingers couldn't grasp it because they no longer seemed to be doing what she wanted.

Her time was running out.

Tara tried to conjure up an image of strength in her mind. In the darkness, Alex's face appeared. Kind, thoughtful Alex. Tara thought of what Blake had done to him. How he had snubbed out a bright light that deserved to shine. And just when Tara could feel consciousness leaving her, she gathered up all her strength, pulled her legs into a fetal position, and kicked them against the closet door with all her might.

SANDRA

CHAPTER 41

Monday, April 7, 2:00 p.m.

"What was that?" Sandra asked, turning around.

"What was what?" Blake closed the door and stepped outside.

"That noise." Sandra pointed inside. "It came from the apartment."

"Probably just the neighbors."

"Inside your apartment?"

"No, next door. It happens all the time." His hand squeezed the doorknob, causing his knuckles to turn white. "I've complained to the landlord about it."

"I've never heard you mention it."

"I don't tell you *everything*, Sandra."

She studied him. "Blake, why are you acting weird?"

"I'm not acting—"

Sandra pushed the front door open and reentered Blake's apartment. She looked around.

"Sandra, seriously? What are you doing?"

"I heard something. A loud bang. I know you heard it, too. Like something fell."

"I did, but I told you. It's not something to get excited about."

Sandra walked past the kitchen farther into the apartment. She opened the bathroom door, closed it, then the bedroom door and stuck her head into the room. It was empty. She was about to close the door, but stopped. "It smells like coffee in here." She looked at the bed. "Did you spill coffee in bed?"

"Yeah." Blake was at her side. "That's why I had the door closed. I was embarrassed. When you knocked on the door, I got startled. That's why it took me so long to get to you. I was trying to clean it up."

Something was weird. It made sense that Blake had taken a long time to open his front door because he had spilled coffee, but Blake never drank or ate anything in bed because he was too afraid of crumbs or stains. And Sandra thought it strange that when he finally *did* let her inside he hadn't returned to the bedroom to finish cleaning it up. Blake never liked leaving a mess. Especially one that would soil his bedsheets.

"Why are you looking at me like that?" he asked her.

"I'm just surprised you left it like this."

"Surprised that I didn't tend to bed linens when my wife is missing and my best friend was standing in my home upset? You must think I'm a shitty person."

"No, Blake, I don't." She glanced around the bedroom. "But it's just . . . Like, look . . . see there?" She pointed to the closet. "It's not fully closed. The Blake I know would never leave his closet door ajar. As opposed to Alex, who rarely shut the closet door and I was forced to stare at his badly hung clothing."

"Yes, Alex and I were very different," Blake said. "That's not breaking news."

"That's not the point." She stepped into the bedroom, but Blake grabbed her arm. "Where are you going?" he asked.

"Hey, stop, Blake! That hurts."

He quickly released his hand. "Sorry."

"I was going to close your closet door."

"Just leave it."

"Why? I know it's bothering you."

"It's not bothering me, Sandra."

"Why are you being so weird?"

"I'm *not* being weird." He let out a long, dramatic sigh. "If you want me to close it, I'll close it then."

Blake walked into his bedroom and began pushing the sliding closet door, but it wouldn't budge. Something was in the way.

"It's stuck?" she asked.

"Yeah, something must be blocking the track on the inside. I'll fix it later."

He came toward her and began ushering her out of the bedroom.

"Why are you pushing me out?" she asked.

"Why? You want to stay in my bedroom with me, Sandra?" Blake raised his eyebrows.

"That's not what I mean, and you know it." She took a step toward the closet, but Blake blocked her way.

"Leave it alone, Sandra."

"Leave what alone?"

"Just leave the bedroom."

"Why? What's with the closet? Is that where the noise came from? Maybe whatever fell is blocking the track, like you said."

"Nothing's with the closet. I'll pick up whatever it is later. I need you to leave *now*."

A chill crept up Sandra's spine. Blake's voice wasn't exactly angry, but it was *close*, bordering on annoyed and impatient. She could probably count on one hand in the past four decades how many times he had sounded this way, and it was usually regarding his mother. "Why are you talking to me like this?"

"Like what?"

"Blake, stop gaslighting me."

He stood there with his arms crossed. "I'm not gaslighting you. You're the one who's acting weird, San. You need to go. Or . . . are you trying to keep me from calling Detective Miller for some reason?"

"Why would I do that?"

"*You* tell *me*."

Sandra's pulse hammered in her brain. Something was very wrong. Blake was wrong. Wailing one moment, angry the next. Sarcastic. *Physical.* Where was her longtime friend? The person she had leaned on over the years? Sensible, logical Blake? "You're right," she said finally. "Maybe it's all starting to get to me, you know?"

Blake's face burst into a smile—another sudden emotional change. "I know." His hand was on her shoulder.

"I'm sorry if I'm acting weird," Sandra said. She reached over and wrapped Blake in a hug. She felt his body relax.

Blake squeezed her tight. "It's okay. We'll get through this. Together."

"I know," Sandra said, releasing him. "Well, I guess I better let you call Detective Miller." She took one step toward the bedroom door, but as Blake moved forward to follow her, she spun around, ran past him, and ripped open the closet door.

Tara's bound body lay crumpled at the bottom of the closet.

"Oh my God, Blake! What have you done?"

She looked into Blake's eyes and expected Angry Blake to return, to yell, to push, to grab her arm again, but he stood there, calmly. Too calmly.

"San, she was trying to kill me," he said. "I had to do something."

Sandra bent down. "Help me get her out of the closet."

"No, San. Don't." He reached for her hand, but she pulled it away.

"Don't touch me," she said, and placed her fingers on Tara's neck. "She's still alive, thank God." She began tugging on Tara's body.

"San, she *killed* Alex."

Sandra stopped pulling and looked at him. "You don't know that, Blake."

"I *do* know that." He pointed to Tara. "She admitted to it in her frenzied state. That she drugged him and she threatened to do the same to me. And *you*. She's unstable. And dangerous. I had to do something."

"You should have called the police."

"The police?!" Blake asked with a laugh. "These days, they let out criminals left and right. I don't have any faith in the police. She *killed* Alex, San. I needed to make sure she was punished for what she's done. I needed to make sure she got what she deserved."

"Why would she do that?" Sandra asked.

"Why do people do anything?" Blake threw up his hands. "Who knows how her twisted mind worked. Maybe she did it for the money. To fund her expensive lifestyle. The designer clothing she wears isn't cheap. Maybe she wanted to hurt you." He slapped his head. "I should have believed you when you said you could sense something between the two of you. Or maybe she's just a fucking crazy bitch!"

Something wasn't making sense. Sandra thought back to the Tara who had shown up at her house that morning. Clearly, she wasn't well. And she definitely looked unstable. And Sandra *had* thought the fentanyl connection was odd. But could what Blake was saying be true? "Why didn't you tell me this when I got here? Why did you want me to think you couldn't find Tara?"

"Because I love you, San, and I didn't want you involved. This was *my* decision. The consequences should be mine alone, if there are any."

Sandra looked at Tara's limp body. "What did you do to her?"

"I used her drugs against *her*. I told you. She's a crazy junkie. Just like Chuck. She's been poisoning me. *Slowly.* That's why I haven't been feeling well. Unlike Alex, who she got rid of quickly."

"What do you mean?"

He reached for her hand. "I know what she did to Alex. She admitted it to me. Told me what she put in Alex's coffee when we were about to ski down the slope in Vermont."

In his coffee? Tears spilled from Sandra's eyes. "No." She shook her head.

"Yes, San. *Yes*. She took from you the one person who made you happy. The one person you shared your life with for decades. I don't know why you care at all about her."

"You should have called the police. You should have told Detective Miller everything. Not *this*." She reached down to pull the duct tape from Tara's mouth, but Blake put his hand on hers and squeezed.

"You and I are all we have left. We need to stick together."

"I can't condone this, Blake. Even Alex would—"

"Oh, enough about Alex!" Blake said, pulling his hand away. He stood up, his nostrils flaring. "You and I were always meant to be together. You know that."

Sandra stared into Blake's face and barely recognized it. He suddenly seemed a stranger. She stood up. "Blake, you're starting to scare me."

"Sandra, you know you love me."

"I do, but—"

"But what? You've said it all our lives."

"And Alex loved you, too."

Blake scoffed. "Alex loved that I played second fiddle to him. He loved that he got the attention. The friends. The girl."

"No. Alex loved *you*. Like a brother."

"A brother who stole his brother's girlfriend?"

"What are you talking about? I was never your girlfriend."

"Oh, so you would give your virginity to just anyone?"

"Blake, we both thought virginity was a burden, so we agreed—"

"*You* agreed, Sandra. *You* agreed." He pressed his index finger into her chest as his voice grew louder. "Not me. You can't look me in the eye and tell me that wasn't meaningful for you. I was *there*. I know it was, which is why I couldn't believe it when you told me you were going on a date with Alex. *Alex?* The football star? How cliché! Do you blame me for crashing the bike that day?"

Goose bumps shot up Sandra's arms. "Wait, what?" The memory flashed into her mind: Sandra sitting on Blake's handlebars. The two of them racing down the block. The sun shining. The wind blowing through her hair. A special moment. Made even more special because Alex Connor had asked her to go to the movies. And she was telling her best friend

MY BEST FRIEND'S WIFE

all about it. Life couldn't have been any more perfect. "You crashed the bike *on purpose?*"

"I wanted to show you how angry I was."

"You wanted to . . . wanted to . . ." Sandra searched his face. "You wanted to *hurt* me, Blake?"

"Oh, please, it was just a scratch."

Information overloaded Sandra's senses as she regarded the last decades of her life through a strange, new lens. Blake crashing the bike on purpose. Blake staying friends with Alex and Sandra through the years not because he loved *them* but because he loved *her*. Blake starting up a business with Alex not because he wanted to work with Alex but because he wanted to work with *her*. Blake wanting to move the business in a different direction than Alex. Blake not wanting to work with Chuck. Blake secretly getting married not because he loved Tara but to get under Sandra's skin because he loved *her*. Blake giving Sandra the wrong phone number for Tara. (Had *he* sent the snowmobile text?) Telling her that Tara didn't want to come to Alex's funeral. That she had pills in her pocket. Making Sandra suspicious of her and her character. So he could blame her for Alex's death? What was it that Tara had said to Sandra at her condo? *You and I never had a chance.*

"Why should Alex get everything he always wanted?" Blake said. "The clients. The girl. *Fuck* him." Sandra flinched as Blake got down in front of her on one knee. "C'mon, Sandra, it has always been you and me. You know how similar we are. We're quiet. Homebodies. We used to make fun of the people-persons like Alex. Thought they were shallow and dumb. You know you love me the way I love you. Remember how jealous you were when I told you that Tara and I were married?"

"Jealous?"

"Yes. When I called you and Alex after Chuck's wedding. It made me so happy to see that. It was a test, don't you see? And you passed!" He reached for her hand, but she pulled it away.

"I don't know what you're taking about. I was shocked, Blake. Not jealous. It was never about you and me. It was always me and Alex."

"I knew you *before* Alex."

"Yes, when we were kids."

"I knew from the first moment I saw you that you and I were supposed to be together," Blake said. "And now with Tara and Alex out of the way, you and I can *finally* be together, Sandra. Tara will get blamed for Alex's murder, and we can live happily ever after."

Sandra didn't believe what she was hearing. "There is no you and I."

"But—"

"No, Blake," Sandra cried. "There never was."

Blake stared blankly at her. Then he stood up, and something changed in his eyes. He leaned forward menacingly, threateningly. "I have waited long enough, Sandra. And I think you have, too."

"*I've* waited long enough?"

"Yes, you know it's true. You deserve to have a biological baby, San. We both know that Alex couldn't give that to you. The truth is, only a *real* man could."

The breath caught in Sandra's throat, and she started to tremble as the revelation finally hit her. Tara hadn't killed Alex. *Blake* did. And Tara had tried to warn her. She glanced at Tara's still body at the bottom of the closet.

"It was excruciating watching you try to adopt," Blake said, his expression again gentle and tender. "I can give you what Alex couldn't, Sandra. A baby." He reached for her hand. "You know you want one."

"Don't touch me," she said, shaking.

Blake took Sandra's hand anyway and squeezed. "Are you with me on this, San?"

She stood there, unable to say anything, wondering if this was truly happening. She looked again inside the closet at Tara.

"Listen, Sandra," Blake said calmly. "This can go one of two ways." He reached into his back pocket and pulled out a small plastic bag of pills.

"What is that?"

"We're meant to be together, Sandra. You and me. But if you don't believe in us the way I do . . ." He wiggled the bag.

"What are you saying?" she asked. "You'll kill yourself?"

"Kill myself?" Blake let out a laugh. "Why would I do that? But Sandra Wilson would, wouldn't she? The poor, bereaved widow? People would say she couldn't live without her beloved Alex, that she couldn't take it when she found out her best friend's wife had killed Alex. And she did away with herself. How very Romeo and Juliet, don't you think?"

Sandra searched Blake's eyes, but the Blake she knew was no longer there. And she was beginning to think he never was.

"I much more prefer plan A," Blake said, putting the pills back into his pocket, "but however you slice it, it gets the job done."

Sandra needed to calm her racing mind. She needed to think. "Blake," she said finally, "if you love me, really love me, you wouldn't do something like that."

"I do love you, San. I've loved you forever. But I won't let anyone else have you. Not anymore. As I said, I've waited long enough." He got down on one knee again. "I'll be good to you, San. You know I will." He let out a laugh. "Maybe my mother will finally get off my back. Our parents will be in-laws. Wouldn't that be great? You know, I think Pam would even be happy for us. She would see. She would see what true love there is between us."

On Blake's dresser, next to the closet, was a photo of her, Blake, and Alex taken at a college party decades ago, the three of them with their arms draped over one another. Sandra had seen the photo hundreds of times before, but it was only now she could see Blake's arm was wrapped around *her*. *Only* around her.

"Will you, San?" Blake asked, his eyes lasered on hers. "Will you be mine?"

Sandra stared at Blake and then back into the closet. At Tara's bound hands. They were stretched, trying, reaching...

"You're right, Blake." She squeezed his hand and nodded. "Everything you're saying makes sense. I don't know why it's taken me so long to see that. I guess when Alex came into my life, it just... obscured everything else."

"He was selfish that way, San." Blake stood up, becoming excited. "Too jokey. Could never understand the seriousness of life or how two people can connect."

"We could have a different kind of life together."

"Yes! We wouldn't have Alex nagging us anymore. Calling us party poopers. We could live our lives the way we choose."

She nodded. "I see that now." She pushed up her glasses and then pointed to Tara. "I think she stopped breathing."

Sandra bent down, pushed Tara's bangs from her forehead, and placed two fingers on her neck.

"Is it finally over?" Blake asked.

"I think so." As Sandra stood up, she reached into the closet, grabbed the baseball bat near Tara's hands, and swung it as hard as she could, the end of the bat catching the top of Blake's head and sending him to the floor.

He lay there, stunned, blood spurting from a widening gash in his head. He touched the bloody spot with his hand and looked at her. "You fucking whore..."

"And this is for Alex, you son of a bitch." She swung at him again as Blake tried to get up, and he hit the bedroom floor hard, his body sprawled out, unmoving.

Sandra raced into the other room, the bat still in her hands, and grabbed her purse. She dialed 9-1-1 and reported an emergency, an attempted murder. When she got back into the bedroom, Blake still lay on the floor, blood oozing from the laceration on his head. Sandra hurried to the closet, reached in, and carefully pulled the duct tape from Tara's mouth. Her lips were blue.

Just like Alex's.

"Hang in there, my friend," Sandra said, sitting next to her on the floor, one hand gripping the bat, the other squeezing Tara's limp hand. "I've got you. I promise."

CHAPTER 42

Saturday, June 14, 10:00 p.m.

The Long Island Music and Entertainment Hall of Fame was rocking. It wasn't the kind of rocking Sandra preferred at 10:00 p.m. on a Saturday night, since it was way past her bedtime, but she was trying to embrace the night owl life.

She surveyed the young people with their hands in the air and their heads nodding to the thumping baseline as Chuck took to the stage wearing a purple graphic T-shirt and jeans ripped along the fronts of his legs. Although this was the first concert she'd ever attended of Rockknot's, Alex said the band's audiences had been growing for the past two years, and she was happy to see wall-to-wall bodies squeezed into the small venue and imagined larger arenas and stadiums to come in the band's future.

The first set lasted about a half hour, and then Chuck excused himself from the stage, announcing there'd be a fifteen-minute "pee break." Sandra couldn't imagine Chuck had anything left to pee—sweat streamed down the sides of his face, matted his hair, and soaked his clothes, his exposed knees glistening in the stage lights. How much body fluid could one skinny rocker hold? He spotted her just as he was about to leave his microphone and smiled.

"Sandra, I'm so glad you came!" Chuck said when he finally managed his way through the audience to get to her. He looked like he wanted to wrap her in a sweat-soaked bear hug but thought better of it, so she leaned forward and hugged him first. *Like she meant it.*

"You sound great up there!" she said.

"Thanks. Saturday night crowds are always amazing." He wiped his forehead. "How are you doing?"

She shrugged. "Okay. Just taking it one day at a time."

He nodded, and something unspoken slipped between them. There was always something unspoken when Sandra spoke to people who knew Alex—like a gaping hole that, if they weren't careful, would swallow them up.

"Hey, man, great show!" said a college-aged dude with blond hair tied in a long ponytail. He shook Chuck's hand.

"Thanks, man. Thanks for coming," Chuck said graciously. "More to come. Stick around." Chuck guided Sandra toward a quieter spot outside the main room, where it was probably twenty degrees cooler. "We can talk better here," he said. "How's Tara?"

Sandra nodded. "She's good. Lucky. At the hospital, the doctors said if treatment had waited any longer or if she had gotten any more fentanyl in her system, things might have been very different."

"That's good to hear." He shook his head. "That was some crazy shit with Blake. Was it true he was making himself sick just so he could pin it on Tara?"

"Yeah." Sandra could hardly believe it herself. Blake hated being sick. The bodily fluids. The disorientation. Little did she know he was *really* sick. In ways she never imagined.

"You were lucky, too, you know," he said, looking at her, concerned.

"I know." Sandra wasn't sure how much Chuck knew, but the media had covered what had happened round the clock for weeks, and would probably cover Blake's trial just as heavily. She couldn't believe Blake was pleading not guilty. He was probably thinking he'd get off, like so many of the other criminals he claimed did. What he didn't know was that Sandra would do everything in her power to make sure that didn't happen.

"I have to be frank with you, San," Chuck said. "I don't know if I would have stopped hitting that guy with that baseball bat."

"My mind was on Tara. Saving Tara. But I *am* thinking of carrying a bat with me all the time now," she said, trying to joke. "I guess I've got some serious trust issues I'm working through."

Chuck smiled awkwardly.

"Well"—she cleared her throat—"now to the reason I'm here..."

"Oh, is this an official visit?"

"Yes, and I don't want to keep you. I know you have limited time between sets, but I got an interesting phone call a couple of weeks ago. From a young woman named Viola Gomez. She's a deejay I met at a marketing meeting I went to..."

With Blake, she wanted to say, but didn't. She knew it would be impossible to erase him from her life entirely. They had been friends for way too long. But she would try to move forward no longer feeling like she needed to include him.

"She said she wanted to meet with me about Napkin Marketing doing her socials for her," Sandra continued. "She said she enjoyed meeting me and... well, thought I was nice and somebody she wanted to work with. Although part of me is wondering if she wants to hire Napkin because of everything that's happened." Sandra shrugged. "Like I said. Trust issues."

"I'm sure it's because she wants to work with you. Who wouldn't?"

"I'm glad to hear you say that." A nervousness flooded through Sandra's belly—a welcome feeling after months of sadness and dread. "I've been thinking a lot over the past two months. Whether I should move. Start over somewhere else. Find a job in the City. But right now the right thing to do feels like staying here. Near my parents. Near Alex's mom. And Viola's call got me thinking of maybe keeping Napkin Marketing going—you know, in addition to my romance stuff. I know it will be a lot of work, but I figure I write most of the marketing materials anyway, and the business is doing well. And it was Alex's baby and—"

Chuck smiled. "You've got me, Sandra."

"You mean, you haven't found anyone to do your marketing yet?"

"I'm with Viola. I haven't found anyone I liked."

Sandra hesitated. "I have to be honest, Chuck. I'm not Alex. No one is. I don't know if I—"

"You're *you*, Sandra. And that's good enough for me."

He stuck out his hand, and they shook on it. Sandra's first business deal as a marketing entrepreneur. It felt good.

Chuck looked past Sandra and waved. "Hey, babe!"

Beatrice sidled up next to Chuck, her protruding belly leading the way, and planted a kiss on his lips. "Great set!" She glanced at Sandra and broke into a wide smile. "Sandra! How nice to see you!"

The crowd began chanting behind them in the main room.

"Well, I'd better go pee and get back up there before there's a mutiny," Chuck said.

"As I've learned these last few months," Bea said, pointing to her belly, "you pee when you can."

"We'll talk, San." Chuck gave Sandra a hug and hurried toward the restrooms.

"You look terrific, Bea," Sandra said. "How are you feeling?"

"Good. You know, *fat*. But the good kind of fat." She laughed. "How are you?" She put her hand on Sandra's arm.

"I'm okay. Moving forward."

"That's all we can do, right?"

The crowd burst into applause, and suddenly Chuck was back onstage. His hair was slicked back as if he had quickly combed it. He grabbed the microphone. "Thank you for sticking around, folks. Who's ready to rock the house?" Whistles and hooting erupted from the audience, which began crowding the stage.

Chuck's eyes spotted Sandra in the back of the room. "This next song goes out to one of the best dudes I ever got the chance to know." He nodded and looked back at his band. "One, two," he called, "one, two, three," and then the distinctive opening piano melody of Journey's "Don't Stop Believin'" filled the jam-packed room.

CHAPTER 43

Sunday, June 15, 11:00 a.m.

Sandra wiped the dirt off the letters of Alex's name on his speckled gravestone and settled back onto her blanket, looking up at the blue sky. It was the first sunny, warm day she could remember in months, with no rain in the forecast. Somewhere, below her, was Alex. She tried not to think about him being alone and in the dark; instead, she imagined the man who had been her foundation since she was a teenager still providing her solid ground.

"Oh, I almost forgot . . ." She reached into her pocket, plucking out one of Chuck's guitar picks. She placed it in the dirt next to the marigolds and zinnias she had planted. "Chuck said he'll stop by next week. He has a new song he wants you to hear."

She patted some loose dirt near a wayward marigold and then, with her index finger, wrote Alex's name in the dirt, the way she used to on her notebook in high school. How excited it had made her feel, placing that looseleaf binder on her desk and letting her fellow students know he was her guy.

She felt the tears coming but willed them to stop. She had promised herself that she wasn't going to cry during these morning visits with Alex, although it was impossible to stop them once she began talking. "I miss you so much." She shook her head and wrapped her arms around herself. "And I'm so, so sorry, Alex. I know you would tell me not to be, but I blame myself. How could I not see Blake for who he was? And what he thought? You could always read people better than I could, although I don't think you saw this coming either. I think love blinded us. Still, I can't help but feel like I should have seen it *for* you. I should have known you were in danger."

A cardinal chirped in a nearby tree, and Sandra wondered if the bird was singing a happy or mournful song. She couldn't tell.

"Blake had been wrong about a lot of things, but I've been doing some thinking these past two months." She stared at the letters of Alex's name as if she were looking into his beautiful blue eyes. "Maybe I *did* take him for granted as a best friend. Maybe I *was* too pushy, or narcissistic, expecting him to let me 'approve' his new wife. I can't believe how hurt I was that he had gotten married without my knowing. It seems so silly now." She looked away, listening for the cardinal's birdsong, but the cemetery was quiet. "You knew all along that Blake should have been leading his own life. Just like we were. I keep wondering: Did I give Blake the wrong signals? Did I make him think I was interested in more than friendship?" She sniffled. "And I worry . . . did you ever feel like *you* weren't enough? Because you were always enough, Alexander Connor. You were everything to me and more. I hope you knew that."

She took a long, deep breath and exhaled. She wanted to talk about happier things. "I'm seeing your mom tonight. Our girls' nights are becoming a regular thing. I think they help us to remember, you know? And to move forward together." The sadness was creeping in again, but she pushed it away. "And did I tell you I've decided to continue the business? Napkin Marketing? I need to work on the legal stuff—you know, getting Blake out of the company. If I have to, I'll start a brand-new business. Not sure what Tara wants to do. I haven't really heard from her since the hospital. I can't say I blame her. What a nightmare to have been mixed up in all this."

Sandra's phone rang. She pulled it from her purse, read the name on her phone screen, and swiped. "Casey?"

"I'm a momma!" said an excited, but exhausted voice on the other end of the line.

"You had the baby?"

"Yes, he came a little early, but he's beautiful and big and almost split me in half." She gave a tired laugh.

"That's so wonderful, Casey."

"Yeah, and I wanted you to be one of the first people I told because . . . I've decided to keep the baby."

Sandra sat up. "You did?"

"Yeah. I think what happened with Alex really, like, affected me. Made me realize that life was messy and anything can happen at any time. I think, before, I was trying to let this pregnancy not interfere with my life, to go on as usual, but I started thinking . . . what if this pregnancy *is*, like, a part of my life? And not a disruptor? I mean, we can't control everything that happens to us, but we can control the things we can control, right? Princeton can wait a year. I'm deferring my admission."

"Wow, how does your mom feel about that?"

"Well, she wasn't happy at first, but now I can't get little Alexander out of her arms." She laughed.

Sandra let out a tiny gasp. "You named the baby Alex?"

"Yeah. I hope that's okay."

Sandra glanced at the letters A-L-E-X-A-N-D-E-R on the gravestone in front of her. The circle of life. "Oh, Casey, Alex would have been so touched."

"I saw him a couple of days after you guys came to my house. I don't know if he mentioned it."

"You did?"

"Yeah, he was meeting with some guy by the Langford Tea Room. Near that music venue."

Casey had been the woman Chuck had seen with Alex from afar? The one Detective Miller had mentioned?

"We didn't talk, like, for long," Casey said, "but he told me he didn't really get a chance to tell me what a great mom you would be when he came to our house. He said the form that you guys filled out didn't really tell your whole story. I could see the intense love in his eyes. All I could think was . . . I want *that*. I want this person who is willing to fight for me the way he was fighting for you. We didn't talk for long because I had an essay to write for English, but it reminded me how much I just liked the way the two of you were. He was so goofy and jokey, and you let him be. You didn't try to dim his light. I could see the two of you loved each other very much and accepted each other for who you were. Just the way he pulled out the desk chair for you in my bedroom and put his hand on your shoulder."

A baby started to cry in the background. Little Alex.

"This one has a set of lungs on him, as my mom likes to say," Casey said. "Who knows? He might change the world."

"I think he already has," Sandra said.

"Will you come and see him?"

"Of course. I'd love to."

"Great. I'll text you the hospital details. I'd better go. He's getting fussy. Goodbye, Sandra."

"Goodbye, Casey."

Sandra disconnected the call and smiled at Alex's gravestone. "Still influencing people, I see. You were an amazing man. And I so, so love you and miss you. See you soon, my love." She pressed her thumb on the A of Alex's name. "Eleven till heaven."

Sandra stood up and folded her blanket. As she walked on the brick path toward her car, her phone rang again. She looked at the screen, surprised, and accepted the call. "Tara?"

"Hi." Pause. "I hope it's okay that I called. You left your number—your *real* number—with my doctor at the hospital. I was glad because I didn't have it." Pause. "I've been meaning to call you. I wasn't sure if you'd want to hear from me."

"Of course I want to hear from you! How are you feeling?"

"I'm better. I've taken a leave of absence from work and I'm going to lay low this summer, but I think I should be back at my desk in the new school year. My colleagues have been so great. And so have my students."

"That's good to hear. You deserve nothing but happiness."

Another pause. "How are *you* doing?"

"Oh, you know . . ." Sandra shrugged, hearing the cardinal singing again from a nearby tree.

"Yeah, I know." Pause. "Sandra, I don't think I properly thanked you for what you did. That took a lot of strength. Facing down Blake like that."

"Well, lucky for you, you had a bat practically in your hands. I only did what you didn't have the chance to do. To be honest, I don't know what our chances would have been if I would have had to rely only on my fists." Sandra laughed at her self-deprecating joke; that was something Alex would have said.

Tara laughed, too. "I'll need to write Rachel Sanberg a thank-you note."

"Rachel Sanberg?"

"It's a long story." Another pause. "But, Sandra, there's a second reason for my call."

Sandra waited for Tara to say something more as she reached her car. She leaned against it, letting the soft breeze caress her cheeks.

Tara cleared her throat. "I'm sure you just want to move forward and put this whole thing behind you. But . . . I was thinking . . . maybe one day, do you . . . do you want to get together and . . . get a cup of coffee or something?"

Sandra smiled. *A cup of coffee.*

A speck of red appeared in the sky as the cardinal flew off a nearby branch, flapping its wings in short bursts until it disappeared into the infinite blue.

"Sure," Sandra said, getting into her car and starting it up. "I'd like that very much."

Acknowledgments

I was folding laundry at home, my mind wandering, as it usually does, when I got an idea for a psychological thriller that would eventually become *My Best Friend's Wife*. Thank you to the following for sharing their knowledge during the writing of this novel: Steven Maluenda, Mike O'Keefe, Meredith Schneider, and the amazing Miffie Seideman, author of *The Grim Reader*. (Note: Any reality missteps in this novel are solely the doing of the author; as I like to say, you can lead a novelist to facts, but you can't make her use them.) Thank you also to Holly Mangin and Jessica Ielmini, my brilliant beta readers; Brittany Dowdle, copyeditor extraordinaire and fellow Futuristic; and, as always, my family, for indulging this novelist's never-ending what-ifs, what-do-you-thinks, do-you-find-this-interestings, and do-you-mind-if-we-order-out-tonights.

About the Author

Dina Santorelli is an award-winning author who lives on Long Island. She was raised in Middle Village, New York, a neighborhood surrounded by cemeteries, which might explain her penchant for thriller and suspense. Sign up today for Dina's newsletter at dinasantorelli.com and receive a free short story that's available only to subscribers.

Also by Dina Santorelli

Baby Grand Trilogy
Baby Grand
Baby Bailino
Baby Carter

The Great Shift Thrillers
The Reformed Man

Standalone Novels
In the Red

Made in United States
North Haven, CT
17 September 2025